Isabella Mumphrey Adventures

Secrets of a Mayan Moon
Secrets of an Aztec Temple
Secrets of a Hopi Blue Star
Secrets of a Christmas Box

Secrets of a Hopi Blue Star

An Isabella Mumphrey Adventure

Book 3

By

Paty Jager

Windtree Press
Hillsboro, OR

This is a work of fiction, Names, characters, places, and incidents either are the product of the author's imagination or are used fictitiously, and any resemblance to actual persons living or dead, business establishments, events, or locales, is entirely coincidental.

SECRETS OF A HOPI BLUE STAR

Contact Information: info@windtreepress.com

Windtree Press
Hillsboro, Oregon
http://windtreepress.com

Cover Art by Christina Keerins
CoveredbyCLKeerins

PUBLISHING HISTORY

First Edition by Windtree Press 2013

Published in the United States of America

ISBN 978-1-952447-56-3

Author's Notes

While researching both the Hopi Tribe and the border between Arizona and Mexico, I came across an elite group of Native American border patrol call Dark Wolves. They were my inspiration for my fictional group called Shadow Eagles.

Special thanks to my awesome daughter and cover artist: Christina Keerins!

Chapter One

Isabella Mumphrey stood in the threshold of her bedroom door. "How long will you be gone this time?" she asked, studying Tino Konstantine's bare, wide shoulders and narrow, firm backside.

He turned, giving her a full view of all his charming assets, including the smile that melted her like a pat of butter on a Phoenix sidewalk.

"*Querida*, you see me more now than when I was undercover for DEA."

Her Venezuelan lover strode toward Isabella, embracing her to his hard chest. "I will only be gone two weeks. The *Malo Perro,* Bad Dog, gang that runs drugs for the Moreno Cartel have been bringing in large shipments across the border. We have to find out where and stop them."

"I know." Isabella inhaled his spicy masculine scent she fell in love with in Guatemala and thought she would never smell again during their missions in Mexico City. "I just don't have any interesting projects to keep me busy while you're gone. Which means I'll miss you all the more." She peered up into his dark chocolate eyes.

"*Pichon*, I'm sure you will dig up something. I am happy the World Intelligence Agency hasn't called you in months." He leaned down, kissed her sweetly. "I cannot concentrate on my work when I worry about you chasing after disreputable people."

She sighed. It was true. Daddy hadn't called her to go on a mission in months. That was part of her boredom. She loved her work as an anthropologist and until her escapade in Guatemala at the *Ch'ujuña* Dig, she was quite satisfied with her job. Now, every day that she worked in her office at the college writing grants to get more money for her department and the few requests for her help and knowledge, her life had become stale.

Tino kissed her again, this time with more passion. Her body hummed, and her mind took the challenge. This was the only part of her life that wasn't stagnant. Since discovering their love in the Guatemalan jungle, they had yet to become tired of one another. At Christmas, Tino gave her an engagement ring, leaving it up to her to pick the wedding date. That was seven months ago. She loved him but was unsure about marriage given their occupations. Her parents made their marriage as undercover operatives work, however, they were in the same organization. She and Tino were apart more than they were together.

Isabella maneuvered Tino against the bed. He tumbled onto the Mayan-print coverlet, dragging her down on top of him.

"When did you say you had to leave?" she asked, shoving his duffel bag closer to the edge to make more room for the antics she had in mind.

"Ten minutes ago. Ezzabella, you always make me late." He cradled her head and pulled her lips to his.

Two weeks. She drifted into the kiss, taking and giving in equal measure.

The sound of Native American drums rolled through the room.

"Hello! Hello!" squawked Alabaster, her cockatoo.

Isabella squirmed out of Tino's embrace and kiss. "I should get that." The interruption annoyed her, but it could be Daddy calling with a mission. And she'd just wished for more excitement than a romp in the bed with Tino.

She fanned her face to ease the heat Tino had injected in her body. Picking up her phone, she recognized the number of the Hopi cultural center. The call had to be from Aunt Una. Isabella couldn't remember the last time she'd talked with her mother's sister.

"Aunt Una?"

"*Loloma*, Isabella. I hope I am not disturbing you." Her aunt's slow wording was indicative of the sedate, spiritual community of the Hopi.

"No, Tino was just getting ready to leave for his job." Isabella stifled a giggle as Tino frowned and grabbed for her. She place her thumb over the phone. "You said you were late."

"Sí. Talk with your aunt, and I will get dressed." He waved his hands in a shooing motion.

"Oh, then this is a bad time to talk?" Una's voice softened with disappointment.

Isabella took the hint. "No, not at all," she said, exiting the bedroom and folding her feet under her as she sat on the couch. She rarely had contact with her family at the reservation. The occasional calls with Una had only started after Isabella had graduated and took control of her life. The same warm feeling she always experienced while talking to Una filled her heart. All her life she'd believed in the power of one's heritage and roots, the comfort she found from this woman's voice proved her theory.

"How is everyone at the village?" She'd only met the extended family once as a child but she still wanted to hear how they were.

The hesitation on her aunt's part sent goose bumps up Isabella's arms. "Is something wrong?"

"Not that I can say on the phone." Aunt Una breathed deeply. "Could you get away from work and come see me at Walpi?"

Before Isabella could answer, Una continued, "You could study drawings on the wall of a recently found cave. Make it a working visit?"

The anxious tone in Una's voice, started Isabella's mind whirling with the possibilities of what her aunt wasn't saying.

"Yes. Tino will be gone for two weeks. I can drive up there tomorrow and stay as long as you need me."

"Thank you! I've had this weighing on my mind and have no one else to call." The relief in Una's voice humbled Isabella that she could bring comfort to her aunt.

"Let me get a pen so you can give me directions to your place." Isabella scrambled off the couch and picked up a pad and pen from her neat and tidy desk in the corner of the room.

"Pen! Pen!" Alabaster said in his gravelly voice while shifting from foot to foot.

"Quiet, Ally." She handed the cockatoo a brazil nut still in the shell from a dish next to his cage.

"Okay, I'm ready." While jotting down the directions from her aunt, Isabella noticed Tino entering the room in her peripheral line of sight. Seeing her aunt was the perfect distraction while Tino was away. She winked at him and ended her conversation.

Tino studied the woman who had captured his heart in a short amount of time. He adored her thick, reddish brown hair, full eyebrows and slim figure. But her intelligence and ease with him, the academic world, and even her new inclusion in the World Intelligence Agency and how she remained so innocent and unassuming had captured his heart. He rubbed his chest, feeling his heart swell. He couldn't believe she wished to spend her life with him, an ex-DEA agent, and now border patrol officer.

He caught Isabella around the waist with one arm as she set the phone on the table. He nipped her ear and whispered, "What did your aunt want?"

Isabella snuggled into his embrace. "She wanted me to come to the reservation and look at a new cave they discovered."

He'd heard that evasive tone before. Tino spun her in his arms, peering into her green eyes. "There is something you are not telling me."

She started to lower her lashes.

"Uh, uh, uh. You are hiding something. I know you better than anyone. What mischief are you getting into, *querida*?" He held her squirming body.

She let out an exasperated sigh and stopped squirming. "Really, that's all she said. She wanted me to make this a working visit. But there was something in her voice. Almost a pleading tone for me to come. I can't explain it."

Tino tipped her face up to read her eyes. "You are worried for your aunt. Go connect with her." He tapped her nose. "But do not get caught up in trouble without checking in with me."

Her troubled expression melted into the seductive siren he'd discovered in the Guatemalan jungle. That woman had been hard to resist and had nearly cost them their lives.

"*Carajo*! You will cause me to age fast."

Isabella hopped up, wrapping her legs around his waist, and kissed him. Her actions and his desire for her won. He carried her into the bedroom to love her thoroughly. What was another hour when he was already thirty minutes late?

Chapter Two

Isabella had only stopped once during the four-hour drive from Phoenix to the Hopi Reservation. The summer desert landscape veiled behind the undulating heat waves rising from the desert floor never ceased to amaze her. Where others saw desolation and endless sameness, she saw the wonders of the life that could live in such arid conditions. Her ancestors, the Hopi, had learned to live with the land and prosper.

The high mesas that cradled the villages of her ancestors rose out of the sandy soil, hoisting the villages heavenward. This was only the second time she'd made this trek to the Hopi reservation. The first was when she was young. Her mother and father had returned to her mother's people for the burial of Isabella's grandmother. It had been a somber rather than a joyful time as her grandmother was sent to the *Maasaw*. The trip had been the first time Isabella ever witnessed the ceremonies and felt a familial closeness. It had been the catalyst to send her on her quest to be an anthropologist specializing in Native American cultures.

Through the years, she'd tried to capture that familial feeling through her work and new discoveries, but she always came away feeling like she still missed many of the pieces. She stopped her Jeep Compass alongside the road and sat, staring at the long arms of the mesa. Her studies of the Hopi only made her more in awe of the people whose blood coursed through her veins. They believed in living a simple life; living off the land and holding their religion close.

Isabella clicked on her blinker even though she'd only seen three cars since turning off the main highway an hour ago at Winslow. She followed her aunt's directions, passing an up-to-date cluster of buildings and turning right onto a dirt road. The road wound at a leisurely pace up the mesa. She studied the stone buildings and metal roofs of the buildings as she drove through Hano and Sichmovi. These villages had adapted some of the twentieth century ways of life. But the people of Walpi, the oldest Hopi settlement, still lived the old way. No phones, no electricity, no plumbing. The residents of Walpi walked to Sichmovi to wash and haul drinking water to their homes. Primitive outhouses sat along the rim of the mesa and town.

Ahead the rock homes and pole ladders came into view.

The sense of coming home overwhelmed Isabella in a way she'd never experienced before. "I know these people are part of my heritage, but why is my heart pounding like after I've made love to Tino?" She pondered this spoken thought as she pulled up to the area reserved outside the village to park vehicles.

Not knowing how long she would need to remain with her aunt, Isabella had packed clothes, toiletries, hiking boots, and her survival vest. She never went anywhere outside the city without her vest. The items stored in the garment had helped her out of several nasty encounters.

She left all these items in the car for now and stepped out with just her notebook tucked into a daypack.

"Isabella."

The soft voice belonged to her aunt. While she hadn't visited over the years, the infrequent contact via the telephone had ingrained her aunt's voice in her memory. Her aunt used the phone at the Hopi cultural center to make phone calls on the days she taught classes.

"Aunt Una, it's so good to see you." Isabella embraced her aunt. The woman was plumper than her sister, who worked to keep a trim figure. But to Isabella it only made her aunt more authentic than her mother.

Tears glistened in the woman's eyes when she stepped out of the embrace.

"What could be so bad it makes you cry?" Isabella wanted to pull the woman back into her arms. She always wondered at the protectiveness and closeness she felt for an aunt she rarely saw.

"These are tears of happiness, not sadness." She grasped Isabella's hand. "It is so good to see you."

A smile spread across Isabella's face, tugging the corners and lightening her heart. "I agree. I've wanted to come see you ever since I started working at the college in Phoenix, but there always seemed to be something that kept me away."

"Now that you have come, you must return more often." Aunt Una led her toward the village. "We do not allow many to see our true hearts, but you, you are one of us and have missed out on so much."

Isabella had studied the Hopi and knew they were a secretive group and believed in keeping their religion and ceremonies to themselves. Even though she had Hopi blood, because she hadn't been raised in the ways, she was considered a *kahopi,* and would only be allowed to see the same ceremonies and Hopi life as that of a tourist.

If her mother hadn't turned her back and ignored her heritage, Isabella could boast she was of the Fire Clan. All children became part of the clan of their mother. She glanced wistfully at the kiva sitting to the side of the village entrance. If she had grown up closer to the Hopi, she could have enjoyed the ceremonies and been allowed into a kiva.

They sauntered by stone structures that had stood against everything the weather could toss at them for over eleven-hundred years.

"This is the home where your mother and I grew." Aunt Una stopped beside a door in one of the rock structures.

Memories of entering this home when they visited her grandmother's burial bombarded Isabella. She'd met cousins and family she'd never known existed. Why had her mother shunned the ways of her family? Why had she lived such a shut-off life from those she loved? Daddy had said it was because of her mother's job working for the World Intelligence Agency, but there was more. Her mother opened herself up to few people, including her daughter.

Isabella stepped into the cool darkness. Her eyes adjusted quickly. The room was much as she remembered. A new tapestry hung from the wall above a bed. The elementary dwelling harkened back to the days when the white settlers came to America.

The absence of electricity or running water gave the place an earthy aura. A loom sat against the wall where she remembered her cousin sleeping in a cot. He would be grown now and out on his own.

"Does Cody still live on the mesa?" Isabella faced her aunt.

She smiled proudly. "Not this mesa. He has a small home down on the valley floor, but he isn't there much. His job keeps him away more than he likes, but he is doing good for our people and many others."

Isabella nodded her head, though she wasn't certain what Cody did. She knew he'd been in the military for a while. With the military background, perhaps he worked as a Hopi police officer.

"This looks a lot like I remembered it from our one trip here."

Aunt Una's expression became haunted, but changed in a blink of an eye, leaving Isabella to wonder if she'd registered the haunted reaction in her aunt's eyes.

"That was a long time ago. I have corn cakes for our lunch. Then I will take you to the cave." Una busied herself, putting the cakes and a pitcher of water on the old wood table covered with a Hopi weaving.

Again, Isabella had the feeling there was more to this visit than the cave and whatever it held.

~*~

Tino pulled his SUV up alongside the others at the end of the road it had taken him several hours to find. The maps Border Patrol gave him didn't include all the roads on the Tohono O'odham reservation along the Arizona/Mexico border.

"I was just getting ready to send a Shadow Eagle out looking for you." Lt. George Melvin of Border Patrol said, slapping Tino on the back. Tino had heard of this elite Native American tracking team under Immigration and Customs Enforcement, but this was his first time working with them.

"If you had given me a reliable map, I would have been on time." Tino stepped forward extending his hand to the first man on his left. "Tino Konstantine."

"Jonny Crow. I head up the Shadow Eagles."

Tino shook hands and extended it to the other three men present.

"Cody Honani." The youngest man in the group had a solid grip and a suspicious expression.

"Tank Halfmoon."

Tino grimaced as the man squeezed his hand. His name suited him. He was taller than any Native American Tino had encountered and his shoulders wouldn't fit through many doorways.

"Ignore, Tank's intimidation. I'm Charlie Taft." The man's good-natured comment and affable face took some of the sting out of the other introductions.

"There are nine on this team, the other five are off duty," Jonny said. "We know this land. Until you become accustom to the landmarks it would be a good idea if you stayed with one of us and not go out scouting on your own."

Lt. Melvin nodded his head. "These men have located what they think is the route the *Malo Perros* have been using to cross the border. You'll go on a patrol tonight and see if you can catch them."

"Are they coming in by foot?" he asked no one in particular.

"They are using human mules. We've found pieces of the burlap they use to wrap the packs," Cody answered. His watchful gaze more wary than the others.

Tino nodded. He'd brought in his share of people packing forty pounds of illegal substances on their backs. Anger bubbled in his gut knowing each person endangered their lives for five hundred dollars, taking all the risk while the cartel reaped the spoils.

"I want to check out the area in daylight and set-up a trap to try and catch them." Jonny motioned to two pickups. "Hop in one of these. Your lieutenant can take your vehicle back to base."

"I'll get my gear." Tino opened the back door of his Tahoe and grabbed his pack, loaded with all the latest surveillance equipment, his weapons, and one of Isabella's survival tins. He would have laughed at her when she handed it to him, if he hadn't watched her get them out of several harrowing instances with the items she kept in a mint tin.

"Hop in here," Cody said, sitting behind the wheel of a faded silver four-by-four truck.

Tino noticed all the others climbing into Jonny's rig.

"Badger will take good care of you," Tank said, drawing his tree-sized leg in and closing the door.

A vehicle was a vehicle, though the other men were in a newer, shiner truck than Cody. Tino shoved his pack down on the floorboard and slid in.

The door barely clicked and the vehicle shot forward, following the plume of dust the other truck kicked up.

"Have you been with Border Patrol long?" Cody, or Badger, as Tank called him, kept his gaze searching the sides of the road.

"About ten months. I was DEA for eight years before that."

"We've worked with Border and DEA before, and Homeland." Cody glanced over then back at the road. "We'll find the traffickers and you can take over from there."

Tino shrugged. In his years of working with DEA, both openly and undercover, he'd learned to ignore distrustful officers of other agencies. Some felt it a slight when they had to work with people from other organizations. But if this group had worked for ICE and with the Department of Homeland Security, they must have skills beyond what technology could do. Which made them the elite and knowledgeable members of this operation.

"How do you know the group we're going to intercept is the *Malo Perros*?" He was more interested in taking down the cartels than some nickel-and-dime dealer.

"We staked out a pick-up site two nights ago and took two suspects into custody. One rolled. He told us about the drop tonight and where he was to deliver it." Cody slowed as the brake lights on the vehicle in front of them flashed.

Tino perked up. This was the most solid evidence he'd come across since taking this job ten months ago. Even though he told Isabella he was glad the WIA hadn't called her, he understood her longing for excitement. Being Border Patrol had long, boring stints as well. Especially when he was used to being on full alert all the time for eight years. But he'd taken this job to be closer to Isabella and it had less risk than his previous job.

"If the informant didn't make the last drop, they may have changed plans." Tino wanted this drop to be effective, but there were so many variables.

"We made sure some of the goods were retrieved and delivered." Cody leveled a steady gaze on him. "We know there are people higher up that must be taken down before this trespassing on sacred ground will be stopped."

Tino nodded. He didn't like anyone getting away with

transporting drugs, but it was a sacrifice that had to be made to capture the people supplying the drugs.

"Did the informant mention any Moreno family member as the drop-off point?" Using his past contacts, Tino had found out Moreno had family in the U.S. and from the word in the drug industry they were his U.S. distributors.

Cody shook his head. "He only gave us the drop, no names." He pulled the truck up beside the other parked truck.

The men climbed out and fussed with packs. Each one donned their packs; slung an M-4 assault rifle over their shoulder; and shoved semi-automatic pistols in their shoulder holsters.

Tino exited the truck, slipped on his pack, and checked the Glock in his shoulder holster and the knife sheathed in his boot.

Crow handed out walkie talkies. "We'll split up, except you." He pointed to Tino. "You'll go with Badger until you become knowledgeable of this country." Crow scanned the horizon. "If you see anything let the rest know. We'll fan out and head toward the known drop site then take up positions around the site."

The men nodded and set out heading southwest.

Cody motioned with his head for Tino to follow him.

It irked that he'd spent years finding his way around South and Central American jungles but these men didn't trust he could find his way around in open country. Tino moved to the left of Cody twenty feet and walked parallel with him through the cactus and sage. The arid climate didn't tax his body as the sweltering jungle had. The moisture dampening his back and brow was his own, not moisture from the atmosphere.

He kept his gaze trained on the ground for tracks. Staring at the grayish-brown sand sprinkled with pebbles, larger rocks, as well as cactus, thorny bushes, and an occasional beetle and scorpion, he wasn't sure he'd be able to see sign of trespassers.

They'd traveled an hour when Cody dropped to his knees.

Tino worked his way over to the other man. "What did you find?"

"I've been following burlap fibers on the mesquite. Then I spotted this."

Two sand-covered pieces of carpet twelve inches long and six inches wide with strips of cloth wrapped around them lay on the ground beside a set of footprints that appeared out of nowhere. Human mules tied the carpet to their feet to hide their footprints.

"Anyway to tell if that's old or new?" Tino made a note to watch the plants for sign. He was used to looking for bent or broken foliage in the jungle, but here the bushes were so full of spines and thorns and far apart, he didn't think people barged through them like they did the lush jungle undergrowth.

Cody shook his head. "What is curious is that he abandoned the carpet and is now making prints for us to follow." He scanned the rises around them. "There could be spotters watching the area to make sure the drop hasn't been compromised."

Tino pulled out his high-tech binoculars and scanned a three-hundred-sixty perimeter. His heart started pumping as he put the binoculars into his pack. "There is a man on the ridge to the north."

Cody nodded and continued on a few paces then knelt with his back to the knoll as if studying something on the ground. He pulled out the walkie talkie. "We have a raven on the knoll to the northeast."

He replaced the radio and stood. "We will continue on following the tracks. They will lead us nowhere near the drop, but it will keep the person watching busy and the others will capture him."

Tino didn't like being the decoy, he wanted in on the action.

"We know exactly where he is. We could split up. I'll circle around behind him."

"Today is not our day to make contact. Today, we are the distraction." Cody kept on marching along the hot desert sand.

Tino let out a long Venezuelan curse and fell in behind the man. Working with the Shadow Eagles was going to take some getting used to. He'd worked as a group before, but everyone also worked as they felt best fit the situation. He was just getting ready to voice his disappointment in the way things were going, when radio static disturbed the desert quiet.

"We have raven. Drop still scheduled. Meet at rendezvous point."

Cody said something Tino didn't understand and continued walking.

Chapter Three

Isabella hid her surprise when Una asked her to drive them to the cave. She'd expected the cave to be within walking distance of the mesa. They drove back down the mesa and through Schmovi and Hano.

"You have cousins who live there and there." Aunt Una pointed to two different residences. "They would like to meet you if you stay long enough."

Family! She'd been dreaming of having cousins to play with her whole childhood. Now, she was an adult and playing was out of the question, but getting to know them would be just as good.

"I'll have to make time."

At the base of the mesa, Una instructed her to turn left. They followed a dirt road around the mesa. The highest speed she could go without the car sounding like it would jiggle to pieces was twenty miles an hour. Nearly an hour had passed when Una leaned forward in her seat.

"There. That wide spot." She pointed. "Pull over and we'll walk from here."

Isabella parked and scanned the area. Stepping out of the air-conditioned car in the arid July heat was like opening an oven ready for a batch of cookies. She moved to the back of her Jeep and opened the hatch, pulling out her vest and two bottles of water. She tucked the waters into her vest pockets.

"What is this?" Una fingered the hem of the fishing vest.

"It's my survival vest. I don't venture out without it." Isabella pulled a rolled-up canvas hat out of a pocket and placed it on her head. "Lead the way."

Una smiled. "You are prepared." She took the lead, following an easy-to-see trail that led up an arroyo. The pebbles scattered across the indention made from years of rain water had Isabella keeping a close eye on where she placed her feet to avoid slipping.

She stopped and scanned the horizon, noting the trail led them to the base of First Mesa, almost directly below Walpi. Anticipation of what she would see had her mind doing mental calisthenics. What could she uncover in this cave? Would it be unknown history? Or a foretelling of the future?

She hadn't been this excited about a discovery since her trip to Guatemala. That discovery had nearly killed her and had killed her mentor. That line of thinking was best left alone. She glanced at her aunt. She couldn't bear the thought her aunt would pull her into something as heinous and evil as the plot hatched by her mentor, Virgil.

Una was Hopi and a blood relative. Isabella loved her aunt and knew the woman loved her. No, her aunt would never lure her into a trap.

The side of the cliff was solid rock. There were the usual nooks and crannies that centuries-old rock developed from the elements, but she didn't see a cave entrance.

"Are you sure we're in the right place?" she asked.

Una smiled and walked up to the cliff. She spread her arms, hovered her hands over the stone, and walked sideways.

Isabella sucked in air as her aunt slid between the rocks and disappeared.

"How?"

She stepped up to the rock wall and slid her hands along the hot, solid rock, side-stepping as Una had. That's when she saw the crevice her aunt had slipped into. No wonder this cave hadn't been found before.

She expected to step into darkness, but cracks and crevices along the rock wall, allowed snips of dim light to filter into the cool, large open area.

"How did you find this?" Isabella dug in her vest and pulled out a small LED flashlight.

"I overheard some of our young people talking about the drawing they saw and knew it was somewhere no one had been before. I asked a niece who is friends with the group. She would not tell me at first because they feel it is their hideaway from their parents. But when I explained it could be an important discovery, she told me."

Isabella peered into Aunt Una's eyes. The sadness was not because the cave had been discovered. "Why did you really bring me here? It wasn't to see these drawings."

Una shook her head. "You will find this," she spread her arms, "of interest. I brought you here because of the group of young people. Two of the boys have been wearing expensive clothing and buying things for their friends." Her dark eyes held a glint of fury in them. "This was after a white girl, the daughter of a teacher, came up missing." Una wrung her hands. "I don't want to think bad of the young people, but I know some go down to the border and carry the drugs over. I now fear they are also kidnapping girls and selling them."

Isabella had a hard time thinking a peaceful Hopi would do anything as heinous as selling another human being. "How can you leap from drug smuggling to human trafficking?"

"I know the young people of this reservation. I work with them at the cultural center. There is a small group who always have more money than the rest. They are the ones who rarely come to ceremonies, who want out of here, but don't want to work the right way to do it. They want quick riches and adventure." Una walked over to a small boulder and sat. "These young people have fallen from their roots. They no longer belong."

She glared up at Isabella. "I will not allow them to dishonor the Hopi way of life."

"What do you want me to do? They won't talk to me." Isabella had her mind not only on the conversation but the interesting carving she found low on the wall. It appeared to be the top of more drawings.

"I have talked to the elders of Walpi. We need to purify our young. We need the Blue Star Kachina to appear and cleanse our people." She shook her head. "I do not know how it will come to be, but I had a vision, and you were standing beside the Blue Star Kachina."

"Una, I know only what I have studied of the Hopi and this is little because the Hopi allow so few white men to know their religion."

Una patted her back. "You will learn everything. You are special. Kele will talk with you. She is your cousin's daughter. It is her friend, Janelle, who is missing. And perhaps your man, Tino, can ask about human trafficking?"

Isabella had her doubts about all that her aunt was hoping she could accomplish. But the markings on the cave wall were different than any she'd studied on the Hopi. She dismissed her aunt's visions and concentrated on what she found under the sand.

Una slid off the rock to her knees beside where Isabella was digging the sand away from the wall.

"What have you found?"

"Some very early carvings. They were made before all this sand sifted into the cave." She handed Una a collapsible cup. "Use this to scoop away the sand."

"What do you not carry in that vest?" Una asked and scooped the silt away from the wall.

Isabella used her hands to pull the loose sand even farther back. Once they had cleared a ditch along the length of the wall, Isabella brushed the grit out of the carved lines and used her phone to take photos.

"These carvings are older than the ones on the top. See how they show the four directions and this…" Isabella traced a drawing of a person with his hands stretched upward, a leader. The details told of a kiva, a ceremonial place south of the Mesa. She sat back on her heels. With the photos, she'd be able to find this place. It would be a new discovery, she felt it in her heart.

Isabella grinned at her aunt. "I'm hungry, let's get dinner and then you can introduce me to Kele."

Una brushed her hands together. "My stomach had the same idea. Come."

~*~

Tino remained still and vigilant. Cody and the others had disappeared into the desert to wait for the drop. He had to admit, the group was well trained and good at what they did. When they said this was the drop site, he'd been skeptical. Now as the lights he'd spotted thirty minutes ago drew near, he realized the Shadow Eagles knew this land better than anyone.

Static from his walkie talkie disrupted his thoughts. "Stay where you are until the prey starts unloading." Jonny Crow's voice floated out of the box fastened to Tino's belt.

He didn't respond and knew the man didn't expect a response.

The SUV chugged over the last rise and down into the ravine. What appeared to be three young men jumped out, scanned the area, and pulled burlap wrapped bundles out of the SUV. Tino's muscles bunched, ready to move in, but Crow didn't give the signal. What is he waiting for? Tino rose. His duty was to capture the three unloading the SUV. He couldn't do that if they finished unloading and left.

"Stay. There are more coming."

The voice at his ear startled Tino. "Carajo!" He whispered. How had the man snuck up so easily?

Cody put a hand on Tino's shoulder. He crouched, pushing Tino down beside him.

"I don't see or hear anything," Tino whispered.

By the moonlight, he saw the narrowed glare on the other man's face.

He knew it was a warning to be quiet. They remained crouched, watching the SUV and three men.

His leg muscles were screaming along with his patience when a low rumble traveled across the quiet from the northwest. Staring in the direction, he caught a glint of moonlight on steel every now and then as the vehicle drove closer.

A lone coyote call echoed over the ravine.

Cody stood. "Now we go," he whispered and pointed to the three men looking in the direction of the approaching vehicle.

Tino followed the Shadow Eagle. They were aptly named. Not only did they have killer tracking skills and keen sight, but the man seemed to disappear into the desert shadows. Tino nearly tripped over Cody, who stopped behind a large cactus, hiding in the shadow.

The approaching vehicle's lights lit up the desert not five feet from their hiding spot. The rumble stopped and the lights blinked out.

Cody moved forward.

Tino followed in a crouched position.

The others stepped out in a circle around the three men and newest arrival.

"Hands in the air!" shouted Crow.

The latest arrival drew a gun. A shot rang out and the sting of gun powder assaulted Tino's nose. The drug trafficker's arm dropped to his side and the gun plopped to the ground. Red seeped onto his shirt near his shoulder as he howled in pain.

Cody lowered his rifle and walked in to help subdue the others who all fell to their knees with their hands behind their heads.

Tino followed. This was the Shadow Eagles' collar, but it was his job to take them back and interrogate them. He stared at the man clutching his injured shoulder. Anglo. He'd hoped to find a member of the Moreno family working this side of the border.

Turning his attention to the other three, Tino stamped down his surprise before the man he recognized turned an angry glare his direction. The young man's eyes flashed with hatred.

"You will die soon!" the young man shouted and started to raise to his feet.

Tank put a hand on Cruz Sanchez's shoulder, holding the man down on his knees.

"You two know each other?" Crow asked, walking up beside Tino.

"Sí, he was an informant for a corrupt DEA agent I worked with in Mexico City." Tino didn't like the thoughts racing through his head. He knew Rico was still alive, but had hoped the man was laying low after officials realized he was working both sides of the drug war. The idea the corrupt DEA agent could be running a drug cartel was not something Tino wanted to think about. The man had connections on both sides of the law. Catching Rico would be harder than taking down the whole cartel.

"Looks like you and this boy will have lots to discuss." Tank jammed the cuffs on Cruz and sat all of the runners in a circle, including the injured man.

The Eagles loaded the burlap bundles into the SUV while Tino took photos of the traffickers, the bundles, and the vehicles. Once the SUV was loaded, they shoved all the men in the back along with the bundles.

Everyone but Cody and Tank slid into the SUV. Crow drove it through the desert and out to a road. Two hours later they pulled into the Shadow Eagle headquarters on the reservation. Tino had contacted Lt. Melvin to meet them.

His superior stood at the door of the building as they led their captives inside.

"Good work," Lt. Melvin said to each Eagle.

Tino stopped in front of the lieutenant. "Sir, one of those men works for former DEA agent Rico Montoya."

Melvin studied him. "How do you know this?"

"My last DEA assignment in Mexico, I was working with Montoya to bring down Paolo Garza. In the end, we discovered that Rico was working both sides. He vanished before we could capture him." Tino had Isabella and another young woman to think about when Rico got away, but it still ate at his pride.

"You think this shipment may have been from Montoya and not Moreno?"

"Sí. Either that or Rico is working for Moreno, in which case, I would say he is trying to take over Moreno's cartel as he was trying with Garza."

Lt. Melvin looked over Tino's shoulder. "Use whatever means you need to find out what you need to know."

Chapter Four

Isabella drove her car away from Walpi. She'd spent three days on the reservation meeting family, visiting with the niece whose friend was missing, and discussing the markings she'd found in the cave with her aunt.

Anticipation tingled down her spine. Aunt Una worried she was making too much of the carvings she found in the cave below the mesa. The carvings represented kivas. Holy ceremonial sites. Isabella believed they were built and used at the start of the Hopi exodus to find a new home. Her aunt had an unsettling dream about the kivas and Isabella. Una argued with Isabella to take someone with her when she visited the area.

Isabella thought about putting in a call to her graduate assistant to meet her at the wildlife refuge where she believed the holy kivas resided. If she did find evidence it would be good to have a witness. However, Jason had taken over her two classes while she was away. She didn't want to endanger his grades and her job for a whim.

She'd be careful and make sure her camera had batteries. While she did tend to get sidetracked while researching, she was always careful when exploring.

Smiling, Isabella thought of her call to Tino. He'd sounded

distracted but had given her the name of his motel in Tucson and said he'd be there tonight when she arrived. She wanted to tell him about the possible holy site and the information Kele gave her about Janelle.

It had taken two trips to see her second cousin before Isabella had gained the girl's confidence and could ask about Kele's friend. At first, Kele had been scared to say anything. Fearful it would get back to the boys that Una felt had a part in the abduction.

Kele said she'd heard the boys say they took something to the border and exchanged it for money. She believed it was her friend. But fear of the boys kept her from going to the authorities. With Una vouching Isabella would get the information to the right people without using Kele's name, she finally broke down weeping and told what she knew.

Isabella would give all the information over to Tino. He was on the Border Patrol and would know where to start or who to give the information to.

During the five-hour drive, she ran the carvings on the cave wall over in her mind. They had similarities to Aztec and Maya drawings. Her mind was alive with all the possibilities this discovery could divulge. She'd spent years trying to find concrete proof the southwestern Native American people were related to the Central and even South American natives. These kivas could hold the clue she needed to piece her theory together and add truth to all the legends and stories.

She arrived at the motel at four-thirty.

Tino's Tahoe wasn't in the parking lot, which meant she didn't have a way to get into the room. Isabella scanned the motel. It was a typical motor inn. The doors to the rooms opened to the outside. No one really watched who came and went.

Did he say his room number? Isabella thought back to their conversation the night before. He hadn't mentioned a number, but he'd looked down on the pool. She got out, slung her pack with her computer over her shoulder, locked the car, and sauntered around the outside of the motel. She found the pool and looked up. There were four rooms directly above the pool with small balconies. She noted where the rooms were located in the building and went back to the parking lot.

Taking the metal stairway up to the second-floor walkway, she found the rooms and did her best to try and peek in the windows. A TV playing in one meant someone was in it. Not Tino's. The next room, she could see the bed unmade and woman's clothes on the floor. Not his either. The next door had a "Do not Disturb" sign.

She smiled.

This was Tino's room. He wouldn't want anyone messing around in his room when he was gone.

Isabella dug into the pocket on her pack and pulled out the lock picks WIA gave her when she joined. She stuck the L-shaped tension wrench into the keyhole and then plucked at the tumblers with the pick. She'd practiced with these items at home every spare moment she had and knew she'd be inside in the same amount of time it could take a sticky lock to open with a key.

Click.

She pulled out the tools and turned the knob. Tino's clean-scented shampoo met her as she stepped over the threshold. She'd picked the right room.

Her heart started galloping at the prospect of being in his arms and discussing all the information she'd learned since he'd left Phoenix.

The room was tidy. His belongings still packed in his duffel bag. Tino was always ready to make an escape.

Isabella set her pack on the end of the bed and wandered into the bathroom. His toiletries were arranged in his shave kit bag ready to be zipped shut and tossed in his duffel. The only place he kept his things put away like a normal person was their apartment. Knowing he felt safe and secure there brought her joy. The last ten or more years of his life, he'd spent too many days and nights fearful for his life and living on the adrenaline of revenge.

She used the facilities and wandered back into the other room. Pulling out her computer, she sat on the bed with her back against the headboard. Might as well do more research while she waited.

~*~

Tino pulled into his usual spot below his motel room door and drew in a deep breath, letting it release slowly. He had to get his head together and not show any of the agitation he felt. Isabella would arrive tonight. He didn't want her reading his anxiousness and grilling him for answers.

He'd thought the days of looking over his shoulder were done.

"Carajo!" He slammed his palm on the steering wheel. Rico will learn he's working border patrol and put a bounty on him. "Sitting here beating up the car will not change things."

He opened the door and grabbed his pack, dragging it out behind him. A shower, clean clothes, and he'd be ready for Isabella.

Tino climbed the stairs to the second floor and stopped. The "Do Not Disturb" sign hung crooked. Granted someone could have bumped it, but after learning Rico was behind one of the largest drug shipments the Border Patrol had ever captured, he wasn't taking any chances. He crouched down and peered at the window. There was a faint light glowing through the crack in the curtains.

Someone was in his room.

He slipped the room key out of his pocket, inserting it slow and quiet. With the patience and stealth he'd developed on the job, he turned the knob and pushed the door past the threshold. He set his pack to the side, shoved the door, and aimed his gun at the person on the bed.

"What do you want?" He growled.

The light bounced. A startled squeak echoed in the dark room.

"Who are you?" Isabella's breathy voice asked.

"Querida, how did you get in here?" Tino stood, grabbed his pack, and flicked on the overhead lights. "And why are you sitting in the dark?"

Relief the intruder was Isabella sent him crossing the room and pulling her into his arms. "It is not good to sneak into my room, I could have hurt you."

"I arrived early and didn't want to find somewhere else to wait." She burrowed into his embrace.

He would never in this lifetime get enough of her scent and warmth. When his heart opened to the intelligent woman in Guatemala, he had developed a need for her greater than anything he'd ever experienced. She was his narcotic.

Tino tipped her lips up and tasted their sweetness. He did not want to leave this earth before he had drunk his fill of Isabella. The thought drew him from the kiss.

"I need to shower. Find a nice place for us to eat dinner." He reluctantly released her. By the sparkle in her eyes she wanted an invitation to join him in the shower.

"I guess we could look up the restaurant afterwards."

She flung her arms around his neck. "I'd love to join you. Now that you're back, I need to get my clothes out of my car."

"Where did you park? I did not see your car." Tino walked to the door with her.

"I parked at the end. I drove the length of the lot looking for your Tahoe."

She gave him a quizzical glance as he pulled the door shut and captured her hand in his.

Isabella smiled at him. "Did you miss me so much you couldn't let me go for the few minutes it takes to get my stuff?"

He kissed her cheek and smiled. "Yes. Every time I leave you, I cannot wait to see you again."

They stopped at her Jeep. Isabella unlocked the back and grabbed the large backpack. Tino took it from her, noticing a map in the back seat folded to the southern part of Arizona. *She knows how to get to Tucson.*

"What is the map for?" he asked, watching her closely as she locked the car.

Her motions stalled only briefly.

"I planned to tell you what I found at the reservation after dinner." Her green eyes lit with excitement didn't waver from his gaze.

Whatever she'd found had her eager to share. Tino sighed and wrapped his arm around her shoulders. "Ezzabella, we have much to discuss but not until I have had a shower and we have eaten."

She leaned her head against him as they climbed the stairs.

Car tires screeched.

Tino stiffened and spun in time to see a dark colored car turn into the motel parking lot. He pushed Isabella ahead of him up the stairs.

"Go! Get to the room!"

He raced after her, inserting the key in the lock and shoving Isabella and her backpack into the room. Tino stood at the door watching the car pull up behind his Tahoe. *What are they waiting for?*

"What's going on?" Isabella asked, peeking over his shoulder.

"I do not know."

"Why did you shove me up the stairs if you don't know?" Her tone said she didn't believe him.

The dark car turned. Tino stepped inside, and closed the door, keeping an eye on them from behind the curtain. If Isabella hadn't been here, he would have confronted the people in the car. He didn't want her connected to him. If Rico found out she was here, there was no telling what the sadistic *pendajo* would do to her.

The car stopped at the office and a man went in.

"Carajo! Grab your stuff, we have to leave out the balcony." Tino grabbed his duffle and pack. Isabella stuffed her computer in her daypack as he shoved his toiletries in his duffle and drew the strings up.

"Hurry! Take your car and meet me two blocks down." He tossed all their bags over the balcony railing.

Isabella stepped over the railing, he grabbed her hands, dangling her closer to the small patch of grass. She looked down, and he released her hands. She dropped, rolled, and started picking up the bags.

He stepped over the railing. Grasped the vertical wrought iron rails, worked his way down the railing to the balcony, and let go, dropping and rolling.

Isabella rounded the corner of the building as he sprang to his feet.

Fists pounding on a door echoed through the opening above.

Tino ducked behind the bushes around the pool and made his way to an alcove that came out onto the main road. Stepping onto the sidewalk, he turned right and kept walking.

Tires crunched on the bit of gravel at the entrance to the motel. He didn't look back, praying it was Isabella. The vehicle drove on by, and he breathed a sigh of relief. Isabella's silver Jeep Compass blinked the brake lights. He kept on walking, watching her turn to the right and pull over another block down.

Tino continued at a calm steady pace, not wanting to catch any attention. He still wore the same camouflage clothing he'd worn the last three days. It wouldn't take a genius to know he hadn't had time to change.

His hand grasped the door handle of the Jeep and he slid in.

Isabella pulled into traffic.

"I think we should find a place to stay that is on the other side of town. Maybe grab something to eat along the way." Her tone was even. Her white-knuckled hands gripping the steering wheel the only giveaway the incident had affected her.

"I like the way you think. And how fast you can act."

"Are those men the reason you came through the door with your gun drawn?"

"Sí. We arrested four men at a drug drop three days ago. One of the men recognized me and I him. He was an informant for Rico."

Her intake of breath proved she understood the danger.

"How did he find out about you so soon?" Isabella reached over, placing her hand on his arm.

"They were put in holding cells in between interrogations. I am sure they have a way of sending messages between riff-raff." He stared at Isabella. "My greater fear is he will learn you are this close to the border."

Her face scrunched.

He knew that reaction. "Tell me you are only here for the night."

"Can we wait until we've had dinner and found a new place to stay?" She nodded toward a large fancy hotel. "I suggest we get a room in there. It has surveillance, valet parking, and restaurants. We won't have to go back out on the streets tonight."

Isabella drove to the breezeway of the hotel.

There was nothing Tino could say or do as a valet opened his door. Tino stepped out and walked to the back of the car. He grabbed his bags while Isabella grabbed hers.

"Getting a night of luxury before you go out hiking in the desert?" the valet asked, his gaze falling on their backpacks and Tino's camouflage clothing.

"Yes!" Isabella smiled at the man and handed her keys over.

Tino could only smile and follow her into the foyer. A valet stepped forward to take their bags.

"No, thank you," Isabella said, holding onto her packs with a tight grip.

Tino just scowled at the young man and he backed off.

"We'd like a room with a king bed, please." Isabella pulled out her wallet.

"Let me—"

She cut him off. "It's better this way."

He understood her meaning. His name wouldn't be in the system. He nodded and scanned the interior for exits. The years of undercover work had ingrained in him to always know your exits from a building.

"Let's go. We have a bird's eye view." Isabella picked up her pack and headed to the elevator.

Tino followed, smiling at her take charge attitude. When he first met her, he never would have dreamed he'd fall for the woman.

On the elevator her cheery expression dissolved. "This should keep you safe tonight. But what about tomorrow? You can't go back to your car, they're probably watching it."

"I'll call the lieutenant and see if I can get a ride back to the reservation tomorrow."

Her dour expression blinked to a high voltage grin. "I can take you to the reservation. I'm headed that way anyway."

His gut knotted. "Why?"

Chapter Five

Isabella knew Tino wasn't going to like her reason, but he had to understand and listen. "The cave Aunt Una took me to see had carvings on the wall that tell of a holy area with kivas that the Hopi used while on their exodus to the fourth world. I believe the kivas are in the Cabeza Prieta National Wildlife refuge."

"No! You cannot go so close to the border. There is as much drug trafficking there as on the reservation. Perhaps more because it is so isolated." Tino clutched her by her upper arms. "Querida, it is not a good idea when we know Rico is behind the drugs I am stopping."

The elevator slowly stopped, bounced once, and the doors opened.

Isabella picked up the pack she'd rested on the floor and walked down the hallway to their room. Inserting the card into the lock, she shoved the door open and dropped her packs on the bed. Her things sunk into the thick comforter.

Tino followed and by the frown furrowing his brow, he wasn't ready to drop the subject.

She wound her arms around his neck after he'd placed his bags on the floor. "Let's shower, eat, and then pick up this conversation." When his eyes held the dark stare she'd come to know as his determined expression, she employed what always worked.

"Please?" She pressed her lips to his and drew him into a deep, sensuous melding of tongues and lips.

Drawing back to get a breath, Isabella forgot why she was kissing Tino senseless. *If it's working on me it should be working on him.*

"Shower?" she asked, arching her brows and pulling her shirt over her head.

"You are a vixen," Tino growled as he followed her into the bathroom and shower.

After making sure the other was thoroughly clean and loved, they dressed and headed down to dinner in the expensive restaurant.

"The atmosphere here is what I needed after days spent in the desert." Tino picked up her hand and kissed her knuckles.

Shivers of delight danced up her arm and settled in her heart. "After all those years you spent in the jungle I would think you would prefer a quiet, less formal atmosphere."

"No. I craved feeling civilized. My job, what I do, makes me feel as barbaric as the animals I capture." His handsome face turned dark and stern.

Isabella turned her hand in his. "Don't think about that right now."

"Tell me about your latest discovery." Tino took a sip of the wine she'd ordered.

"Una actually called me to come to see the cave for another reason." She didn't want to bring up unpleasantness after she'd told Tino to think of things other than his work, but this felt like the right time to talk to him. Before he returned all his attention to work and staying alive.

"Really? Then why are you searching for a holy spot down here?" His eyebrow arched.

"Because I want you to deal with what she told me while I search for the kivas." She picked up her fork and took a bite of her salmon. Chewing gave her a moment to collect her thoughts.

"You want me to deal with what she told you? Why me?"

"Because it may have to do with human trafficking."

"That's the feds, F.B.I. and ICE, not Border Patrol." He set his utensils down. "What does your aunt know about human trafficking?"

"She knows very little. But she realized something was wrong and that my second cousin, Kele, might know something. Kele's friend, who is the daughter of a Caucasian teacher, is missing. My niece believes two boys, young men, really, from the reservation had a hand in her disappearance. But Kele fears saying anything to anyone. These two particular boys don't follow the beliefs and pacifism of the Hopi. They are only out for as much money as they can make. And not by legal means."

"How does this lead to human trafficking?" Tino took another sip of his wine as he watched her.

She had him hooked. "Kele heard the boys talking about delivering something to the border right after her friend went missing. And they were flashing lots of money. This friend is blonde, light skin tone, and petite. The exact type that gets bought and sold like cattle." She couldn't hold back the contempt she felt toward the men who made money dealing in sex slaves.

"Does she know where on the border?" Tino leaned forward.

"No, she only knows the two were at the school dance the night her friend went missing, and then they were back at school on Monday and waving around the money."

"Are the law and the parents looking at these two?"

"No, not really. According to Kele, they have alibis for their time over the weekend, but Kele and her friends didn't see them all weekend." She shook her head. "There isn't strong law enforcement at the reservation. And the parents are battling to get more exposure, but it's the usual—officials think she ran away."

"Was that something she'd done before?"

"No. Kele said her friend was excited about an upcoming school play she was auditioning for and had never talked about running away."

"I'll run this by the lieutenant and have him pass it off to other organizations."

"Thank you." She meant every syllable of the two words. Once Tino found an injustice, like her, he couldn't let it go. He would make sure something happened with this information.

"But they can't go to Kele for information. I promised no one would ask her more questions. She's fearful the boys will discover she gave me information and she'll be punished."

He sighed. "You know that is tying the officials' hands if they cannot talk to all the people involved."

"I know, but if I hadn't promised, she wouldn't have talked to me."

"You worked your charms on her." Tino smiled and pushed his plate to the center of the table. "Ready to go to our room?"

"Yes. We need to make plans to get you back to work tomorrow." She pushed her chair back, and Tino rose to hold it as she stood.

"I have plans for you, but they have nothing to do with my job."

His whispered innuendo sent her heart racing and her blood sizzling.

Once in the elevator, they moved into a heated embrace. The doors opened. She glanced at the digital number above the door and noted it wasn't their floor, then glanced at the couple getting on.

Isabella turned to Tino's side and buried her head into his shoulder. She didn't usually get embarrassed by her actions, but she knew the man as one of the trustees of her university and didn't want him recognizing her.

Isabella remained tucked against Tino until the elevator stopped at their floor. She continued to stay snuggled in his arms as they exited. Once the doors slid closed, she breathed a sigh of relief.

"Not that I mind you clinging to me, but why were you hiding?" Tino opened their room door.

"I know that man. He's a trustee at the University."

"So kissing me is against your school's policy?" His eyebrow arched as he started unbuttoning her blouse.

"No, but I was nearly devouring you. I didn't want word to get back to the University that I go to other cities and maul men in elevators."

His hands spread her shirt and cupped her bare breasts. She sighed. No matter how many times he touched her intimately, she remained astonished that he found her attractive. Her high metabolism left her thin and wanting for womanly curves and assets.

"I see." Tino maneuvered her to the bed, where he made quick work of undressing her. "How about you show me exactly how you maul a man."

Isabella grabbed him by the shirt front and pulled him down on top of her. He wanted mauled, but she was in the mood for slow lingering kisses and caresses. She set the stage by slowly undressing Tino and taking matters into her hands—literally.

"Querida, how could I go so many years not knowing your touch

38

when it pleases me so?"

She kissed his chest, releasing his shaft and sliding him down her body, so he could give her aching nipples some attention.

"Oh!" Sparks of delight shot to her extremities. "Perhaps you and I were destined to meet and those years you spent looking prepared you for…Oh! Your talents to…Tino, you need to…"

"Sí!" He moved down her body, kissing, leaving a hot, wet trail of kisses.

"No!" She twined her hand in his hair, tugging to get him to fill her not…

She shuddered and shattered as his masterful tongue teased her genital area.

Chuckling, he slid up and into her body, bringing even more shattering revelations to her body and mind. They moved in a fast-slow rhythm of a sensual dance, until both exploded, whispering endearments.

"Ezzabella, you are a wonder every time we make love." Tino kissed the vivacious woman he loved firmly on the lips and rolled her to his side. She'd told him to wait to discuss her traveling to the wildlife refuge until after dinner. Dinner was over, and he had to make her see heading back to Phoenix was the only safe thing for her to do.

He glided a hand up and down her arm as her fingers twirled in the hair on his chest. "I know you have made a wonderful discovery." She stiffened in his arms. "But right now with Rico working the border, it would be best to go back to the University and set up an exploration group to come down here and look for this holy site. It would be better for you to come back with a group and not be exploring the desert alone."

She pushed out of his arms and sat up, peering down at him. "I only have assumptions and my gut telling me this is something special. I can't justify the money to bring an exploratory team down here until I prove there is something more concrete."

Tino grasped her arms and rolled, dragging her on top of him. He cradled her head in his hands. "Then wait until I have some free days. I will go with you to get your proof." He kissed her, willing all his love and fear into the kiss.

Her body grew limp, and she returned the kisses. She will give in. She knows it is best. He deepened the kiss and rolled her underneath him. He still wondered at how this woman sparked his desire like no other when she was the complete opposite of all the women he'd dated in the past. Where all the other women were curvy and voluptuous, Isabella had only enough meat on her bones to hold her together and make her a strong adversary at martial arts.

They made love, again, and soon Isabella was asleep. Tino held her in his arms and prayed she didn't slip out during the night and head straight for trouble.

Chapter Six

Isabella woke knowing Tino would be hard to convince to let her go to the refuge. He was reluctant to take a shower, and she noticed he only did so after taking her car keys into the bathroom with him.

She smiled. He knew her too well. Once she was on the trail of a historical discovery, she had a one-track mind. Right now it was to talk Tino into accepting her traveling to the refuge.

Tino walked out of the bathroom. "Your turn. I'll order breakfast while you're showering."

She kissed him, breathing in his shampoo and shave cream. "I'm starved so order plenty." Once in the bathroom, she turned on the fan and the shower, then pulled her cell phone out of her clean clothes. She punched in her assistant's icon and waited for Jason to answer.

"I thought you were out of town?" he said immediately.

"I am. I need you to call me in twenty minutes and say you will meet me at Aljo, Arizona tomorrow." It was sneaky, but she knew there was no way Tino would allow her to continue if he thought she would be alone.

"Why?" Jason was going to be a fine anthropologist. He asked lots of questions.

"I need my fiancé to know I won't be going into the refuge

alone." She lowered her voice when it sounded like Tino walked toward the bathroom.

"So you want me to meet you there tomorrow? You know I'm already covering your two classes this week because you said you had family business."

"I don't want you to come. Just tell Tino that you are. That way he won't worry about me." She sighed. The women she'd had for assistants had been easier to work with. "Just call in twenty." She hung up from the call and jumped in the shower.

After the shower she dressed, braided her wet hair, and stepped out of the bathroom.

"I was beginning to think you were going to stay in there all day rather than discuss your plans." Tino sat at the desk with two trays of food.

Isabella sat on the end of the bed. Tino handed her a tray. She picked up a crispy piece of bacon and enjoyed the salty goodness.

"I called the lieutenant. He agrees we should leave my vehicle at the motel for a day or so, but he cannot spare anyone in this area to give me a ride to the reservation." Tino watched her as he took a sip of coffee.

"I said I'd give you a ride." Isabella picked up a forkful of eggs.

"If not for the investigation, I would rent a car and send you home. A rental will not be paid for by the agency, and I do not want to deal with getting the vehicle back on time." A stern expression, much like the first time they didn't see eye-to-eye, marred his handsome face. "I will have you drive me to the reservation headquarters. But after you drop me off, I want you headed straight back to Phoenix."

The sound of Native drums cutoff her reply. She grabbed her phone from her back pocket. "Hi Jason. Yes, Aljo, Arizona, tomorrow."

"What plans are you making?" Tino motioned for her to stop talking.

"Hold on a minute." Looking as innocent as she could muster, Isabella turned her attention to Tino. "What?"

"What are you planning with your assistant?"

"Jason will meet me at Aljo, the entry to the wildlife refuge, tomorrow. That way I won't be going in alone."

Tino narrowed his eyes and grasped the phone. He stared at the name then held the phone to his ear.

"Hello, Jason?" He listened. "Sí, I know you are Dr. Mumphrey's assistant."

Isabella's nerves bounced and shimmied. She hoped Jason didn't spill that she asked him to call her.

"You're meeting her at the refuge headquarters tomorrow?" His eyes remained skeptical. "Sí, good-bye."

Tino stared at her as he held her phone. "He had to go. He said he will call you later for more details."

Tino placed her phone on the desk and leaned toward her. "Querida, this is not a game. Rico tried to kill us before. He will not be happy until we are dead."

She knew the danger. She also knew she wasn't going to live her life in fear. "We'll be careful. I'm a trained agent. I know what to do in tough situations."

He placed a palm on her cheek. "But Jason does not know you are an agent and what does he know of dealing with the likes of Rico?"

Guilt slammed her in the gut like a round kick. "I promise if the refuge headquarters says there has been more than normal incidents of smugglers, we won't go into the refuge."

"This does not make me happy, but I will defer to your best judgment." He sat back in the chair and poked at his food. "Eat. You will have a long drive today if you plan to be at Aljo tonight. The roads on the reservation cannot be traveled as fast as the highways."

Isabella found swallowing her breakfast hard. She was withholding important information from Tino. She should tell him the truth or go to Phoenix and put an exploratory team together. But she couldn't deal with another of her projects being set to the side until there was more money to fund it. If she had proof they would find money.

They both ate only half the food Tino ordered. The conversation stayed on safe topics like, did she want him to drive to the reservation headquarters, and calling to have the car brought around.

~*~

Isabella watched the city drift behind them as they headed southwest on Highway 86. She didn't want to ride in silence, it gave her too much time to think about all that could go wrong with her plan and reflect on the man that had escaped in Mexico City.

43

"Do you work with a partner?" She twisted in the seat to watch Tino.

"Not a partner. On the reservation I work with a team of elite trackers from various tribes." He grinned and glanced her direction.

She smiled back. He knew that would get her attention. "Why didn't you tell me this earlier?"

"I haven't had a chance with all your news and the quick escape from the motel."

"Tell me about them. What are they called?" She twisted as much as the seat belt would allow to give Tino her full attention.

"I am working with an elite tracking team called Shadow Eagles. I have met four so far. The leader is Jonny Crow. A large, quiet man named Tank Halfmoon. Charlie Taft is an easy-going man. The last one, I spent the most time with, but feel I understand the least. His name is Cody Honani. They call him Badger."

Tingles skittered across Isabella's arms. There couldn't be more than one person with that name. "Really? Cody Honani?"

Tino stared at her. "Sí, that was how he said his name." He scowled. "Why?"

"That's Una's son. My cousin." She'd never been this excited to meet someone. Finally, she would get to meet a cousin she barely remembered from her grandmother's funeral. He was older. In his teens already when her family visited Walpi.

Tino shook his head. "He is not very friendly. He is sullen and wary."

"I'm sure he's only that way when on the job." Isabella couldn't believe it. She'd meet her adult cousin. He was an enigma on their one visit. He stayed to the edges of the family and aloof when she tried to talk to him. All the others were friendly and excited to meet her. She thought back to that short visit so long ago.

She remembered waking and hearing Daddy and Cody in an argument outside the house. The next day Daddy loaded her and mother into the car, and they left with only a good-bye to Una. She never saw Cody again. What could that argument have been about? Had her father tried to straighten Cody out about something? Or had Daddy offered to help them with money? Her uncle had died when Cody was twelve. Una had worked at the agency offices for an extra income ever since.

"You are quiet." Tino reached across, taking her hand in his and squeezing.

"Just trying to remember Cody. It was a long time ago that we met. It was my only other time at Walpi until a few days ago."

"Why have you not visited more?"

"When Mother married my dad she gave up her Hopi roots and became *kahopi*, no longer Hopi. Marrying my father and ignoring her roots, she became White in their eyes." She squeezed Tino's hand. "I've never heard her regret that decision. She is so analytical that she didn't understand the spiritualism that is a huge part of her people."

"You are analytical as well, but you also feel with your heart." Tino kissed her knuckles.

She smiled. The first time they met, Tino had discovered more about her than she knew herself. "True. Daddy says my heart will cause me unbearable pain someday."

"Is he referring to me?" Tino's defensive tone made her chuckle.

"No!" She thought hard. "I'm not sure what he means by it."

Signs for the Tohono O'odham reservation marked the boundary. Another thirty minutes and they pulled off Hwy 86 onto a dirt road. A short distance up the road Tino steered her Jeep into a parking lot with a single-story stucco building. The only signs revealing this was a police station were the two words above the nondescript door.

Isabella slipped out of the car before Tino could tell her to stay put. She stretched and scanned the parking lot and front of the building.

Tino opened the back of the car and pulled out his bags.

"We heard you lost your wheels but didn't expect you to come rolling in with a pretty lady." The wide grinning face of the Indian man walking toward them made Isabella smile back.

She held out her hand. "I'm going to take a stab and say you're Charlie."

He grinned even broader. "You mean that silent, wary man of yours talked about us?"

"I can be very persuasive when I want to know what he's been doing while away."

The man belly laughed and wiped the tears from the corners of his eyes. "I like your lady." He grasped her outstretched hand. "Charlie Taft."

Isabella started to introduce herself.

"Dr. Isabella Mumphrey," Tino said, giving emphasis to the doctor.

"Just call me Isabella," she said, winking and shaking hands with Charlie.

"I have my stuff, you can go now," Tino said, parking his bags at Charlie's feet and taking her by the elbow.

She deftly stepped around him. "I'd like to meet Cody. Where can I find him?"

Charlie's grin broadened. "He tell you about our young warrior and you want to meet him?"

Tino growled and Isabella couldn't hold the laughter gurgling in her throat.

"No. He's my cousin."

Charlie scanned her again and nodded slightly. "I see the resemblance."

But instead of saying where Cody was he turned to Tino. "You didn't say you knew Cody's family."

Tino's face darkened. He didn't like to talk about Isabella or his family to anyone. "I did not know he was related until I told Ezzabella his name."

Charlie turned back to Isabella. "He called in this morning asking for vacation. Not sure when he'll be back. Sorry."

She hadn't realized how much she was looking forward to seeing Cody until she'd learned he wasn't available. Her elation deflated like a blown tire. But her determination to continue her quest to find the ceremonial kivas remained strong and steadfast.

"Then I guess I'll be heading on." She walked to the driver's door.

Tino caught up to her before she could slip into the driver's seat. He settled an arm around her shoulders and leaned close.

"Querida," he said in a low voice for only her to hear, "call your assistant and head back to Phoenix. I fear for you until we can find and stop Rico."

She placed a hand on his cheek. "You need to worry more for you. You are the threat to him, not me. I'm going to look around. When I find what I need to get the university to back funding, I'll head straight to Phoenix."

He shook his head. "Do not investigate anything. Look for your kivas and get out of there."

Isabella pressed her lips to his, lingering in the sweet heat of a "see you later" kiss. She drew back and slid down into the driver's seat. "I will do my best to leave the area as quickly as possible."

She drove out of the parking lot, staring at Tino in the rearview mirror. He remained in the same spot until she could no longer see him. She understood his worry, but it was no different than if Daddy had called and sent her on a WIA mission. In fact, this was much simpler. All she had to do was get to the area where she suspected the kivas to be and document them.

Chapter Seven

Tino watched the Jeep disappear. He had a sinking feeling he was watching his future dissolve into the hot desert heat.

"You're lucky Cody didn't see you kiss his cousin like that."

Tino turned to find Charlie still standing in the parking lot.

"I don't think he will have much to say since the two have not seen one another in years." Tino walked over, picked up his packs, and headed to the door of the Tohono O'odham Police Station.

"She didn't look full blood. But the eyes and gestures showed they are family."

Charlie used a tone that offered Tino a chance to explain. But it wasn't his life to explain. It was up to Cody and Isabella.

He continued into the building, ignoring the man following him. In a small room off the hallway, he dropped his bags and continued to Jonny Crow's office.

The Shadow Eagle leader was in a conversation on the phone.

Tino continued on down the hall to the holding rooms. If he was lucky, he'd get more information out of the mule who'd recognized him.

Nodding to the officer watching the holding cells, Tino entered the hallway and stopped. Empty. He made an abrupt about-face and marched back to Crow's office.

"Where are the mules we brought in?" Tino didn't have time for pleasantries.

Crow leaned back in his chair, removing the reading glasses perched on the end of his nose. "DEA arrived yesterday after you left. They hauled the lot of them off."

"Carajo!" Tino slammed his fist against the doorjamb. Once DEA started interrogating them, he'd never learn where Rico was hiding.

"You have been taking this bust personally. Care to tell me why?" Crow crossed his arms, studying Tino.

The Shadow Eagles had a right to know they were in the middle of a vendetta, but he still had a hard time sharing with anyone other than Isabella. He didn't want to drag anyone else into his own little war, but he needed the help of this man to keep any other mules who knew him under wraps.

"The mule, Cruz Sanchez, knows me from my days as a DEA agent. A rotten DEA agent used Sanchez as an informant, and it looks like is now using him to move drugs. My last mission, in Mexico City, I exposed Rico Montoya as a corrupt agent. He has sworn to kill me and my fiancée who was also in Mexico City at the time. Last night three men broke into my motel room."

Crow leaned forward. "Did you apprehend them?"

Tino shook his head. "No. My fiancée was there, and I did not want her in the middle. We left before the men arrived. We passed by the motel on our way out of town. They were waiting for my return."

"Where is your fiancée now?"

Crow's concerned expression eased a bit of the gnawing dread in Tino's gut. Then he remembered where she was headed and couldn't bite back a Venezuelan curse.

Crow's eyebrows shot up.

"She is headed to the Cabeza Prieta Wildlife Refuge."

"That's next to the border. Didn't you tell her of the danger for her being so near the border?" Crow's stunned gaze bore into him.

"Sí, I told her. She is hard to dissuade when she believes she is on the trail of ancient discoveries."

"What does your woman do?"

"She is a doctor of anthropology. Her aunt took her to a cave with carvings that Isabella believes are linked to kivas hidden in the refuge." Tino ran a hand over his face. "She becomes single-minded when she is on the trail of her ancestors."

"Your fiancée is Indian?" Crow's expression became more animated.

"She says a quarter Hopi, but her aunt is full." Tino shrugged. It had never mattered to him so he hadn't contemplated the discrepancy.

"That must be why Cody was so interested in you." Crow nodded and sat back in his chair.

"I did not tell him who my fiancée is." Tino frowned. "Unless his mother had said my name…" That must have been why the man had watched him so close and been so aloof.

It was Crow's turn to frown. "Why would Cody's mother know you?"

"She is the aunt who sent Isabella on this foolish hunt." If he had Isabella's aunt's phone number he would call her right now and ask her to stop her niece.

Jonny Crow smiled, showing his wide white teeth. "You tell good stories. Are you sure you don't have some Indian in you?"

Tino shook his head. When would he find someone to understand how serious it was to find Rico?

"I am going to call a friend at DEA and see if they learned anything from the mules. I do not want to be surprised by Rico." He spun about and found Cody standing next to Charlie listening intently. Perfect! All he needed was to have Isabella's cousin lay into him for not stopping her.

Tino entered the hall. Cody stalked toward him, motioning for them to step into an empty office. Tino squared his shoulders and strode into the room, shutting the door behind him. He didn't need the others to hear this conversation.

Cody stepped forward. "I knew who you were when you joined us. My mother had mentioned your name."

Tino nodded. He'd figured as much.

The man's eyes darkened with anger. "I will not have another non-Hopi, hurt my family. Charlie says you and Isabella are close. I can't change who she loves, but I can make sure she isn't hurt."

"I will not hurt Isabella. But she is in danger. Your mother told her of a cave, and she found carvings that have her headed to the Cabeza Prieta Wildlife Refuge down by the border. We, Isabella and I, revealed a rogue DEA agent last year. I have reason to believe he is part of one of the cartels running drugs through this reservation. He is also out for revenge against myself and Isabella."

Cody stared so long without uttering a word, Tino wondered if the man had fallen asleep with his eyes open.

Finally, the man spoke. "My mother told me she feared for Isabella. Not because of this man you talk about but because of a dream she had." Cody crossed his arms and sat on the edge of the desk. "As soon as my mother told me, I asked for vacation days. I'll go to the refuge and keep track of Isabella."

Relief welled in Tino's chest. With her cousin looking out for her, he could continue to gather information to bring down Rico and keep her safe.

He held a hand out to Cody. "I would be forever in debt to you for watching over Isabella. Your cousin is not easy to keep up with or watch over. I have been with her on two occasions when we were in many perilous situations. She can fend for herself most resourcefully, but she is too trusting."

Cody shook hands. "She sounds like my mother. Too trusting."

The dark brooding mask Tino had witnessed on the man's face before reappeared.

"I'll leave immediately and catch up with Isabella. I'll call and let you know I've made contact." Cody strode to the door. He turned back before he opened the door. "I can see you care for Isabella. I will do my best to keep her from harm."

Tino nodded. "She is my heart."

~*~

Isabella pulled into the parking lot of the Cabeza Prieta Wildlife Refuge office. A niggling sense of guilt shimmied across her shoulder blades as she sent a text to Tino saying she arrived at the office and was filling out the paperwork to enter the refuge. Omitting whether her assistant was with her or not. She didn't get a response which meant Tino either was out of range of a cell tower or had his phone turned off.

She didn't hesitate to sign the Hold Harmless Agreement saying she understood the dangers and wouldn't sue them if drug runners caused her harm. With the paperwork filled out, she climbed back into her car and headed to the refuge following a highway that cut through the Organ Pipe Cactus National Monument and into the southeastern corner of Cabeza Prieta. This route would put her practically on the Mexico border on a dirt road called El Camino Del Diablo, but the area she wanted to hike was in the Agua Dulce Mountains in the southeast corner of the refuge.

This expedition was falling into place. Only two days before no one was allowed in this area due to the impressive pronghorn program that kept the public away from the breeding grounds of the Sonora Pronghorn from April to mid-July.

According to her research, the carvings, and the notes she had on the travels of the clans, the Agua Dulce Mountains had to be the area of the ceremonial kivas from the cave at First Mesa.

Once Isabella crossed into the refuge, she drove a few more miles on El Diablo before finding a dusty pull-out. She studied the map given to her at the office. This road was blocked a couple miles west and where it veered down close to the border. Only Border Patrol was allowed in this area. Now would have been a perfect time to have Tino with her. He could have helped her through the blockade.

She shrugged. So far she'd managed to puzzle out difficult situations. This one was easier than previous predicaments.

Isabella folded the map open to the corner of the refuge where she wanted to go and shoved it into her survival vest pocket before exiting the vehicle. At the back of the Jeep, she shoved her day pack into her larger backpack along with eight quarts of water. The ranger at the refuge office made it clear water was an essential to walk about in the desert in July. There were designated water holes for the animals but it was preferred that humans stay away from those areas if at all possible.

Isabella shrugged into her backpack, locked the car, and walked southwest through the scrub brush and cacti, heading straight for the Agua Dolce Mountains. The sun beat down on her shoulders and canvas hat as she trudged through the sandy soil. She skirted areas with small circular mounds around quarter-sized holes not wanting to risk gathering ants on her shoes and socks.

She tried to keep her sight trained on the mountains ahead of her as she walked through washes, but not watching the ground could result in a sprained ankle. Holes the size of rabbits and large enough for a coyote littered the ground. Twenty feet away she spotted an owl standing near a hole. Many creatures of the desert lived underground where it was cool and shaded from the hot sun.

Plans to hike to the base of the mountain by dark didn't look promising. The sun was setting. Gold, yellow, and orange heralded the deep blue of night over the desert. Sitting in the middle of the desert without a way to hide wasn't an appealing thought. The drug smugglers and illegals moved at night when it was cooler and less chance of being caught. She didn't want to be stumbled over.

Isabella kept on walking using the twinkling stars and the moon to light her way through the shadowy saguaro and cholla cactus. An owl hooted not far from her path. She stopped and scanned the area. Instead of finding the owl on the ground, the glint of moonlight off its eyes when it blinked, brought her gaze up to a hole in a saguaro.

She stopped, pulled an energy bar from her pack, and watched the owl as she ate. The mountains grew closer, but she still had another thirty minutes to get to their base. At least now that the sun had set, she didn't have the scorching rays beating down on her. The evening wasn't cool, but cooler.

Shoving the wrapper into the empty vest pocket reserved for trash, she continued on, dodging cactus, making a straight line for the mountains in front of her. As the evening cooled, creatures came to life. A rabbit hopped across her path and the yip of a coyote sent a shiver down her spine. During the daylight she'd felt alone, now the desert came to life and she listened to the sounds.

She stopped.

The sound of a small engine invaded the tranquility of nature's sounds. Turning slowly, she pinpointed the direction. It was to the east of her. Hopefully, it stayed in the distance. But to be safe, she dug into her pack and pulled out the sheathed knife she took from a man in Guatemala. The fourteen-inch knife had been hidden in her pack to avoid explaining such a weapon.

Holding the carved handle as she slid it into the outside pocket alongside a water bottle steeled her confidence. Shouldering her pack, she continued with renewed vigor. There would be a place near the base of the mountain to relax and be hidden from entities who would do her harm.

Chapter Eight

Tino cursed and paced the parking lot at the Tohono O'odham Police Station. Cody hadn't contacted him about catching up with Isabella and both their phones went straight to voice mail.

He should have never let her go. He cursed again and stared up into the night sky. A star fell from the darkness and he wished harder than he'd ever wished for anything in his life. "Please keep Ezzabella safe."

"Konstantine, grab your gear, we have word of immigrants stranded." Crow walked toward his truck.

There wasn't time to worry about Isabella. It was his job as a border patrol officer to help the stranded UDAs, undocumented aliens, and stop the drug traffickers. He had to pray Isabella found her information and returned to Phoenix without incident.

~*~

Isabella slid her pack to the ground behind a large boulder and settled next to it. The last half mile had felt like three miles. The sand had been deep, but she didn't want to veer from her course and run into the vehicle that had remained on the perimeter of her hearing.

She drank half a bottle of water, then pulled out dried cherries and jerky. Her stomach had rumbled the last fifteen minutes. Times like this she wished she didn't have such a high metabolism and could go for days without food like Tino.

Now that she was concealed behind the boulder, she pulled out her small LED flashlight and studied her notes and the detailed topographical map she'd printed before heading to the refuge. She was north of where she believed the kiva resided. There was mention of a life-giving spring in the vicinity of the kiva.

From the map it looked like there were several ravines and washes she could follow to get to the other side of the mountains.

"What are you doing?"

The gruff voice and interruption of the natural sounds jolted her to her feet, with her hands in defense pose and her feet balanced to throw a kick. Since Guatemala she'd found what she'd once thought of as good exercise had become her most lethal weapon. She thanked her Daddy for suggesting she take Taekwondo lessons.

Her eyes became accustomed to the darkness and she found the interloper. A broad-shouldered man slightly taller than her five ten. His facial features were shadowed.

"Who are you?" she asked in a stern tone not relaxing a bit.

"I'm the person getting you the hell out of here." The man stepped closer.

She let loose with a round kick. In a blink of an eye her backside came down hard onto the sand. She scrambled to her feet. Once up, she realized the man wasn't making a move to attack. He stood with his feet apart, his arms crossed over his chest.

Isabella pushed wayward strands of hair out of her face and studied the man. Who could he be? Someone sent by Rico? Fear slithered through her veins, sending a shiver through her body. The sadistic man would like nothing better than to use her as bait to lure out Tino and kill them both.

Her foot touched her pack. In one swift move she bent and came up with the knife in her hand. "I don't know who you are, but I'm not going anywhere with you." She pointed the tip of the fourteen-inch, broad blade at the intruder.

The man shrugged. "Tino said you would put up a fight. I am prepared."

Her suspicions sprouted anew at the mention of Tino. "Tino sent you?" Why would he send this man? How did she know this wasn't a ploy to get her to go along?

"Yes. He said you wouldn't be easy to persuade to leave whatever you were doing." The man uncrossed his arms and crouched. "Isabella, you're safe with me. I'm Cody Honani."

Her legs crumpled and she sank to the sand, stabbing the knife into the ground beside her. Even though she was relieved to know this man was family, she had to be sure. "What is your mother's clan?"

White, even teeth gleamed in the moonlight as he smiled. "Fire."

She nodded. "When did your mother's mother die?"

The smile vanished. "Twenty years ago my *soi*, grandmother, was put into the earth."

Isabella's chest ached. This was Cody, her cousin. She threw herself at him, hugging him tight.

"Hey!" He peeled her arms from around him and set her away. "What was that for?"

"I've wanted a cousin to talk to my whole life and now here you are, when I could use a friend." She settled back against her pack and held out the package of jerky to him. "Want some?"

He didn't hesitate to pluck a piece of the dried meat from the package. Biting the end off, he chewed then waved his hand. "This is crazy."

"What?"

"You out here alone. There are drug traffickers and UDA's out here that would steal your pack and leave you for dead and that's the good news. You could find yourself beat up or used before they decide to leave you for dead."

Now, she not only had Tino lecturing her, she had Cody. Maybe not having close family was a good idea. "I know the risks. But if I find what I think I will, it will all be worth it. Our ancestors help us to see who we are and give us clues to our future."

He took another bite and chewed as he studied her.

Something about the intensity of his gaze made her uneasy. What was he seeing? Thinking?

"Water?" She held a bottle out to him.

"Got some." He pulled a pack and an assault rifle into view.

"Are you expecting trouble?" She raised an eyebrow.

"There is always trouble in this part of the world." He unscrewed the top to his water and took a long drink.

She had to feel him out and see if he planned to drag her kicking and screaming back to Tino or if she could get him to help her find the kiva.

"How did you find me?" She plucked another piece of jerky and chewed on it, waiting.

"Mother called last night. She was worried about you running around down here alone. I called in some vacation time, planning to catch up to you after I took care of paperwork. Then I overheard Tino telling my boss you were headed here today. I jumped in my pickup and followed your tracks."

Isabella laughed. "Followed my tracks! How could you follow my tracks on a highway?"

He raised his water bottle to his lips, swallowed, and peered at her. "I knew you were headed to this refuge. I asked at the wildlife office to see your papers. You had to fill out where you were going. I came the most direct route, which I knew you would take in your haste to get to something that has been hidden for hundreds of years."

She half snorted, half laughed. "How did you know I would be in a hurry?"

He shook his head slightly. "You have rushed everything in your life. Grade school, high school, college, your masters' degree—everything, perhaps even Tino."

"How do you know all of this? From Mother? Aunt Una?" She took a defensive tone, not liking that he had brought up a subject she had wondered about herself. Had she jumped into Tino's arms because he was the first man to show an interest in her?

He shook his head. "I've been keeping my eye on you little sister."

Her head jerked, snapping her gaze to his. "What do you mean little sister?"

His wide shoulders rose and fell. "All girls, cousins and such, from my mother's side are my sisters. All boys are my brothers."

"Oh." She knew that, but for some reason, it hadn't sounded like he was referring to her in that way. It had felt more familial. She studied his features. His eyes, nose, and cheeks reminded her of looking in the mirror. His face was a bit broader, but they had many similarities, much like her aunt, his mother.

"If I had siblings I wonder if they would have mirrored me as much as you do." Her smile wavered when he flinched.

His dark eyes peered into hers as if searching.

"What do you want to know?" she asked, beginning to think he had something he wanted to tell her.

"You're stronger than I imagined you would be." His gaze remained steady, unblinking.

"And you're nicer than I thought you'd be." Two could play this game.

"Why? I never was mean to you." His gaze narrowed, and his chin jutted out in defiance.

"I heard you arguing with Daddy when we were at the reservation for grandma's funeral." She squared her shoulders and continued. "You stormed off, and Daddy made us leave early. I figured you said something mean about his being Caucasian and shouldn't be at the ceremony."

His handsome face glowered, and his eyes sparked with rage. "I wasn't mad at him because of who he was, I was mad at him because he wouldn't tell you the truth and seek justice for our mother."

Her thoughts tumbled and stumbled over one another. "What do you mean tell me the truth? Why should he seek justice for your mother?"

"Not my mother, our mother." His gaze bore into hers. "My mother is also your mother."

Isabella used the full moon's glow to stare into his eyes. The dark orbs reflected intense honesty and belief.

"I don't..." What did he mean his mother was her mother? Thoughts and images swirled in her mind. Her childhood. Her mother's distant emotions. Then the intense connection she felt hugging Una. Could it be? But how? Why?

"How is your mother my mother?" Her hands shook. She clasped them together in her lap and studied the face in front of her. That would explain their similarities much clearer than cousins. It would also explain her connection to Una.

"The truth is ugly. Are you sure you want to hear it?" The venom in his words, drew her even deeper into wanting to know how he could claim they were siblings.

"Yes. No." She gathered her courage. If he was telling the truth she needed to know. "Yes, I want to know. I've felt an outsider in my family my whole life. I need to know the truth no matter what." Her words were said with more conviction than her heart held. Her belly quivered with fear of the unknown. Was learning the truth better than wallowing in the self-doubt and insecurity of the family she knew?

Cody peered into her eyes. "Are you sure?"

"If you swear you're telling me the truth, then I need to hear it." Even as she said the words and knew she had to hear, her stomach knotted.

Cody's concerned face became stern. "I have never told anything other than the truth. What I tell you is the truth as I know it and as it was told to me. When I was five my father and mother delivered my mother's weaving to a store in Phoenix. I stayed with my cousins at Hano. On the way home, Father was tired and swerved. A county deputy pulled them over and said he would give my father a drunk driving violation and throw him in jail without bail if my mother didn't give her body to him." The rage in Cody's voice tore at her heart.

Isabella reached out to him, taking hold of his hand.

"My father refused to allow this. The cop beat him and shoved him in the police car. My mother didn't want my father to be taken to jail for something he didn't do. In those days, as now, we battled with prejudice and injustice. She offered herself to the officer." He looked away as a tear trickled from the corner of his eye.

Her heart tore for Una. To be raped was more violent than to be killed. The victim lived with the reminder and fear their whole life. And to allow it to save another…She swallowed the lump of emotion bobbing in her throat.

"The Hopi way does not believe in violence, but she allowed that man to take her body, so she would have her husband. Her way of life." He wiped at the tears on his cheek.

"When she realized she was pregnant, she had no choice. We do not take the life of innocents and if the officer found out, he would have made sure you did not live."

Anger scorched her lungs and her thoughts. The man violated Una and then would have made sure the child he'd conceived did not live. Nausea snuffed out the anger. Her life began with an act of violence and hatred. How could Una look at her?

Cody continued, "Mother is a healer. She made up the story her sister was pregnant and not well. She would stay with her until the child was born. When you were born, Ana and Theodore took you in as theirs. Mother came home and missed you every day."

Cody turned his weary gaze back to her.

Isabella saw the truth in his eyes. He hurt for the past his mother endured and the secrets he had to keep. She ached for all of them. Cody, his father, their mother, her mother, and Daddy. The truth they kept from her, and the distance her birth had put on the whole family.

He cleared his throat. "When my father was dying he told me never to allow another man to take what was mine. Just because you are Hopi does not make you weak." A sardonic smile stole his good looks. "His death is when I learned the truth I had a sister, and why I joined the military. I wanted to be strong and know how to take care of your biological father should I meet him one day."

Her insides quivered as she asked, "And have you? Met him?"

He released her hand and turned his face away. "It's hard not to run into him periodically. He is now a sheriff."

"Does he know who you are?" she asked softly. Her thoughts swirled and tumbled in her head. Cody had no reason to lie to her. The anger and resentment he felt toward the man who raped his mother hadn't soured his view on law enforcement or he wouldn't be a Shadow Eagle.

She stared into his eyes. It would be cruel to tell her this if it wasn't true. Everything she'd ever heard about Cody he wasn't cruel. He cared for family. She had to believe he told the truth.

"No, I've been careful to hide my emotions around him. I don't want him discovering you exist. You would be a problem he would make go away. He is still as corrupt as all those years ago. Only now he has more authority."

"So you won't tell me who he is?" Did she want to know? Part of her didn't wish to ever see such a cruel man. Then there was the part of her who could not let an injustice go. Could this inherent trait reside in her due to her start in life? She wouldn't need Cody to give her the man's name. There weren't that many sheriffs that Cody would come in contact with in his line of work. She would find them all and one by one deduce which was her biological father. She had no familial pull to know him, knowing how he took her mother to conceive her. But she would like to keep tabs on his dealings and bring about justice for her mother and herself.

She was, however, curious. "Is he married? Does he have children?"

"After what he did to our mother, who knows how many bastards he's sired." Cody winced. "I am not referring to you, my sister. You are of our mother's people. You are pure of heart."

Understanding Cody's anger was like understanding the revenge Tino harbored. She felt his deep-seated need to avenge his mother…their mother, but he also held life dear. It was the Hopi way.

"Do I have half-siblings?" she asked.

"I only know of one child from this man's marriage. He is as bad as his father. But while his father pretends to be legal, Wesley does not hide his illegal involvement. His mother is an invalid from a fall."

Cody wasn't painting a very pretty portrait of her biological father or half-brother. She'd focus on knowing Una was her mother and Cody her brother. Something she wouldn't be able to acknowledge beyond the two of them, but she now knew why she'd felt so out of place with Mother and Daddy. They had raised her out of duty. Daddy had loved her with the veracity of a biological father, he just didn't have time for her. His career came first. Mother had remained aloof. Would she have been a better mother to a biological child? Somehow, she didn't think so. Her mother was too analytical. How Daddy brought out her passionate side had intrigued Isabella since she was old enough to know what it was and see it in her mother.

A sweet sadness filled her chest. Tino brought out the passion in her as Daddy brought out the passion in her mother. Having a man in their life that loved them completely was a trait they shared. Yet while her mother showed passion for Daddy, Isabella was able to feel passionate about everything in her life, including her reserved mother.

"How are you feeling? I just turned your world upside down." Cody put a hand on her shoulder.

"I want to believe you because deep down it feels right knowing my biological mother is Una. But why didn't she turn the deputy in? Why hide the pregnancy? No one would have known that I wasn't conceived of your father and mother." The fact her mother more or less shunned her was frustrating.

Cody shook his head. "It would have been mother and father's word against a deputy. Who do you think the authorities would believe?"

"But they could have found others he'd forced himself on and made a case." She believed in fighting and digging for the truth.

"My parents lived on a reservation. They lived off the money from mother's weaving, the government payments, and what father could grow. They didn't have money to fight."

"What about going to the counsel?" She couldn't believe there hadn't been a way to bring about justice. "Justice can't work if people don't come forward."

Cody laughed. "Sister, there is only justice for those who can afford it." He waved at her pack and rolled out yoga mat. "You don't know how hard it is to feed and clothe a child when you have so little. I had a wonderful, loving childhood, but I owned more clothing as a solider than I did growing up. You were lucky to be raised by Theodore and Ana."

"I may have had things, but I never felt like I had their complete love." She dropped her gaze to her hand gliding back and forth over the yoga mat. "I would have rather had less things and more love." Her heart, while feeling slighted for having missed out on a life with Una and Cody, was lighter, freer. Many questions she'd dissected to death over the years now made sense. She'd been as analytical about her life as her mother—fake mother—had been about everything in her life.

"Your mother, our mother, could have kept me. How would the man have ever found out?" She wanted to believe what her parents, Una, Mother and Daddy, thought they were doing what was best, but it hurt no one had told her the truth.

"You've seen yourself in the mirror. Do you look full blood Hopi?" He shook his head. "There would have been questions. How would mother have answered without someone finding out the truth? It was better to have Aunt Ana take you in."

"I should have been told the truth long ago. I don't know who to be the most angry with." Learning who her true family really was had her off balance, but the fact no one in her life cared enough to tell her the truth hurt with a depth of betrayal she'd never experienced before.

Cody placed a hand on her shoulder. "I'll always tell you the truth. I wanted to tell you the truth when grandmother passed."

She squeezed his hand on her shoulder. "My job is dealing with the truth and appreciating its worth." Which brought her thoughts back to why she was sitting in the middle of a desert.

"Tomorrow, are you going to help me find the holy kiva or are you going to wait for me here?"

"I am going to throw you over my shoulder and haul you back to Phoenix." He leaned forward. "This isn't a safe place for anyone, but right now with some vengeance-seeking drug dealer out to take down Tino and you, this is even more dangerous for you."

Shamutz! Tino had told him about Rico. She'd hoped he hadn't heard that bit of unsavory information. "All the more reason for you to come along with me. Two of us searching will be faster and safer." She grinned to project more confidence than she felt. When she'd started out she'd only thought of getting the information, now with her burly brother insisting she return, the threat of danger felt real.

"We'll discuss it in the morning." Cody batted his pack a few times, then leaned back and pulled his hat over his eyes.

Isabella dug around for her toothbrush. She picked up a bottle of water and walked away.

"Where you going?" Cody asked.

"To brush my teeth and think without you stomping on my thoughts." She stalked farther away than she'd planned. His keeping watch only made her more determined to make sure she didn't get carted back to Phoenix. Why would traffickers be up in the mountains? Across the flat expanse of desert was the quicker, easier course to haul things, not going through the ravines and passes of the mountains.

Thinking of the traffickers, her thoughts circled to the vile man Cody said fathered her. Her heart ached for Una and what she must have experienced that night. But why send me away? Isabella dropped to her knees, hugging her arms tight around her torso. She wanted to cry for the missed opportunity of the loving childhood she'd always dreamed of, but the tears trickling down her cheeks were for her biological mother, who'd suffered so much.

Chapter Nine

Tino spent the night hauling in ten UDAs. By the time he'd finished the paperwork and had them in a holding cell, he was ready to drop onto a cot in the back room and sleep until they received another call or he started his shift.

"Konstantine, you have a call." Tank leaned against the door frame, filling the opening.

Tino ran a hand over his face and nodded.

"Line one," Tank said, and shoved out of the doorway.

Tino picked up the receiver and punched the blinking light on the phone with his index finger. "Konstantine."

"We just broke Cruz. Rico has already taken over one cartel and is planning a trip to the states to do business with another. Word is he plans to cross the border and meet with buyers."

Hearing his contact at DEA say the news he'd been dreading, bile rose in Tino's throat. He swallowed, shoving his anger and fear for Isabella back down in his gut to sour. "Did Cruz elaborate on whether Rico knows where I am?"

The silence told him more than any words could.

"You might want to take a vacation. According to Cruz there is a reward to the man who brings Rico your head. And I don't think he meant attached to your body."

Tino swore. "What about Dr. Mumphrey. Did he mention her?"

"No, he only had colorful descriptions of what was to be done to you."

Muchas gracias, Dios. Tino sent up a reverent prayer. "I do not care what they wish to do to me as long as they do not harm Dr. Mumphrey. Rico's anger must remain on me and no one else. Thank you for calling." He replaced the phone and shuffled down the hall to the cot.

Where were Isabella and Cody? He'd tried both their phones several times during the day. They had to be away from any cell towers, which could be anywhere in the Cabeza Prieta refuge. He placed an arm over his eyes to hide from the sunlight streaming through the window and to hide his thoughts from anyone passing by.

He must tell the others about the bounty on him. It wouldn't be fair to go out in the reservation with the Shadow Eagles without the team knowing he was a wanted man and they could get caught in the crossfire.

~*~

Isabella woke with a kink in her neck and cold, stiff muscles. The stars still shone in the sky, but the moon was descending toward the horizon. She rotated her head this way and that, stretching her neck muscles and waking her mind.

Cody's breathing remained slow, even, and deep. He'd pulled a flannel shirt out of his pack at some point. It draped across his body like a blanket. How much sleep did he get while working? That he slept so sound when he thought she was in danger meant he was either very tired or not as worried about her as he'd made out.

She'd caution on the side he made things sound worse to get her to go back with him. Not happening. Stretching, her toes skittered pebbles across the hard ground. The sound resembled a herd of cattle to her, but Cody didn't flinch.

She stood, picked up her pack, making as little noise as possible, and walked away from the sleeping man on tiptoes.

Once she'd put a good distance between them, Isabella quickened her pace and didn't watch as closely where she placed her feet. She wanted distance between them before Cody realized she'd continued without him.

Daylight washed down into the ravine she'd been traveling in for the last three hours. The easy to travel washout ran north and south. This had made her decision to remain in the ravine and follow the route southward—toward the area she believed the kiva would be found. She stopped, took a drink, and consulted her notes. The kiva was near a spring. Once she made her way through the highest mountains, walking along the ridges would give her a better vantage point to see a spring.

Isabella set her pack down and pulled out an energy bar and dried fruit. She was already hot and soon the sun would beat down into the ravine baking her. The best strategy would be to walk on the shadiest side of the ravine and take shelter from the sun during the hottest part of the day. Sleep a little and then resume walking when there was shade again.

With her plan in place, she donned her pack and continued along the shady side of the ravine. Her legs became rubbery when the crevice she followed started ascending toward the mountain peak. Checking her topographical map, she discovered there was only one way to the other side. Over the top.

"Now would be a good time to take that mid-day break." She unscrewed the lid on her second jug of water and wiped at the sweat beading her brow and trickling down the back of her neck.

"Now would be a good time to get a spanking."

She started at Cody's deep, angry voice. Looking back the way she'd come, there stood her brother, his hands on his hips, glaring at her.

"Why the hell did you sneak away from me?" He dropped his pack next to hers and lowered his body to the ground on the other side.

"I'm not going back to Phoenix until I've satisfied my curiosity about the kiva." She offered her water bottle to him.

He took it, swallowed several times, and handed it back. His dark brown eyes peered straight into hers.

"What makes you think I wouldn't help you find the kiva?"

Her mouth dropped open. Many reasons came to mind, but she said, "You didn't seem amenable to the task last night. Spouting you were taking me back to Phoenix."

"I had time to think about it. I'd like to see if you and mother did unearth some ancient ceremonial site." He smiled.

For the first time she saw a bit of the young man she remembered all those years ago. And a bit of herself in the twinkling eyes and interest in their ancestors.

"You won't haul me back to Tino or Phoenix before I've had a chance to try and find the kiva?"

"On our walk this morning, I noted we are the only humans who have crossed this mountain. That tells me we should be safe while you explore."

He'd just said the best thing she'd heard out of him since they met. She threw her arms around his neck, hugging him. "I'm glad you're with me. If we are siblings as you say, we can work on bonding." Pushing away from him, she noticed uncertainty in his eyes.

"Don't you want to get to know me better?" She pulled out dried fruit and jerky, offering him a share. "My whole childhood, I dreamed of having siblings and cousins and getting to know them."

He took the offered food and watched her. "Why didn't you come see us?"

She shrugged. "When I was younger Mother and Daddy didn't have time to bring me to the reservation and when I began my studies, I used all my spare time to accelerate my learning." Guilt stung her heart. "I told myself after I moved to Phoenix the first free weekend I had I'd drive up to Walpi and visit family." She glanced up at his face. He studied her much like she studied ancient carvings. "I'll confess, I wasn't sure how I'd be received, and always came up with an excuse to stay home. Aunt Una…Mother calling broke the fears for me. The family I've met so far have been wonderful, and I see my fears were unwarranted."

Cody pulled out his water bottle. He offered it to her. She shook her head. He swallowed and recapped the bottle. "You have always been welcome."

"I know that now. But Mother never…she never talked about her childhood, about family. I know she had a different father than your mother. A Caucasian man but she never speaks of him."

Cody's face clouded. His eyes darkened and his eyelids lowered as if he didn't want to show his emotions.

Why would he appear upset at the mention of her mother's father? "Is there more you aren't telling me? Who was my grandfather?" An inkling of dread swirled in her mind. Had Mother been conceived the same way?

"I promised I would tell you the truth." Cody stared off then leveled his gaze on her. "Our grandmother fell for a sweet-talking traveling man who came through the reservation selling wares. She was married and tried to pass Ana off as our grandfather's daughter, but he was wise enough to see the Whiteman traits. Mother said Ana was always treated like kahopi even before she left the reservation. She couldn't wait to get away and live a Whiteman's life."

"Yet, she willingly took me in." The thought her mother may have cared enough to take in her illegitimate niece gave Isabella a bit of hope for closeness between them.

"Mother said it was because Ana knew how deep it hurt to not be accepted and feared what would happen should you stay here and the truth come out." Cody shrugged. "I think it was her persuasion that allowed Mother to give you to Ana."

Her head spun with all the new information she'd accumulated over the past twenty-four hours. She wanted to believe Cody and see herself and her life in a different light, but her analytical self needed more proof, more facts.

Cody stood. "Sitting here talking won't find the kiva. How far to the area you plan to search?"

"We have to climb to the top, and then I'll be able to look on the other side and search for a spring. According to documents and the carvings, there was a spring located close to the kiva."

He nodded. "Let's go. Maybe we can get cell service on the top of the mountain."

She knew he wanted to check in with Tino, but she'd rather wait until after her return to tell him she'd started out alone.

~*~

Isabella stood on top of the mountain. Using her palm-sized binoculars, she scanned the arroyos, crevices, and mounds. A small copse of green bushes and cluster of birds looked like a promising spot to search for the spring.

Cody cursed. "Not enough signal to place a call. A text might get through. You want to send a message to Tino?"

She shook her head and caught a flash of light on a ridge to their right. Raising the binoculars, she zeroed in on the spot. Two ATVs, all-terrain vehicles, with metal boxes strapped on the back ran along

68

the ridge, headed toward her spring. Should she tell Cody and have him hustle her back to the vehicles or keep quiet and stay away from that ridge?

"What are you staring at so intently?" He pulled out his own set of binoculars and aimed them at the other ridge.

"We have company," she said, pocketing the binoculars and heading down the slope.

"Whoa!" Cody grabbed her arm. "We discussed this. You aren't going anywhere near the likes I just saw on that ridge."

She crammed her hands on her hips. "No, *you* said I wasn't. I didn't have any say in the matter."

"Because I've had the training to deal with the likes of those two, you haven't."

She smiled. Should she tell him? Yes. If he knew her training, he'd be less likely to drag her kicking and screaming out of here.

"There's something you don't know about me—"

"Tino told me you're single-minded when it comes to your profession. I know. But your life is more important than some artifacts that have been hidden for hundreds of years." He interrupted.

"No. I mean, yes, I am single-minded when I'm on the trail of history. But what you don't know, I'm proficient at Taekwondo, I'm certified to carry a gun, and I'm an agent for World Intelligence Agency." She smiled up at him as she watched him process the new information.

His eyes narrowed. "Taekwondo did you a lot of good when I caught up to you."

Her heart sunk, remembering how he'd dropped her on her butt when she'd thrown a round kick.

He shoved his binoculars into the pocket of his cargo pants. "I can't believe they pulled you into the espionage shit they do."

This reaction wasn't what she'd expected. "Excuse me? They didn't pull me in, I had to beg to be trained and join."

"Why? Why would you want to live the life that took you away from us, your family?"

His tortured appeal struck her heart and her mind.

"I did it because I wanted to be closer to Mother and Daddy. And after the events in Guatemala when I met Tino, I felt I'd earned my spot in the agency." She wasn't sure he'd understand the rush she got from puzzling out a successful conclusion to an assignment.

"Are you closer? Have you worked on an assignment with them?" The disdain in his voice carried to his eyes.

"No, of course, I haven't been on an assignment with them. That would be ludicrous to have a whole family in danger."

"Really," he said sarcastically.

"Ohhhh," she said through clenched teeth. How was she to get through to him? "We can argue about the contradictions later. I told you my credentials so you wouldn't think I'm helpless. I'm trained in covert ops and know how to take care of myself." She pivoted and headed down the side of the mountain. If they didn't stop for anything longer than a swallow of water, they'd make the area she believed to be the spring by dark.

"You might think you can handle yourself, but you haven't come up across drug dealers." Cody's voice carried to her.

She laughed. "Tino and I infiltrated a drug lord in Mexico City last year." An icy shiver ran down her back. "I know how nasty those people can be." Rico was out to get Tino and possibly her. The Shadow Eagles had better be as good as Tino said. He'd need expert protection to stay out of Rico's hands.

Chapter Ten

Tino woke with a start.

"Come on. We have word there's a drop happening tonight." Charlie's round face peered down at him. "You don't look so good. Maybe you should skip this one."

"No. I'm coming. Give me a minute then gather everyone. I have information they all need to hear before we hit the desert." Tino sat up and swung his feet over the side of the cot.

Charlie headed to the door and tossed over his shoulder, "We have two guys you haven't met with us tonight."

Tino nodded and stood. Muscles protested. He should lighten his pack and stop sleeping on this cot. Rotating one shoulder and then the other, he slowly loosened up. He splashed water on his face, downed two pain relievers, and picked up his pack. Sleep had hit him like a sledgehammer, and he'd remained dead to the world. He checked his watch. Five hours he'd been out.

Charlie, Tank, and Jonny all stood just outside the building. Two men he'd yet to meet leaned against Crow's pickup. One was short and wiry. The other tall, slender, and possibly the youngest member of the Shadow Eagles.

"Charlie said you wanted to talk to us," Crow said, nodding to

Charlie.

"Sí." Tino held his hand out to the smaller of the two men. "Tino Konstantine."

The younger man's eyes narrowed slightly before he caught himself.

"Alfred Mongwau. I've heard you are learning this country better than most newcomers." The small man had a firm grip and a calculating gaze.

Tino glanced at the three men he'd been working with. They all smiled like proud parents. "I have good teachers."

He offered his hand to the younger man. "Tino—"

The man interrupted, "Konstantine, yeah, I heard."

"Percy..." Crow admonished.

"I'm Percy Arnold." He dismissed Tino's handshake. "I heard there is a bounty out on his head." Percy pointed to Tino.

"Sí. That is what I learned as well and wanted to tell all of you. If you do not wish to take me on your sweeps, I will understand. But I will be out there doing my job."

Crow slapped Tino on the back. "You're less likely to get killed if we tag along. Load up!"

Everyone headed for the three vehicles in the parking lot.

Tino caught up to Crow. "Anything I need to know about this outing?"

"Alfred found tracks last night that we believe will lead us to a drop site. We're splitting up into three vehicles to drive some of the roads that cross the trail and see if there are any new prints."

Tino nodded and climbed in the truck with Crow. Tank and Charlie drove off in the second pickup and Alfred and Percy in the third.

The slight narrowing of Percy's eyes when Tino said his name had been recognition. But was it because the man feared being with someone with a bounty on them or because he wished to collect the bounty?

"What do you know about Percy?" Tino asked nonchalantly.

Crow cast a glance his way. "Not much. He sent in a request to be part of the Shadow Eagles. His background was checked, his talents assessed, and here he is." Crow unwrapped a stick of gum. "I have to admit, I wasn't keen on having someone so young in the group, but

ICE vouched for him and that's who we work for."

Tino took all the information in. "He seemed a bit hotheaded."

"Yeah, that's one of the things that bothers me."

They continued on in silence for an hour before Crow slowed the vehicle. Cruising along at five miles per hour, they scanned both sides of the road looking for sign of something other than animals crossing the dirt road.

A walkie-talkie squawked. "We found something." Charlie gave the coordinates, and Crow pushed his foot down on the accelerator.

Fifteen minutes later, Crow stopped the truck next to Charlie.

"What did you find?" Crow stepped out of the pickup.

"Fresh tracks, looks like mules. Deep indentions. Four people." He nodded to the east. "Tank headed that way. Thinks he can circle in front of them."

"I'll go around from the west," Tino offered.

"No. You stay with someone. More eyes makes it easier to spot your enemy." Crow turned to Alfred and Percy. "You go that way." He pointed to Percy. "The rest of us will keep pressure on them from back here."

The youngest member shot Tino a scowl and loped off the direction he was given.

Tino knew these men believed they could keep him safe, but the only way to find safety was to capture a mule or runner who knew where to find Rico.

They spread out with thirty feet between them watching for signs that told them the mules were still ahead of them. To his left, Charlie stopped and raised his binoculars. He stared toward a knoll two miles away.

Charlie lowered the binoculars and spoke into the walkie-talkie.

Tino didn't understand a word, but understood the motions Crow made indicating they were begin watched from the knoll. Had they seen Tank head that direction? Tino remained alert as they continued across the hot sand, pebbles, and brush. Heat rose from the ground, baking him from the top and the bottom. The nose-stinging tang of the creosote bushes irritated his eyes.

Kneeling behind a bush, he pulled out a canteen and drank deep. How desperate must the UDAs and mules be to walk through this incendiary country in summer? This was why there were so many deaths. Desperate people paid money to get escorted across the border and desert by "coyotes" only to find the "coyotes" didn't care how many made it alive.

Over half the group of UDAs he'd rounded up last night had heat stroke and the rest were on the verge. The coyote told them he was going for water and left them. He probably saw a patrol in the area and lit out, leaving the UDAs to fend for themselves. They resided in a shady holding center this morning with all the water they wanted. But would soon be headed back over the border in a bus.

His walkie-talkie crackled. "Tino. You okay?"

He hadn't planned to sit in the shade musing over the night before. "Coming," he replied and tucked his canteen back in his pack.

Before standing, he glanced at the base of the bushes around him and noticed a burlap pack not thirty feet away. Rather than let the lookout on the knoll see him walk to the discarded pack, he remained crouched and duck walked over to the bundle.

He poked the burlap with his rifle barrel. The object didn't budge easily. He pulled his knife out of his boot sheath and slit the burlap. White powder sifted into the sand. This was worth more than a bundle of marijuana. This was a manufactured drug.

Shrugging out of his pack, he dug in a pocket for a Nik kit. The one-by-two-inch plastic bag with two chemical ampoules would determine if the substance was cocaine. He stuck the tip of his knife in the substance and tapped the blade to drop the power into the kit. A clip sealed the bag. He broke one ampoule inside the packet and shook. Waited thirty seconds, then broke the second ampoule. The liquid in the packet turned pink. Cocaine.

He grabbed the walkie-talkie to contact Crow. A pair of boots came into view.

"Just getting ready to call. I noticed this pack, but didn't want the lookout on the hill to know I'd found it." He held up the Nik kit. "Cocaine."

Alfred gave a slight nod and spoke into his walkie-talkie in a language Tino suspected was Tohono O'odham. The reply was just as foreign.

"Crow says to grab it. That is worth more than marijuana. They may try to get it back."

That had been Tino's thoughts as well. He grabbed the bundle and stood, making sure the lookout for the mules could see him put it in his backpack. The act put another target on his back.

"You want me to take that?" Alfred asked as if he had the same thoughts.

"I'm already a target, no sense in splitting up the surveillance." He forced his lips into a smile. If Isabella knew how much danger he'd placed himself in… That wasn't a topic he wanted to dwell on. She knew his life was full of danger. He also believed that was half of her infatuation for him. He was everything she'd lacked in her life before her trip to Guatemala.

"We better hurry and catch up with the others." Alfred set out at a fast clip, his short legs striding right along.

Tino shrugged into his pack and followed. At least carrying the cocaine and knowing someone could make an attempt to get it felt more proactive than scouring the desert for signs of mules.

~*~

Golden hues bathed the sky and the desert ridge Isabella descended, heading toward the small copse of mesquite trees that had to be the spring.

The cool mountain air made her shiver. The higher they climbed, the more layers of clothes she'd added. The unexpected plant life around the spring welled the hope she might just be in the right place. Isabella spun in a slow circle, searching the side of the ridge where she stood and the one across the ravine for anything that might prove to be a kiva

"This looks like the perfect place to set up base camp," Isabella said, dropping her pack.

"Base camp?" Cody placed his pack on the ground and stared at her.

"Yes, base camp. We can sleep here and head out from here each morning searching for the kiva." She pulled a small cloth out of her pack and dipped it in the spring water. The cool cloth washed away the dried sweat and set her mind charging in different directions. First she would recheck her notes and the carvings.

"How long do you expect to be out here?" Cody pulled binoculars from his pack and scanned the ridge across from them.

"Either until I find something or my food runs out." She dug her journal from her vest pocket and studied her notes.

"You couldn't have brought more than enough food for a couple of days."

The wistfulness in her brother's voice made her smile. She didn't look up as she uttered,

"I have enough for a week."

"A week!" He stomped over to where she sat. "If you stay out here a week, Tino will come looking for you if you don't find a way to contact him and let him know you're alive."

She glanced up at the concern on Cody's face. "He'll be too busy trying to find Rico. I know him. He won't rest until the man who has sworn to kill us both is behind bars or dead." She frowned. "He takes vengeance seriously."

"Vengeance?" Cody sat on the ground near her and pulled out a water bottle.

"He takes people he loves being killed or threatened as a personal affront to him." She returned her attention to her notes. "He won't come looking for me until he's captured Rico."

"And you think it will take him longer than a week to find this Rico?"

"No, it will take that long for Rico to show his hand." She shivered. She had no doubt Rico was plotting to kill Tino and then find her. He was a crafty, psychotic killer.

"Pull your nose out of the book and tell me about this Rico." Cody sat on his bottom with his legs crossed, facing her.

She closed the journal and sighed. "There isn't much to tell other than Rico was Tino's contact in the DEA while he infiltrated the drug lord he was out to bring down. I was there on a W.I.A. mission and breached the bubble the drug lord kept around him. It wasn't until Tino and I were both completing our assignments that we discovered Rico was a corrupt DEA agent playing both sides. He was trying to take over the drug lord's cartel. Rico got away. And now he seems to be in charge of one of the cartels that is running drugs through the Tohono O'odham reservation."

Peering into Cody's eyes, she saw the gamut of emotions swirling within him. Anger, fear, disgust, and resolve.

"This isn't your battle. It's between Tino and I and Rico. I prefer to let Tino deal with Rico." Reality, she preferred to deal with history and not the here and now. The here and now made her feel paralyzed because she couldn't project an outcome. History she already knew and only wished to add to what the world knew.

"It is my battle when my family is being threatened." Cody's eyes glistened with rage.

"I won't have someone else who is dear to me get in the middle of this mess." She saw her words fell on deaf ears. The determined jut of his chin and jaw muscle flexing, proved he was already planning a way to get into the mess.

Shamutz! She wouldn't be able to talk him out of whatever he was thinking. But she could keep him away from harm the longer it took her to find the kiva. Right now she wanted to divert his attention.

"Our mother had a vision and believes I am part of the Blue Star prophecy." She dug in her backpack and pulled out a package of jerky, offering it to Cody.

"Many of Mother's visions have come true." He took several pieces and chewed.

She could see it would take a deeper conversation to get him to switch the thoughts in his mind. "She said I was standing beside the Blue Star Kachina. I'm not sure why I'd be standing by an immortal being. If her visions are correct then the kiva I am looking for could have something to do with the prophecy."

This caught his attention. "The prophecy is centuries old. No one knows what it is only that it will purify and cleanse our people, and hopefully the world." He looked dubious. "Mother has many visions. You standing beside a kachina doll dressed for the Blue Star prophecy could mean Mother had been thinking about the prophecy not that you have anything to do with it."

"But you believe in our mother's visions. You said so earlier. Now you see why it is so important for me to find this kiva?"

His head barely tipped in a nod. "Many of the Hopi religious truths have come true. But for mother to believe you will find the Blue Star prophecy…" He studied her a moment. "If you are correct about what you'll find, it could mean a lot for mankind."

Her lips curved into a smile. She not only got him thinking of a greater good, he no longer looked dark and deadly.

"According to my notes, we'll head north along the side of this ridge tomorrow." Isabella rechecked all her notes until it grew too dark to see. She didn't want to use a flashlight in case the people they'd witnessed earlier were still around. Rolling out her yoga mat to sleep on and then her down sleeping bag, she prayed the men they saw had left the mountain range.

~*~

Isabella woke from a deep sleep. She lay on her back, staring up at stars and listening. There it was. The sound that had woken her. A distant drone of small engines. She rolled over to see if Cody was awake. His pad and sleeping bag were empty.

She sat up. Using the moonlight, she searched the shadows around the camp for Cody. Fear dried her mouth at the notion he'd taken off in search of the vehicles. She picked up her vest that had been folded for her pillow and slipped the garment on. Next, she pulled her daypack out of her larger pack and slipped her revolver into her daypack.

Better to be prepared.

With stealth, she stood and walked in the direction of the humming vehicles. She slowly climbed the ridge, ducking behind bushes to keep from being seen if the people she approached had night vision. If Cody had caught up to the riders, he would be outnumbered. She'd be his backup.

She dodged behind a darker bush. An arm clamped around her shoulder and her mouth. Defensive maneuvers were instinctive. She slammed her heel onto the top of the assailant's foot as her fist met his soft male parts.

"Ooph! Shit, sister, it's me." Cody groaned.

Contrition hit her, knocking her as breathless as Cody. She gulped in air and fought for words to convey her mortification. Whispering, she apologized, "I'm sorry! I didn't know it was you. I...I, oh my... Did I hurt you?"

He sucked in air through clenched teeth. His hand on her shoulder gripped tightly as he dealt with the blow she'd landed to his testicles.

"I really am sorry." She infused sincere apology into her words.

"What are you doing here?" He hissed in a clipped tone.

"I heard vehicles and saw you were gone. I thought you might need help."

"Not this kind of help." He released her shoulder and lowered to the ground. "That's one hell of a punch you landed, sister."

She registered the pride in his voice.

"I told you I can take care of myself." She punched his arm amicably.

"I believe you now." He stilled. "You hear that?"

Isabella listened. "What?"

"That's it. Nothing. They either drove far enough away we can't hear them or they stopped." He shoved something at her. "Here, look through these, I had them in my sights before you showed up."

"Were they Border Patrol?" She grasped the binoculars, put them to her eyes, and the world turned green but brighter.

"No, they weren't border. One Caucasian. One Hispanic. They had boxes on their ATVs filled with food and water."

"Food?" She scanned the area ahead of them but didn't see anything other than plants.

"Yeah. It could have been a UDA drop site they're headed to."

"I don't see anything." She looked down at Cody. "You ready to head back to camp?"

"Yes." He stood and shuffled for a bit but was walking normal by the time they reached the camp.

"Hey!" Isabella couldn't believe the mess. Their belongings were strewn about the area. Her sleep pad was in pieces and her sleeping bag ripped with feathers spilling out.

Cody flipped on a flashlight and studied the scene. "This is what we get for sleeping near a waterhole. Looks like javelinas were through here while we were gone."

Isabella picked up her belongings, noting the animals had ruined most of her food supply along with her yoga pad.

Chapter Eleven

Tino wasn't sure if he felt fortunate or disappointed. No one made an attempt to get the bundle of cocaine from him. Which spared him any harm, but meant they weren't any closer to nailing the group carting it over the border.

The vehicles pulled into the Tohono O'odham station as the sun was rising.

Crow stopped the pickup and watched Tino. "You want to come crash at my place instead of sleeping on that cot?"

The idea of a bed was appealing, but he couldn't put Crow and his family at risk. If Rico had someone tailing him, he was safer at the police station.

"Thank you, but the cot and I are becoming friends." He smiled, patted Crow's shoulder and shoved himself and his pack out of the vehicle.

"See you tonight." Crow drove off, leaving Tino standing in the parking lot, wishing he knew where the hell Isabella was and if Cody had caught up to her.

He entered the station. The small shift of office help and local officials glanced up then went back to their work. They had all become used to his staggering in about this time, taking a shower, and falling asleep on the cot in the back room.

Tino locked himself in the small bathroom with a shower and dug through his belongings for something that was clean. He made note to ask about a laundromat. His hand bumped his phone. Maybe Isabella or Cody left a message. He pressed the "on" button and while the phone went through the motions of turning on, he stripped and started the water.

Glancing down at the phone, he noted there were messages. He snatched it up and clicked through. They were all from Isabella's father.

"¡Coño!" He didn't need Mr. Mumphrey wondering about his daughter. The urge to shut his phone back off warred with wanting to have it on in case Isabella did contact him. He placed the phone on the counter and stepped into the shower. Handling Isabella's father wouldn't be pleasant. Washing the sweat and sand off his body before he delved into that conversation would put him in a better frame of mind.

His phone buzzed as Tino stepped out of the shower. He wrapped a towel around his waist and plucked the phone from the counter.

Mr. Mumphrey. Tino cleared his throat and opened the phone connection.

"Hello."

"Tino, this is Theodore Mumphrey."

"Sí."

"I've been trying to call my daughter and there's no answer." The man's tone demanded an answer.

"She is looking for an ancestral kiva." Better to keep the particulars, like she was dangerously close to the Mexican border out of the conversation.

"That doesn't explain why I can't contact her by phone. She is in the states, isn't she?"

"Sí. Her aunt took her to see a cave and while there Ezzabella discovered something no one else had found. She is following that lead with her cousin, Cody."

"Shit!"

The force of the expletive from Mumphrey's mouth, caught Tino off guard. "Sir, why would that be bad?"

"I'll track her down using the GPS on her phone."

The line went dead. Why would Isabella's father not want her to be under the care of her cousin? And why hadn't I thought to track her using the GPS on her phone?

Tino dried, dressed, and hauled his belongings to the back room. He walked back out to the office area. "Would you see if you could get a location via GPS on this phone please?" He handed the officer Isabella's phone number and information.

"Is this official business?" the man asked.

"Sí, the woman is in danger, and Cody Honani is guarding her." Tino headed back down the hall and spun around. "Come wake me when you find out where they are."

The man nodded. Tino reversed direction and made a straight line for the backroom and the cot.

~*~

Once daylight lit up the side of the ridge, Isabella stood, stretching and working out the kinks from sleeping in an upright position. Without her pad to keep her head from wallowing in the sand, she couldn't bring herself to lie prone on the ground. Instead, she'd slipped into the remains of her sleeping bag and propped her back against a tree.

She began a search of the area and found half-a-dozen unopened energy bars and two water bottles that didn't have tooth punctures. Cody came back from an outing with one package of unmolested jerky.

"They must have dropped this when they heard us returning." He tossed the package on the pile of food she'd found. "This isn't going to keep us alive very long."

She'd spent a good amount of the night trying to decide whether she should scrub the trip and come back later with Tino or live off the land and continue with her search. Since it wasn't just her life on the line, she'd decided Cody should have some say.

"We have two options."

"Two?" He raised an eyebrow as if to say there was only one option.

She scowled at him. "Yes. We can walk out of here today, and I'll come back with more supplies and help, or we can live off the land and at least see if we can find the kiva." She preferred the second but would go with what Cody wanted. He had a job he couldn't miss. She had someone to fill in for her.

Cody sat down, watching her. "I took seven days of vacation. We've used up two, so you have three days to look for the kiva, then we'll have to head back."

Isabella threw herself at Cody and hugged him tight. "Thank you!" She meant it from the tips of her toes.

"You're welcome. I'll set up some snares while we're searching today. Jack rabbit isn't the easiest to eat but it will be better than nothing."

"We're on a refuge. We shouldn't eat the animals or start a fire." Isabella had battled with that half the night as well. A refuge was for the animals to feel safe.

"They aren't going to jail us for eating a jack rabbit. I don't plan to take down a pronghorn or sheep." He smiled, "And I'm pretty sure if we come across a rattler, which are fine eating, they won't begrudge us a meal of one of those."

She wasn't sure she'd be able to eat snake but with her metabolism, she'd go through the little bit of food that was left just today. "Let's go." If she stayed busy she'd think less about her stomach. Her daypack in place, she headed north.

A hand landed on her shoulder. "Wait. That's the direction we saw the vehicles last night."

"I know, but the kiva is most likely north or south of the spring."

"Let's go south today." Cody grasped her shoulders making her do an about-face.

"Fine, but we'll go that way tomorrow."

"Not if we find the kiva this way."

He grinned and she couldn't help grinning back. This was the kind of camaraderie she'd missed growing up. Someone who looked out for you and you could trust to have your back. The more she saw of Cody and felt his trust the more she believed his story that they were siblings. Not that she thought he'd lie about such a thing, but her analytical side spent a good deal of the night categorizing what he said and linking it to events in her life so far. She wasn't ready to concede her complete trust in him, but she slowly found herself believing his story.

Even though she was walking south, she didn't want him to think she gave in easily.

"I mapped out our route north, it won't be as quick without a plan." She glanced over her shoulder.

Cody shook his head. "Even if there was a flag flying on a slope to the north directing us to the kiva, we aren't going that way today."

She laughed and continued on, scanning the terrain for a mound that appeared manmade. "You know if we split up, we'd cover more ground," she said after an hour of Cody wandering along behind her.

"We aren't splitting up. Besides, you know what you're looking for, I don't."

She'd noticed while her gaze was on the terrain around them, his gaze scanned the upper regions of their ridge and the one adjacent. He watched for traffickers.

"Do you think a patrol comes through here?" She stopped and took a drink from the bottle she'd refilled at the spring, then held it out to Cody.

"This time of year, they probably do. It's more likely the traffickers would use this route because it is less likely to be seen and cooler than the desert floor." He handed the bottle back.

She shed her outer long-sleeved shirt and tied it around her waist.

"That's an interesting vest you wear. I noticed you had it on when you assaulted me last night." Cody rubbed his crotch and scowled.

Isabella couldn't help laughing. "I said I was sorry. You shouldn't grab me." She patted a pocket on the vest. "This goes with me whenever I head out of the city. It's my survival vest."

"Survival Vest?"

"Yes. I have everything I need to get out of any situation in this vest." She strode away from Cody, renewing her evaluation of the area around them. "There are some interesting rocks over there."

Three large orange boulders pressed against the side of the ravine. Up close, the boulders resembled each other in size, color, and smoothness. She ran her hand over the first one, walking sideways, feeling the contour of the boulder as its spherical shape curved from the side of the cliff around to the boulder next to it. There was enough space between the middle rock and the one on its left for her to squeeze between the rocks.

She took off her day pack and handed it to Cody. With a bit of squeezing, she worked her way between the two smooth, unyielding boulders and stepped into darkness. Flipping up the flap on a pocket of her vest, she pulled out her LED flashlight. The bright beam blinded her a moment. When her eyes adjusted, she found herself in a small cavern. Rustling above her head stilled her heart.

Fearful of what she'd find, Isabella refused to look up and stood frozen.

"Isabella, where are you?" Cody's voice echoed into the small cave. "I can't fit. Are you okay?"

She tried to blank out the sounds above her. The smell, the sounds, and the hair on her neck prickling, told her it was bats. Her biggest fear. And even more so after she and Tino were attacked by vampire bats in Guatemala.

Backing toward the boulders, she slipped a hand between the rocks and slowly slid back out into the sunshine. Only once her whole body was heated by the sun did her breathing resume to normal.

"What was in there? You're white as milk." Cody grabbed her arm and let her over to a rock the right height to sit on. He lowered her onto the seat.

"It's a cave or cavern, I didn't take time to shine the flashlight all around." With trembling hands, she pulled out her water bottle and took a sip. "There's bats," she said softly.

"Probably. This refuge has a large population of long-nosed bats. They pollinate the cactus and eat the fruit."

"Thank you, Mr. Encyclopedia." Isabella couldn't believe how excited his voice sounded over flying rodents. She knew the long-nose bat was one of the prides of the refuge. She'd shoved aside the thought she might come in contact with them.

"They aren't going to hurt you. They like prickly cactus and other cactus flowers." He laughed. "Though right now you're annoyed enough you could be sprouting spines."

She wanted to say something pithy but seeing the jovial face and teasing eyes, she could only smile back. This was the first sign of pure happiness she'd witnessed on her brother's face. Allowing him to tease her had brought out a side to him she liked.

"I don't like bats. In Guatemala, Tino and I were chased out of a cave by large vampire bats. Tino had open wounds and the scent of blood had made them…" She couldn't finish. The reminder brought on a bout of shivers.

"Sister." Cody crouched next to her, putting an arm over her shoulders. "I can guarantee these bats are only a few inches long and will not attack."

His attempt to comfort her, struck her heart. He would have made a wonderful brother growing up as the younger sibling behind him. All their cousins must love and respect him.

She looked into his sincere gaze. "I really do want to check this cave out. It could have markings that will direct us to the kiva."

"How do you suggest I get in there? I can't shrink to your puny size."

"Hey!" She tossed his arm off her shoulder and stood. "That isn't nice. I'm not puny, I'm just right." Her gaze travelled up and down his body. "You on the other hand should have been named bear instead of badger."

He laughed. "What is your idea, that I dig us in?"

The word dig slapped her mind into gear. "Yes! We will dig our way in."

Cody stared at her. "How?"

She walked over to the boulder on the left side of the opening. "We dig the sand out from under this side and it will roll away from the other boulder making the gap larger." She began scooping the sand with her hands.

"Let me. I have larger hands." Cody sank down beside her and together they scooped sand and pebbles away from the bottom of the boulder.

After a significant hole was dug, they began working to pull the sand out from under the boulder to allow it to roll into the hole they'd made. The large rock teetered toward their dug hole. Isabella grabbed Cody's shirt, pulling him down on his bottom to be out of the path of the boulder as it rolled sideways. It moved a bit and settled. They continued digging.

The third time the boulder rolled, she inspected the opening. "I think you can fit now," she said, stepping sideways through the enlarged gap.

Cody shoved his rifle and pack through the opening. She grabbed hold and waited for him to squeeze sideways into the cave. The fluttering overhead was drowned out by Cody's grunts. Once he stood inside the cave, they turned on flashlights.

"This is something else. Do you think the boulders were put there for a reason?" Cody moved about, his flashlight beam exploring the walls.

"I think there is a reason they are covering the entrance. Look. There. It continues into the ridge." The cooler air prompted Isabella to pull on her long-sleeved shirt. The farther they walked into the passageway the cooler and damper the air became. The walls narrowed down to a passage only wide enough for one person at a time. She was thankful the bats didn't use the tunnel to sleep. If they had been hanging from the lower ceiling, she wouldn't have been able to continue.

"We must be passing by the spring," she said, pointing the beam of the flashlight down at the slick muddy floor of the passage. Her footing slipped. Arms spread, she braced against the walls to keep from falling down.

"Watch your step." Cody caught one of her arms helping to steady her.

She nodded and pulled her feet back under her before cautiously stepping through the mud. Only minutes later she again walked on the packed dry dirt like before the muddy area.

"How far do you think we've gone?" Her light bounced off a pile of rocks. It appeared to be the end of the passage.

"We've traveled about two miles, I'd say." Cody moved up close behind her to peer over her shoulder. "Looks like the end of your exploration."

"I need to think." Isabella sat in the passageway, staring at the blockade and pulled out an energy bar. She handed it to Cody. Another rummage in her daypack supplied her with one more. The last one. She peeled back the paper, took a bite, and studied the pile of rocks.

"These aren't a natural barrier."

"What do you mean?"

Isabella glanced at Cody. "These were placed here. Someone wants it to look like we can't get through."

"Who do you mean by someone?" A scowl furrowed Cody's brow.

She shrugged. "I'm not sure. It depends on how long the rocks have been here. Could be the Hopi. Could be someone much older or much newer." Shoving the wrapper into her pocket, she took a long swallow of water, capped the bottle, and shoved it into her pack.

"It's like a puzzle. Find the right piece and you have the way in." She stood, placing her hands on the rocks. Yes, they were definitely set here to make people think they couldn't pass. Light from her flashlight showed the contours of each rock. One had what appeared to be a handle, smooth there the fingers would grip.

Isabella gripped the rock. "Step back in case I'm wrong."

"What about you?" Cody moved closer instead of farther down the passage.

"Someone will need to tell my parents and Tino where I'm buried." She smiled and hoped that wasn't what would happen.

"How about I pull the rock. You're more important to our culture than I am."

His words thrilled and saddened her.

"Every human is important. I have to do this because I've figured out the puzzle." She glanced over her shoulder. "Go on. Back up."

"How do you know that rock will even do anything?" Cody stood his ground.

"I don't. But if it does happen to be the rock that's holding the whole wall up, we don't both need to be hurt."

"I agree. But I thought you were a genius or something." Cody grabbed her arm, propelling her down the tunnel out of harm's way, and grasped the rock. "I'm bigger and can take a beating better than you can."

Her heart hammered in her chest, standing out of the way and watching Cody place his hand on the rock. *Please, let that be the right stone.*

Chapter Twelve

Inch by aggravating inch, Cody slowly pulled the rock loose as they both watched the wall to see if any other rocks moved.

Once he held the rock in his hand and nothing happened, she hurried forward.

Voices whispered through the hole. Isabella leaned down and peered into the darkness beyond the rock wall. The smell of unwashed bodies and waste assaulted her nose. The sounds of sorrow and defeat echoed in the air. Crying, whispers, and whimpering. There were people on the other side

"What did you find?" Cody's voice boomed like thunder to her anxious conscience.

"Shhh." She whispered. "There are people over there. They sound frightened and sad."

"Let me see." He stuck his head up to the hole and pulled back. "Whew. I see what you mean. It reeks in there. Damn, I wish I'd brought my night vision binocs."

Isabella pulled him down the passage ten feet so they could talk without being heard. "We have decisions to make. Quietly make a hole in this barrier and see if we can get them out, or one of us stays here and watches while the other gets the Border Patrol."

Cody shook his head. "I don't care for either, but I know we need to stay together. My vote is we both go find the Border Patrol."

"But what if they get moved? Someone needs to remain here to listen in." She wasn't going to leave the people suffering in that chamber.

"I don't like this. You don't have food and you could be found and then what?" Cody grasped her lower arm. "The best thing is for both of us to go find help. I can't leave you here. Mother and Tino would never forgive me."

"I'll be fine." She tried to ease his hand off her arm. "I'll stay on this side of the rocks, take notes, and wait for your return."

His grip tightened. "No. We'll both go for help. Once this is cleaned up, we'll come back and look for the kiva."

"I'm not a porcelain doll or fragile-minded. I can keep surveillance until you return." She yanked her arm from his grasp.

"I said you'll come with me." He grabbed her wrist, pulling her away from the chamber and back the way they came in.

"Stop!" She dug her heels into the dirt, but she wasn't strong enough to escape his grip or his pull. Finally, she followed. It was ridiculous to fight him. He was doing what he was trained to do: protect the innocent. The only problem; she wasn't innocent. After surviving nearly becoming a human sacrifice, she didn't think there was anything else that could terrify her more.

Eventually, he released her wrist and stopped, pressing his body against the side of the passage. "Go ahead of me."

"I'm not that childish I would turn around and run back," she said, brushing by him and taking the lead. She picked up the pace. If they were going to help those people, they needed to contact authorities quickly. There was no telling when they would be moved and then they may never be found.

Soon they were slipping through the mud. Isabella wanted to run but knew they also would need to conserve their energy since she didn't have any food left and she had yet to see Cody eat anything other than what she'd provided.

They entered the first chamber. The flutter of wings hurried her steps across the twenty feet to the light shining through the rocks. Out in the sunlight, she glanced up at the sky. From the angle of the sun and shadows it was mid-day. They'd have to walk all night to get back to the cars by morning.

She turned her toes northward and started out.

"Not that way."

Spinning around, she found Cody headed down the ridge to the south.

"What are you doing? Our cars are north."

He stopped and glanced over his shoulder. "But we're more likely to run into authorities down close to the border than heading to the vehicles." He strode away from her.

His pace was fast, but once she ran and caught up, she matched him stride for stride.

"We keep this up the sun is going to burn us out."

"Don't think about the sun. Think about something cool and refreshing. Like the spring or a mountain stream." His gait didn't slacken.

She knew a mind could make a person believe anything. Images of a stream not far from her favorite boarding school played through her mind. She walked barefoot to the bank and through the cold, clear water. Minnows swam in schools around her feet, tickling her toes and ankles.

"Oomph?" She ran into Cody's back. Her images had been so vivid she'd walked without seeing what was around her. Pressing her hands against his back to push away, his taut muscles revealed she'd missed something.

She grasped his arm to peek around, but he held her behind him.

"What do you have behind you?"

The heavy Mexican accent sent apprehension skidding across her shoulder blades. This wasn't a border patrol guard.

"We are hiking through the refuge and aren't looking for trouble." Cody tensed.

The sound of several pairs of approaching feet registered as did the slight drone of an engine in the distance. No wonder he'd stopped and not confronted the person.

It was better to show herself. She knew the only person who found her appealing was Tino, so she didn't worry about them making advances.

Cody's arm shot out as a Hispanic man tried to walk by him.

"It's okay. They know I'm here." She stepped from behind Cody and was shocked to see four men holding assault weapons. No wonder Cody had come to a complete stop.

"If you are only hiking why are you carrying a rifle? There is no hunting in the refuge." The same voice as spoke before came from a man in the middle of the pack.

She estimated his age at mid-thirties. His clothing reeked high-end and his hair was elegantly styled. He had to be the head of the organization they'd just walked into.

"I could ask all of you the same question." Cody didn't move to grab the rifle slung over his shoulder.

Cody wasn't dressed in camouflage. He did look like a normal hiker other than the rifle and the gun she knew was strapped to his leg under his baggy cargo pants.

"Search him!" the head man said.

Two men moved forward, one with his rifle aimed at Cody, the other taking the rifle and patting him down. This led to him finding the gun tucked in the ankle holster.

"*Mi amigo*, you are heavily armed for a hiker," the leader said.

"You never know what kind of animals you'll run into out here." Cody glared at the leader.

The man who took Cody's weapons started for her.

Again, Cody stopped him from touching her.

His protectiveness would get him injured or killed.

"I don't have any weapons. My friend was only protecting me." Isabella didn't allow her gaze to stray to Cody. She didn't want anyone to know he was related. If these men perchance knew Rico she didn't want to put Cody in danger.

"You can have the guns if you'll just let us continue on our way." She didn't want to appear in too big of a hurry, but she also didn't want to give the men any time to decide they may have seen something they shouldn't.

The sound of the motor grew closer. All heads turned to the sound of the approaching vehicle. When the men with the guns didn't appear nervous, she realized help wasn't coming.

~*~

Tino woke. He checked his watch. "¡Coño!" He'd slept his usual five hours without anyone waking him. That meant they hadn't located Isabella or Cody via GPS. Had Isabella's father been able to pinpoint

92

where they were?

He swung his legs over the side of the cot and sat. Scrubbing a hand over his face, he argued with himself. Did he need to call Mumphrey and see what he knew? That would be the same as saying I lost your daughter, the woman I promised you I would care for. But WIA had better resources than the Tohono O'odham police.

Against his pride but knowing it was the right thing to do, he picked up his cell phone and punched in Theodore Mumphrey's phone number.

"Have you heard anything?" the man asked, sounding more unsure than Tino had ever heard him before.

"No, sir. I was hoping you had learned more about her location. You have more resources than I do as a border patrol officer." It was no longer a matter of worrying how the man felt about him. They needed to work together to find Isabella.

"I know she went to the Cabeza Prieta Wildlife Refuge in the southwest corner of the Arizona."

The man on the other end of the line cursed. "There isn't a cell tower around there for miles. Why did you allow this?"

Tino couldn't stop the scoff that built in his throat and spit out between his teeth. "You know your daughter. I forbid her to go, which only made her more determined. I could not go because Rico Montoya, the traitor DEA agent from Mexico City has a bounty on my head. I wished to stay far from Isabella. That is why her cousin went after her."

"After?"

Of course, he would hear that word. "Sí. When I told Cody where she had gone, he hurried after her. I am sure they are together, hunting for the kiva and are well. But it does bother me to not have any communication with them."

"So you have no idea where in the refuge they could be?"

"No, sir."

Charlie stuck his head in.

Tino nodded. "Sir, I have to go. My shift is starting. I'm sure we will hear from Isabella soon."

"I know I will." The phone clicked.

He believes I have failed his daughter. Tino shook off the rejection like he'd done all the insults he'd garnered while growing up

Venezuelan in the United States. He'd been called every slang term there was for a Hispanic person and derided for refusing to become a U.S. citizen. His father had political reasons for leaving Venezuela, but that hadn't meant the family didn't take pride in their heritage.

Right now he had to believe in Isabella's abilities to always land on her feet like a feisty feline. Her courage and ingenuity were two of her attributes that he admired most. She will be fine. Her father will go hell-bent into the desert to find her, and she'll be sitting in the kiva sketching the site.

Tino smiled at the thought and quickly donned his clothing and snatched up his gear.

The office was a flurry of motion.

"What's happening?" he asked, stopping at Jonny Crow's office door.

"We have UDAs claiming they witnessed a killing. We're taking one of them with us to find the spot." Crow rose and came around his desk.

Tino's heart raced. He knew Isabella was at the refuge but fear clamped his gut. "Who was the victim?"

"They said it was a man."

His insides quivered with relief. "Let's go." He led the way out of the station.

They all climbed into two vehicles along with a young Hispanic man. Tino learned his name was Manuel.

They drove for two hours on one of the main roads, before Crow slowed and turned down one of the lesser-used roads.

Manuel's head was practically spinning on his neck as he talked and took in the view from all angles.

His arm came up. "There. Over there is the place."

"Are you sure?" Crow asked.

"Sí, we had stopped in the shade of the many bushes there." He pointed to a large clump of creosote plants. "We heard shouting and feared it was Border Patrol. I hid and walked toward the shouting to see. It was three men with terrain vehicles. They stood staring angry at one man." He gulped. "The man closest to him, said something and then shot the other three times." His eyes grew rounder. "I was scared. I dropped to the ground so they would not see me. When I heard the vehicles leave, I stood up and ran back to my family. We hurried away."

"You have not seen the man we are looking for?" Tino asked, wondering why they would shoot a man out here in the middle of nowhere. They had to know he would eventually be found.

Crow braked to a stop.

Birds flew up and a coyote ran away, leaving a torn body and clothing.

He'd seen other bodies that animals had torn into before they were found. The scene didn't bother him. There was something familiar about the clothes and particularly the shoes. His mind wasn't grasping onto why they were familiar.

"Stay," Crow told Manuel.

The man was all too happy to remain in the vehicle. Everyone else piled out and cautiously approached the body.

"Look for tracks. We need to gather evidence." Crow handed Charlie a camera. Tank started a perimeter search of the area, picking up bits and pieces of the clothing, dropping them into evidence bags.

Crow and Tino walked over to the body and looked down. The eyes had been pecked out. Even with the vacant eye sockets, Tino knew the man. Cruz Sanchez.

"We know him." Tino nodded to the body.

"He's the man who threatened you." Crow put on rubber gloves and began checking pockets. He found a folded slip of paper in the front shirt pocket. His eyebrows rose and his brow furrowed, reading the paper.

"Put on gloves and read this," he ordered Tino.

The tone of his voice pushed Tino instantly to action. He donned rubber gloves and took the paper.

THIS MAN FAILED. THE NEXT ONE WILL NOT.

Tino knew who left the message.

Rico.

Chapter Thirteen

Isabella's breath stalled when an ATV rolled up. A young Caucasian woman sat in front of a man driving the all-terrain vehicle. The young woman's hands were tied, a rag separated her lips, bruises bloomed on a cheek, and a red gash resided above her angry eyes.

"She needs medical attention." Isabella stepped toward the vehicle. Cody grabbed her arm and two of the men stepped in front of her.

"What are you doing with these gringos?" the man on the vehicle asked.

Isabella found his use of the word gringos interesting since he was Caucasian.

"They stumbled across us," The well-dressed man said. "He was carrying these." He motioned for the man who took Cody's weapons to bring them forward.

"I see." The man on the ATV studied Cody, frowned, then aimed his gaze on Isabella. She didn't like the way his eyes lit up while viewing her. "We better hang on to them until *Chaca* moves the merchandise."

Chaca was a word for top dog or boss. Which meant the Hispanic well-dressed man wasn't the man in charge.

Isabella glanced toward Cody. The muscle in his jaw was twitching. Typical male. He was plotting how to get away. She didn't want to get away. The bound young woman on the vehicle gave Isabella reason to believe this group was headed to the chamber she and Cody had found. If they took her and Cody to the chamber, they could help free the women.

The men on foot shoved a rifle barrel into Cody's back and herded him ahead of the pack. The other men surrounded her like walls, moving her after Cody. The man with the girl on the vehicle drove behind. The constant drone of the ATV was the only sound other than their feet skittering pebbles as they walked.

Using her shirt-tail, Isabella wiped at the sweat beading her brow. Luckily, the sun would soon set, and she'd be thankful for the shirt she refused to take off. If the men became curious about her vest, they would discover all her hidden escape tools.

Cody glanced back now and then, keeping tabs on her. She'd smile. The frown on his brow and determination in his eyes proved he thought of escape.

She didn't want to escape. Instead she watched and assessed the dynamics of the men. The man on the ATV and the well-dressed Hispanic man appeared to think they were running the show. This could work in their favor at some point.

Their course over the ridge took them directly above the three boulders and entrance to the cave. She only glanced down long enough to make sure it was impossible to notice the opening they'd made. The gray of dusk descended on them as they neared the spring. She argued with herself over whether to deny the packs in plain view were their belongings or fess up.

Cody walked right on by, but the man holding the rifle on him ordered him to stop.

"What is this?" the Hispanic man asked. "Who has been camping here?" His gaze flicked from her to Cody and back to her.

He obviously felt she was the weaker of the two and most likely to be coerced into talking.

The man smiled, reminding her of a snake about to strike. "Señorita, I am a reasonable man. I have not hurt you or your friend. But I will, if you do not tell me the truth."

"We camped here last night and were using it as a base camp while we hiked around." She didn't see where that information would get them in trouble.

"I see. And why is everything so neat and tidy? Only the two back packs. No food, nothing set-up as if you planned to return?" He moved closer, his breath smelled of stale cigars.

"We were visited by javelinas once already. We decided to pack everything up and put the packs where we hoped they couldn't get to our stuff."

The men all laughed.

"What did the javelinas do? Did they scare you?" He leaned in closer as darkness settled over the area.

"They ate most of our food and tore up my sleeping mat." Isabella kept her tone conversational and her eyes away from her pack. It held her phone, her knife, and her revolver. The best scenario would be these men leaving their packs behind to the javelinas.

"Paco, grab both the packs." The Hispanic man pivoted and stared at Cody.

Isabella held her breath hoping Cody didn't do anything irrational. He remained stone faced and stoic. His military training and ancestry was his advantage. She hoped she held up as well.

They continued marching north, climbing slightly up the side of the ravine. It wasn't until the man in front ordered Cody to stop that she saw a ladder sticking out of a hole in the ground.

The kiva! Her heart pounded against her ribs like a raging gorilla. They were using the sacred ceremonial kiva to harbor women they stole and sold. The agony she felt over this sacred ground being used in such a way stopped her breathing. This was an affront to the gods and the Hopi people.

The man on the ATV stopped next to the ladder. "José, go down first, light the lantern, and we'll send Paco down so there are two of you when we send our captives down."

The man giving orders was American. He had a bit of a southwestern twang. The others in the group had Hispanic backgrounds. Isabella focused on deciphering the moods, attitudes, and pecking order of the men. The more she could discern, the better to figure out the weakest link in the group.

Light beamed out of the hole. Paco climbed down the ladder.

"Ready," said a voice from below.

"Your turn," said the man dressed more like a business man than a kidnapper. "Luis, give our guest a hand."

The man who had been holding a gun on her, pressed it against Cody's back, moving him toward the ladder.

"Amigo, you can climb down or we can toss your body down, your choice."

For as suave as the man looked, he tended to have a violent streak to him.

Cody glanced at her and then started down the ladder.

"Señorita, you are next." He smiled and waved his rifle toward the hole.

A quick thought ran through her head. If she could get to the bottom, pull the ladder down and she and Cody knock out the men at the bottom, they could round up the people in the chamber, take down the rock barrier and lead them out.

But what about the woman on the ATV?

No, she would get them all free. Her feet touched the floor and she turned. The gasp that whooshed out couldn't be stopped when she saw the young women in cages. Their hair was straggly and dirty. Some clung to the bars, their eyes beseeching her. Others were huddled in corners as if hoping no one would see them. Her heart went out to each and every one of them.

She would get them out.

Her resolve must have shone in her eyes. Cody caught her attention and gave a slight shake of his head. She quickly lowered her eyes to the floor and moved toward him. It wouldn't do to have the men see the fire this scene had built in her.

The elegantly-clad man stepped off the ladder and immediately picked up a bucket with a ladle and began offering it to each of the captives.

Luis came down the ladder. The chamber, while being a good thirty feet across, was becoming crowded. The young woman from the ATV came down, her hands still bound. As soon as she stepped off the ladder, her leg came around in a nicely thrown round kick, connecting with Luis' leg.

Before Isabella or Cody could react, Paco had an arm around the girl and a gun pressed to her side. The anger sparking in the girl's eyes told Isabella this would be the person to help her get the rest out of here. She just had to find a way to talk with her. Right now she tried to catch the young woman's gaze, to show her they were there to help.

It was the elegant Hispanic man who came over, cupped her bruised cheek, and clucked.

"Sweet one, you bring all this hurt to yourself. If you would relax and let us care for you, you will see how kind we can be."

Isabella couldn't hold her tongue. "These women don't look well taken care of."

"Ah, you have fire as well. I thought you might."

"Emilio, stop trying to sway them with your genteelness. It ain't going to happen." The man from the ATV landed with a thud as he jumped off the third rung from the floor.

"Wes, you can get more with kindness than this." Emilio gently ran his fingertips over the gash on the girl's forehead.

"She did that herself. Ever since she came to, she's been a hellcat." Wes grabbed the girl by the arm and walked to a cage. "Bring that one, too." He nodded toward Isabella.

Emilio took her hand as if they were lovers going on a walk. "Come, you will make a fine addition."

She pulled her hand out of his and walked to the open cage. As soon as she passed the threshold, the door clicked behind her. The girl watched her with wary eyes. Isabella walked up to her, took the rag from her mouth, and started untying the knots binding the girl's hands.

In a hushed voice she whispered, "We'll get out of here, just don't antagonize them."

The girl watched her closely. She must have witnessed the resolve in Isabella's eyes. Her head bobbed slightly once.

In a bit louder voice, she said, "I'm Isabella, what's your name?"

"Sky."

"Can I get some water to clean up her gash?" Isabella asked, turning to the men. She'd figured they would tie up Cody. That didn't shock her. But they were already going through the packs. She didn't know if Cody had his credentials on him like she did, but the minute they saw all their weapons the men would know they weren't typical hikers.

Emilio picked up a bottle of water and brought it over to her. "It is kind of you to help."

The way he kept his gaze on her, rattled Isabella. What did he see or what was he trying to convey?

"Thank you." She took the bottle and turned back to Sky. "Let's get that gash cleaned up before you get an infection."

Isabella ripped off the bottom half of the T-shirt she had on under her long-sleeved shirt and vest. Sky's eyes widened when she saw the vest, but she didn't say a word. Isabella left her outer shirt undone so she could reach things without the men noticing.

Leaning toward Sky to wash the gash, she whispered, "Take the tin in the front right pocket and slip it under you."

The girl deftly reached in, snagging the tin and slipping it under her body.

"When I finish, find a place to hide it in here."

Sky nodded.

"It appears you two are more than recreational hikers," Wes said.

Isabella glanced over her shoulder. Wes stood over Cody who had his wrists and ankles bound. She handed the water to Sky and stood.

"What are you talking about?" she asked, standing at the door of the cage. If she could keep the man's attention split, there was a better chance of their getting out of here. She also didn't want all his distrust and anger to be focused on Cody.

Wes walked toward the cage. "You don't look like a threat."

"Why would you say that?" Her attention remained riveted on Wes, but her mind was circling around all the scenarios that would get them all out of here.

He held up her revolver. "Why would a hiker have a Glock?"

"For snakes." She scowled. "The two-legged kind."

He laughed and then narrowed his eyes. "This kind of weapon is favored by cops. You a cop?"

She shook her head. No lying would be needed. "No, I'm not a cop. I just like having a weapon that will do the job."

He watched her for a long minute and spun around to Cody. Wes sniffed. "You smell like a cop to me. Perhaps, you gave your girlfriend a present of this big revolver."

Cody stared the man square in the eyes. "I didn't give her the gun. If she brought it with her that's the first I've seen of it."

Wes lashed out striking Cody alongside the head. "Don't lie to me! The weapons my men took from you are all military grade.

You're either a cop or Border Patrol."

Isabella couldn't stop the squeak that emitted when Wes hit Cody.

"He's not a cop or Border Patrol. That's no way to treat a man who gave his service to this country." She didn't care if she gained the man's anger, it would give Cody time to regroup from the hit he took.

Wes swung around and stalked toward her cage. "One thing my country has taught me is you take what you want. What I want is money and power. Falling in with Emilio and Chaca are the best ways to get there before I'm too old to enjoy it."

"So kidnapping and selling innocent women makes you feel powerful?" She glared back at him. "I'm sure the people you want to impress won't see it that way. They'll see it as cowardly."

"Why you!" He reached for the lock on the cage.

"Wes, the señorita, she is getting you riled up on purpose, no?" Emilio grasped Wes by the shoulders. "You, Paco, and Luis go see what is keeping Chaca."

Wes sent Isabella a nasty glare before heading up the ladder. The other two men followed.

Once the other men left the chamber the mood changed. Emilio walked over to Cody and crouched beside him.

"Amigo, you may not be a cop or Border Patrol, but I do believe you are a threat." He glanced toward Isabella. "If you want your friend to be safe, you will not give us problems, no?"

She couldn't see if Cody agreed because Emilio's body hid Cody's head. Why were they holding the women here? She scanned the other cages. They were two to a cage, three cages beside the one she and Sky were in. Seven women she had to get out of here.

Coughing in the cage next to her caught her attention. She walked over and put a hand on the woman's back. The cough sounded and rattled the woman's ribs like bronchitis.

"This woman needs a doctor," she said, peering over her shoulder at Emilio, who leaned against a wall watching her.

"She will be tended when she is sold."

"That could be too late." Isabella stood and walked to the front of the cage.

"That will be the buyer's problem. She is already spoken for." Emilio scanned the length of Isabella. "You would bring a high price with your youthful look. Unfortunately, you have too much intelligence. Our buyers wouldn't want to be continually dealing with you."

"In that case, you should let me go." She knew he wouldn't but couldn't help herself.

"No, no, señorita. You are too clever to be let loose. You would find your way back and ruin everything."

"So you either plan to keep me down here indefinitely or kill me?" She wouldn't go down without a fight.

Her thoughts must have been revealed in her eyes. Emilio smiled. "I like your fire. If you are lucky, I will persuade Chaca to let me have you."

A shiver crawled up her back and settled in a knot of tension at the base of her skull. She saw beyond his soft words to the cruel man hidden behind his sophisticated façade.

"You might as well shoot me now." The words came out tough, while her mind cried out she wasn't ready to die. She needed time to try to help Cody and these women. And she wasn't ready to say good-bye to life and Tino.

Emilio laughed loudly. "I do like your fire."

Chapter Fourteen

Tino stood guard over the body along with Crow as they waited for the reservation police to arrive and take over the investigation. A border patrol copter had buzzed by once.

Was this a threat or was there a sniper sitting on a knoll waiting for a chance to shoot? Crow had the same idea and had dispatched Tank and Charlie to do recon.

"Why don't you go see if Manuel can think of anything else he heard the men say?" Crow patted Tino's shoulder.

"I doubt Rico said much. He is a player. He uses people like tissue. They are only worth his time as long as they are giving him information or making him money." He kicked at pebbles near his toes. The only good news about this killing, Rico was focused on him and would not be looking for Isabella.

"Go speak with him. He may have heard more than he told us." Crow held his rifle at the ready. "Go."

Tino walked over to the pickup.

The man inside jumped as if someone electrified his seat.

"You are jumpy," Tino said, sliding into the front passenger side of the four-door pickup.

"Sí. I do not see a man killed often." Manuel shook his head. "Not even back home."

"Tell me everything you heard." Tino put his rifle on the seat beside him and shifted in the seat to peer into the back.

"Why does it matter now?" Manuel's gaze looked everywhere but at Tino.

"This man was in my custody a week ago. Now he is dead. We need to know why he was killed."

Manuel visibly shook. "I have nothing to tell."

This man was hiding something. Tino leaned over the seat, grabbing the *pendejo*, jackass, by the shirt front. "You are not telling me all. Either you heard something that has you scared or you are working for the man who killed Cruz."

Manuel's eyes widened at the name.

"Oh, you did not know it was Cruz Sanchez who was shot?" Tino tightened his grip. "It is interesting that you know the name. Now I am positive you are working for Rico Montoya."

The man's body shook harder. He put a trembling hand to his mouth.

Tino jerked his hand down and found a small pill clutched in his fingers.

"¡Coño! You will not kill yourself before I have found out all I want to know!" Tino grasped both the man's hands and hit the horn on the pickup.

Crow ran over. "What's up?"

"Manuel is on Rico's payroll. He tried to swallow this." Tino handed the pill over to Crow, who bagged and tagged it. Tino put cuffs on Manuel, binding his hands behind his back and hooking his feet to the metal leg of the front seat.

He wanted to get the man back to headquarters for interrogation, but they had to wait for the Reservation police and Tank and Charlie to return.

~*~

Isabella tried her best to comfort the woman who sat up against the bars to get relief from her coughing. "I'm Isabella." She put her hand on the woman's back. The woman flinched and pulled away from her touch. The reaction to physical touch revealed the woman may have been sexually abused.

"Where are you from?" Isabella asked quietly. Taking in the six feet by six feet cage with blankets on the ground for beds and a bucket in a corner to use as a toilet.

"Detroit, I'm Judy," the woman replied between coughs.

"How did you get clear down here?" Isabella offered her the bottle of water she'd used to clean Sky's gash.

"I was visiting a friend in Mexico City." She shot a glance at Emilio. "He saw me in a bar and bought me a drink. The next thing I know, I'm down in this hell hole." She coughed uncontrollably.

"How long have you been down here?" Isabella had to get a bearing on how soon they needed to make a move.

"I think a week." She nodded to her cage mate. The woman hadn't moved since Isabella arrived. "Suri has been here for two weeks, she thinks. She's not a strong person. I don't know if she'll be well once she leaves." Judy's concern for the other woman showed even though the women had been treated poorly they still held compassion.

Isabella stood and crossed the three steps over to Sky, taking a seat on the blanket beside the woman. She studied the cages. They were in three foot sections, narrow enough to fit through the opening, with long-shafted locks used as pins to hold the panels together.

"How did you end up here?" Isabella asked Sky, keeping her voice low.

José appeared to be dozing. Emilio was playing a game of cards. The click and slap of the cards was comforting and irritating at the same time.

"I was partying with some college friends in Puerta Vallarta. A nice-looking Latino man came over to our table, we talked and danced. My friends wandered on to another bar and the next thing I know I wake up straddling that quad with that Neanderthal. He's the one that smacked me around when I tried to get away." Anger sparked in Sky's eyes. "There is no way in hell I'll be sold to some rich bastard who'll use me for his morbid fetishes." Her voice rose.

"Shhh. We'll get out of here. Just keep calm. Cody and I will find a way." Isabella cast a glance toward Emilio. If only he'd leave, she was pretty sure she could get out of the cage and take care of José.

Emilio looked at his watch, stacked the cards, and headed for the ladder. He tapped José on the shoulder, waking the man, and climbed the ladder.

Isabella dug her tin out from under the blanket where Sky hid it.

She took out the two magnetized sewing needles and sat with her back to the chamber. Using the tin and lid as pliers, she bent one needle into an L-shape and made small waves in the end of the other one.

"Keep this handy in case I get caught," she whispered to Sky and handed over the tin.

Isabella stood, stretched, and walked to the cage door.

Cody's head tipped down as if he slept, but she saw his gaze following her movements. She nodded toward José, sitting on an upturned wooden box. The man's head bobbed and his eyelids were slowly lowering. Cody nodded.

Isabella put the L-shaped needle into the lock and held tension on the needle. With the wavy needle, she slowly and quietly worked the tumblers until the tension gave way and the lock popped open. Sky stood beside her. Isabella handed the lock to the other woman, and softly swung the door open.

A metal on metal creak echoed through the silence.

José came up off the box. Isabella jumped, executing a flying side kick. Her foot connected with his chest, slamming him against the wall. His head hit the wall with a thunk, and he slumped over the box he'd been sitting on.

She landed with both feet on the floor. That was the first time she'd used that maneuver to actually take out a true adversary and not a sparring partner.

The women started to chatter.

"Shhh! Emilio is up there somewhere. Let me get Cody loose." Isabella hurried to Cody. She grabbed her knife from the side of her pack and sliced through the ropes binding him.

He grabbed up his weapons. "What's your plan?"

She looked at the rock wall they'd discovered. "We have two choices. You go up the ladder and hope to surprise Emilio, or we quickly remove rocks, get you free to go for help, and I'll see about getting the women out.

Sky stood at Judy's cage, cursing and trying to pick the lock.

"I'm not leaving without you. We're all going out through the tunnel." Cody started moving the rocks.

Isabella and Cody made a hole large enough for a person to slither through.

"José, Chaca is on his way." Emilio's voice boomed down into the chamber.

"We can't all get out before he comes down or this Chaca arrives." Isabella grabbed Cody's arm. "Go! Bring back help. I'll stay and help the women."

"I won't leave you!" Cody said, taking a firm stance.

"This is our only chance to get help. Go. You can move faster without me or the women. Bring back the authorities." She thrust his rifle into his hands and turned him, pushing him toward the hole.

His gaze slid over the cages and women with their faces pressed up against the bars. Sky was still working on the same lock.

He shook his head. "I don't like leaving you here."

Sky glanced up from the lock. "Go, I think I hear him coming back."

"We can't all get out of here without being caught. Go, you're the best chance these women have of getting free." Isabella put on a braver front than she felt. She would love to slide out through that hole with Cody, but she couldn't leave these women behind. She could at least keep them hopeful and make sure no one ratted on how Cody escaped.

"I'm going to close this back up so we can use it for our escape if the chance arises." She gave him another nudge toward the hole. "Go. You'll be back with help by morning."

"You're very brave and I'm proud to call you sister." Cody squeezed her shoulder and wiggled his body through the hole.

"Come help me." Isabella called Sky over.

The two women worked quickly replacing the rocks.

"Why did you let him go alone?" Sky asked as they set the last stones in place.

Isabella staged her pack and the knife next to the ropes that had bound Cody. "Come on. We need to get back in the cell."

Once they were both back in the locked cage, she sat in the corner near Judy.

"When the time is right, we'll use that wall as our exit. We don't know what direction this Chaca person is coming from and with this many people and several who are not well, we would not have been able to move fast enough to get away." She patted Judy's knee. "Cody will bring back officials. But if the chance arises we will all leave here, together."

"Is Cody your brother? Is that why you believe he will bring back help?" Judy asked.

She wanted to tell the woman he was her brother but too many lives would be endangered by the truth. "He's my friend and he is part of an elite law enforcement team. He'll be able to get through to help easier alone than with a bunch of women trailing after him." She made light of the women slowing him down but it weighed heavy on her mind. She had yet to visit with the women in the far cages.

"Do you know who those women are and how they got here?" she asked Judy.

"They were pretty much drugged and ended up here as well. All from tourist spots in Mexico." She nodded to Suri. "She is the only one I don't know how she ended up here. Marie in the cage next to us told me Suri's name and how long she's been here. She hasn't said a word to me since I've been here."

Isabella didn't like what she was hearing. Suri would be their Achilles heel when they made their move.

"When we go for the escape, Judy, if you can manage, you and Marie will have to make sure Suri is with us. Sky and I will be busy conducting the escape."

Judy nodded. "I'll let Marie know."

"Thanks."

"José, I can see the lights getting closer." Emilio's foot appeared through the hole in the kiva. He descended the ladder and scanned the chamber. He let loose a stream of curses in Spanish and shook José.

"What happened?" Emilio sat José straight on the box and held his face between his hands. "Where is the man?"

José stared at Emilio.

Sky started to snicker. Isabella touched her arm and shook her head. Emilio didn't need to get the notion the women had anything to do with Cody getting away. She leaned her head back against the cave wall, pretending she was asleep. But her lashes were raised enough to watch the man's actions.

"Where is the man?" Emilio stalked over to the pack, the knife, and the cut ropes. "How did he get these?"

José rose to his feet, swayed, and sat back down on the box. He moaned and grasped his head in his hands.

Emilio turned in a circle. "How did he get out of here?"

Isabella held her breath when Emilio walked over to the rock wall and stared at it. Did I get the stones back correctly? Are there any telltale signs the rocks were moved?

He placed his hand on a rock and shoved.

She watched in terror. If the rock budged or another fell their escape would be hampered.

Nothing moved.

Emilio walked back to the ladder and stared up. He pivoted and marched over to the cage.

"You, wake up," he ordered.

Sky flinched. Isabella opened her eyes slowly and pretended to be surprised at her surroundings.

"Whe—?" She turned to Sky, winked with the eye away from Emilio, and turned a slack-jawed face his direction. "What do you want?"

"You know what I want señorita. How did your man get out of here?"

She glanced at the spot where Cody had been tied up and feigned surprise. "Where'd he go? And without me!" She sprung to her feet. "That lying…he said if I went on this hike with him it would prove I loved him." She spun back toward Sky, smiled and jammed her hands on her hips as she swung back around. "The first sign of trouble and he takes off like his butt's on fire." She tried for an indignant expression while on the inside she was leaping with joy. The longer she kept Emilio entertained the farther away Cody traveled.

"Señorita, you are a poor actress, no?"

Emilio's hand came through the bars so fast she didn't have time to jump back. He grasped her shirt front and pulled her up against the bars.

The air whooshed out of her lungs at the impact. Fear spiraled before she caught her breath and fought down the fear with anger. She'd not allow herself to make the mistake of getting close enough for him to touch her again.

"I know you had something to do with his escape. You are too clever to pretend you do not know where he went." His other hand grasped the back of her head, pressing her face through the bars.

She struggled to hold her head back from the crushing impact of the bars against her cheekbones. Anger had to fuel her and not allow fear to creep in.

"I will personally take care of your boyfriend when we catch him. And because you think you are so smart, I will make you watch, then take care of you." His face came forward as if to force a kiss on her.

Isabella spit in his face. He released her so fast, her body tumbled backwards onto the hard floor.

"You will pay for your insolence!" Emilio wiped his sleeve across his face and glared at her.

Sky dove to her rescue. "Are you okay?"

Her backside ached from the impact of hitting the solid floor. Her cheeks hurt from being crushed against the bars. And her pride hurt that she'd allowed his nastiness to provoke her.

Chapter Fifteen

Tino sat in the interrogation room with Manuel and Crow. They'd questioned the man for an hour and he was uncooperative.

Tank stuck his head in the room. "There's a call for you."

"I am busy. Take a name and number, I will call back," Tino said, frustrated they had accomplished nothing with the interview.

"He said he could get me tossed out of the Shadow Eagles if I didn't make sure you answered the phone." Tank made a grimace. "He seems to know a lot of people."

"¡Cono!" Tino slammed his hands on the table. It had to be Isabella's father. The man liked to use his connections to make things happen his way. He glared at Manuel. "When I come back you better have answers or I'll send you back to Rico along with a rumor you are turning against him."

Tino stalked out of the interview room and into an empty office.

Tank followed. "Who is this guy?"

"My future father-in-law."

Tank grimaced. "Line three."

Tino nodded, picked up the receiver, and stabbed the blinking three. "Tino."

"Where the hell have you been?"

"Dodging bullets. Did you find out where Isabella and Cody are?" He wasn't in the mood for a lecture from Mumphrey.

"No. We've been working since I talked to you trying to piece together their movements via the GPS in both their phones, but they aren't within signal distance of a tower."

"Did you ask at the Cabeza Prieta refuge if she filed a trip log?" He'd learned that it was required in the parks along the border. That way patrol and wildlife officials could keep tabs on the civilians using the parks.

"Yes, I have a couple of men on the ground looking and Border Patrol has a copter in the air. She and Cody seem to have vanished."

Tino's chest constricted. The only way he knew they could have vanished was if they were dead or taken by Rico. "Keep me in the loop. I will come help if necessary."

"Same goes. If you hear from her, call. I don't care what time it is."

"Sí."

The phone went dead. Tino sat contemplating his options. He could head out now and be at the park by nightfall. He'd get the coordinates of Mumphrey's men and help them look. But his gut told him he'd find her quicker if Manuel talked. He pushed away from the desk and headed back to the interview room.

Before opening the door, he took three deep breaths, put a smile on his face, and opened the door.

"Good news, Manuel. I found an informant who has agreed to take you to Rico. He'll explain how you did a good job of getting me out to Cruz's body and then couldn't go through with killing me." Tino grabbed a chair, turned it, straddled the seat, and crossed his arms over the back.

The man across the table squeaked and squirmed. "You cannot do that. You would be part of my murder."

"I didn't hear a word he said," Crow announced, standing. "Fact, I think I need to use the latrine."

"No, you cannot make me go with this person. I have rights."

"The only way I'll spare you is if you tell me everything you know about Rico's business and where I can find him."

~*~

The sound of several motorized vehicles echoed down into the

113

kiva.

Instead of sleeping, Isabella had studied the walls and noticed carvings on the one opposite the cage. She couldn't see them from her cage, but she was sure they would tell the story of the fourth world exodus of the Hopi. She wished she could have found this place before these men had brought such disgrace to it.

Voices carried down into the chamber. Feet appeared and one by one, four men descended the ladder. When the last one turned around, Isabella's heart lodged in her throat and chills of fear snaked through her veins.

Shamutz! Rico Montoya shook hands with Emilio.

The one man Tino had feared she'd meet was standing not twenty feet from her. She had nowhere to hide and feared she'd just sealed Tino's fate.

Sky tapped her on the shoulder. "What's wrong?" she asked quietly.

Isabella shook her head. She didn't want to speak or be noticed.

"Wes told me you had a man and a woman you found sneaking around." Rico cast a gaze about the chamber. "Where are they?"

Emilio sent a glare Isabella's direction. "The man escaped while I was up top contacting you." He waved an arm at José, who still nursed his head. "He appears to have cut himself loose, rendered José senseless, and I fear he must have climbed the ladder and got away while my back was to the hole."

Rico's eyes flashed. He back-handed Emilio. "You know how I feel about imbeciles."

"Yes, Chaca."

Chaca! Rico was the boss of the smuggling operation? She remained with her back slightly towards the men. As if she didn't care what they were talking about. Sky faced her, watching.

"Did you send anyone after him?" Rico stood nearly touching noses with Emilio.

"I had no one to send." Emilio didn't back down to Rico.

Was he looking to take over? Could she use him to her advantage?

"Which is the woman?" Rico turned to the cages.

Isabella's heart raced and her hands turned cold. What would he do when he recognized her?

Emilio stalked to the cage and pointed. "This one. She is trouble."

Rico stepped up to the cage. "Turn around!" he ordered.

She swallowed twice, squared her shoulders, and faced the man. "Hello, Rico."

His face turned scarlet. His mouth opened and shut for several seconds.

"You know this woman?" Emilio stepped between them, capturing Rico's attention.

She mentally thanked Emilio. The interruption gave her more time to figure out how to approach the man who wanted her and her lover dead.

"The man with her. Was he Latino?" Rico pointed at her but his attention was fully on Emilio.

"No. He was Indian. Why?" Emilio insisted, pushing ever closer to Rico.

Chaca shoved him out of the way. "Who did you pull into your little games this time, Dr. Mumphrey?"

There was a collective gasp from the women and Emilio.

"I don't know what you're talking about." She had the presence of mind to stay far enough away from the bars that no one could make a grab for her.

"Last time we met you had a DEA agent wrapped around your finger as you stuck your nose into my business." Rico snarled. "Has he told you I have a bounty on his head?"

"He might have mentioned it in passing. He isn't scared." She remained nonchalant, not sure how to handle the man to get the others out of this mess. "When did you take up human trafficking or is this an old occupation?"

Rico laughed. "So cool and calm. You didn't answer my question. What brings you to my smugglers cave?"

"This chamber we're in? I was looking for an ancient Hopi ceremonial kiva." She waved her arms. "This one to be exact. You do know by holding these women against their will you have angered the gods. I wouldn't doubt that you will soon have all kinds of trouble coming down on you."

She decided to use a little mythology and legends to see if his men might have a bit of superstition in them. The past had proven Rico had no conscience. Glancing past Rico and Emilio, she saw the other men backing toward the ladder. Rustling behind drew her attention to Suri, who watched with bright eyes. Superstition had brought her out of her shell.

Again, Rico laughed. "You will not use your knowledge to trick me." He drew a cigarillo out of his pocket, put it in his mouth, and lit the end. Puffing, dispensing small clouds of smoke in the chamber, he watched her. His eyes narrowed.

"I now have you to draw out your lover. Emilio where are her belongings?"

Emilio motioned to her pack and the knife beside it. Rico crouched, digging through the change of clothes and sundry toiletries.

He looked up, watching her. "Where is the vest?"

Emilio stared at him. "What vest?"

"Dr. Mumphrey goes nowhere without a fishing vest full of her tricks." Rico stood. "Get her out here."

Emilio pulled a key from his pocket and unlocked the door.

Isabella shook off his hand when he grabbed for her. "I'm not stupid. There are six of you and one of me." She stepped out of the cage.

Rico pointed to her shirt front. "Unbutton your shirt!"

Staring him in the eyes, she unbuttoned her shirt, revealing her vest.

Triumph shone in Rico's eyes as he pointed. "That is her vest of tricks. Take it off."

She drew the long-sleeved shirt off first, sticking it between her legs. What was still in her vest? Her identification, but Rico knew who she was. Wrappers, her journal, first-aid kit, luckily she'd passed off the survival tin. As long as Rico didn't know about it, she was good.

"Hurry up." Rico held out his hand.

Heaving a defeated sigh, for his sake, Isabella took off the vest and handed it to him.

Emilio stepped up beside him. "I do not see what is so special about the vest?"

"I do not know either, but it will be my bait to get a man I have wanted dead for ten months into my hands." He smiled, his dark gaze glinting with malice. "This will be my bait to bring your lover to me."

He turned to Emilio. "Put her back in the cage."

"I am glad I am not your lover or you. Rico does not play nice with people he wants to kill." Emilio shoved her in the cage and snapped the lock shut.

She didn't want to appear desperate, but she needed to hear what he said to two of the men who had arrived with him. She grasped the bars and tried to listen.

Rico handed her vest to one of the men and said something. They both disappeared up the ladder.

How long before they'd get her vest to Tino? Would he think he could come on his own? Fear she'd just handed Tino to Rico froze her heart and her feet.

Sky pulled her into a hug. "Who are you really?" she whispered.

Isabella hugged her back and allowed the woman to lead her to the corner by Judy.

Suri was snuggled next to the coughing woman. "Will the Indian's ancestors hurt us?" she asked in a small shy voice.

Isabella tamped her fear down. She had to remain calm and in control to get out of here and stop Tino.

"No. They aren't mad at us. It's the men who are using a sacred site for evil that they will make pay." She wasn't above spinning a good legend to bring the woman to follow orders.

"Who are you?" Sky insisted again.

"I am Isabella Mumphrey, doctor of anthropology at the University in Phoenix. I came down here looking for this kiva. I just stumbled upon it in an awkward way." If Cody had let her come this direction yesterday, they possibly would have found the kiva and the women and had them out of here before Emilio and his group arrived.

She studied the conversation between Emilio and Rico. They were in a deep discussion.

"How often has Rico visited here?" she asked Judy.

"This is the first time I've seen him."

"They must be getting ready to move or sell you." Isabella glanced down the wall at the other four women she'd yet to meet. "Fill the others in on what I've told you and have them listen to all the conversations they can and relay the information." She peered into Judy eyes, then Suri's. "I promise I will get you out of here. It will just take some time to figure out how."

They nodded and moved to the other corner of their cage to relay the information.

"You are determined to get us out," Sky observed.

Isabella smiled. "I've done everything I've set my mine to thus far. I don't want to ruin my streak." She watched Rico and the other man who came with him climb the ladder. "We better get some sleep. Tomorrow might bring our freedom."

Sky nodded and laid down on the blanket by the wall.

Isabella remained sitting, her head tipped against the wall, calculating when Tino would arrive. It would be within twenty-four hours, she had no doubt.

Chapter Sixteen

Tino had the list of places Rico stayed according to Manuel, who had become cooperative once he realized Tino had no compunction of sending him straight back to Rico as a snitch. His contact at DEA promised to send people to several of the sites. He also called in a favor with acquaintances over at ICE. With any luck, they'd have Rico in custody by tomorrow and he could hunt down Isabella.

One of the civilian women who worked the office knocked on the open door.

"Sí?"

"This arrived for you." She placed a small package on his desk.

"Was it hand delivered?" He noticed there wasn't a return address and just his name in black felt marker.

"Yes. Some Hispanic man walked in, said it was for you, and walked out."

Tino rounded the desk. "How long ago?"

"Ten or fifteen minutes. I waited until I saw the light on the phone go off."

"¡Carajo!" He stared at the package. It appeared to be flimsy. "What did it feel like?" Most bombs were in boxes.

"It felt like clothing and possibly a book." Her face reddened.

"You were trying to figure out what I would have delivered to me at the station?"

Her lashes lowered in embarrassment. "Yes. You've been living here. I imagined you ordered clothes."

He pointed to just his name. "But there is no address. How would a store know to send me clothes?"

She shrugged.

"Ask Crow to come in here please." Tino sat back down at the desk and moved the package around with a letter opener. Did he open it? Was it a trap sent to him from Rico? His nerves and desire to rip it open and find out had his mind buzzing.

"Sharon said you wanted to see me." Crow leaned against the door jamb.

"This package was delivered by hand for me." Tino used the letter opener to shove the package across the desk.

Crow pushed away from the doorframe and approached the desk. "I see. Not your typical wrapping for a bomb."

"That's what I thought. Grab some rubber gloves and masks and meet me behind the building."

The man nodded and exited.

Tino dusted the envelope for prints. He picked up several sets and placed them in an evidence bag. Once he collected the fingerprints and took several photos of the package, he carried it out the back door.

Crow, Tank, and Charlie all stood by a utility spool about thirty feet from the back door.

He placed the package on the spool, donned the rubber gloves and mask, and motioned for the others to back up. Flicking open his knife, Tino sliced the end off the package and using the blade lifted the wrapping.

The faded olive green color started his hands trembling. He picked up the other end of the package, tipping it. His worse fear slammed into him with more impact than if there had been a bomb in the package.

"No!" He grasped the edges of the spool with both hands to keep him on his feet as he stared down at Isabella's survival vest and journal. A folded paper stuck out of the top of the journal.

Crow came up beside him and pulled the note from the book. "I have Dr. Mumphrey. If you want her to live, you will meet me tonight at these coordinates. Come alone or she will die in front of your eyes. Rico." Crow read the note aloud. He put a hand on Tino's shoulder. "We know where he is, we'll find him first."

Tino shook his head. "No. He will be close to the spot where he plans to kill me." He ripped the note from Crow's hand, picked up Isabella's belongings and stormed back into the building. He pulled up the coordinates on the computer. Rico was in the southeast corner of the refuge. In a mountain range.

"You aren't planning to go in there alone, are you?" Tank asked.

"No, I'm taking all my resources with me. I'm pretty sure Rico will have his men and he won't let Isabella go. He'll kill me and then her or vice versa. I'd be stupid to think he'd let her go."

"We'll go with you," Crow said.

"I appreciate the offer. I like being backed up by people I trust." Tino picked up the phone. "I'll make calls for backup while you get the equipment ready. We'll need to get moving to get there early and set up."

The three men left and the first call Tino made was to Isabella's father. He had a right to know his daughter was in danger.

~*~

Isabella woke with a stiff neck and grumbling stomach. Emilio stood next to the cage watching her. She slowly rotated her head left and right. A toothbrush would have been nice, along with a trip to a restroom. She glanced at the bucket in the corner. There was no way she'd use it with the man staring at her.

"Do you feed us or do your clients like women with their ribs sticking out?" she asked.

Emilio shoved away from the cage, rummaged in one of the boxes, and tossed a handful of granola bars into the cage and moved down the line. The other women scrambled to gather the food. Isabella took her time, picking the bars up and handing Sky half.

Sitting beside the other woman, she opened a wrapper and took a bite. Her body wasn't used to so little fuel. Hopefully, when she needed to use her muscles they would perform.

"Sometime today, I need to get the wire in my tin out and string it around my waist. I may need it when they take me out of the cage," she whispered to Sky.

"How do you know they'll take you out?"

"If Rico sent my vest to Tino, he will come. Rico will want me there to antagonize Tino."

She took a bite, chewed, and had a hard time swallowing despite her grumbling stomach. Tino would come. She prayed to all the deities she'd ever studied that he came with backup.

"We need water to wash down these bars," she called to Emilio.

The perturbed expression revealed he didn't like waiting on the women. The task must have usually fallen on a lower man in the chain. His actions spoke more than his words. He didn't like being left in charge of the women. He would rather be with Rico discovering his enemies.

He walked over to the cage with a bottle of water. Isabella stood and met him, standing back far enough only to grasp the bottle.

"You should be out there checking on shipments and handling the money, not here babysitting us." She unscrewed the lid and tipped the bottle to her lips.

His eyes narrowed. "What do you know?"

She sighed, screwing the lid back on. "That you are better than the likes of José." The underling was still groggy from her attack. He leaned against a wall, his eyes closed, moaning now and then.

"What are you trying to do? Maybe get me to leave so you can find a way out?" He slashed a hand through the air. "I do not usually babysit women, but I know what will happen if I disobey Rico. I will miss my chance."

"Your chance to take over?"

His eyes widened a moment before settling into a scowl.

"Yes, I know what you want. Tonight, when he tries to enact his revenge on my fiancé and me, you could catch Rico off guard and make yourself the Chaca." She pivoted and walked over to Sky, handing her the bottle. Crossing her legs, she sat facing the cage door. Emilio remained deep in thought.

Perhaps, she'd put enough of an idea in his mind that he could be beneficial.

"What was that all about?" Sky asked after taking a long draw on the water.

"Just setting things in place to hopefully give Tino and I an edge." Isabella scooted toward Judy and Suri's cage. "Emilio, the other women need water too."

He jumped at her voice, then absent-mindedly passed out two bottles to each cage.

Yes, he was thinking about how to take advantage of Rico's obsession with Tino.

Chapter Seventeen

Tino called Border Patrol to have agents from the wildlife refuge meet him at the Cabeza Prieta visitor center. Before he could contact ICE, he received a call from them asking where to converge. Their contacting him had to be the work of Isabella's father. Tino also had the full force of the Shadow Eagles behind him. They drove to the refuge in two pickups.

Halfway to the visitor's center, Tino's phone rang. He looked at the caller ID and immediately responded. "Where are you? Do you have Ezzabella?"

"I'm at the border with several border patrol officers. I don't have Isabella. She refused to leave the others." Cody's tired voice did little to bolster Tino's attitude.

"What do you mean she refused to leave? We are headed to the refuge visitor center. Rico Montoya has her and wants to meet with me."

Cody cursed. "I knew I should have forced her to come with me. We were caught by human traffickers. They are holding seven women in the kiva Isabella was searching for." Cody cursed, again. "When we had the chance to leave, Isabella and I, she told me to get out and bring back help. She wasn't leaving the others. One woman isn't well."

Tino could see Isabella persuading Cody to leave her. She'd persuaded him to allow her to handle being a human sacrifice and he loved her. "Rico has asked me to meet him alone in the Agua Dulce Mountains."

"That's where he's holding Isabella and the women. I'm headed that way with Border Patrol."

"Stay out of sight. If Rico sees you, he'll kill Isabella before I can stop him." Tino clicked the off button and stared out the window.

"Was that Cody?" Crow asked.

"Sí. He left Isabella alone to come for help."

"Then we know where to surprise Montoya."

"He will not be there. It is where they are holding women to sell." Tino turned his attention to the head of the Shadow Eagles. "Cody is headed back to free the women he and Isabella found. If he is discovered before we arrive, Isabella is dead."

"The traffickers may have moved the women if they know Cody got away."

"True. Then *mi pichon*, my dove, risked her life for nothing."

~*~

At the refuge visitor center, Tino discussed the mission with the border patrol for the refuge and discovered the coordinates Cody gave for the prisoned women were a mile south of the coordinates Rico had given him.

"This is good," Tino said. "We will be able to keep all our forces close together."

"But we'll have to go in from all different directions. If this body of men moves in as one, they'll know we are gunning for them," offered one of the refuge border patrolmen.

"Sí. I agree. We do not want to allow them to see us." Tino feared if Rico saw it was a trap, he'd kill Isabella and wait for another time to deal with Tino.

"We have a surveillance truck moving to a high point in the mountains. We should have a pretty good eye on the coordinates from there. It's too risky flying copters in the area," Lt. Rodgers of Border Patrol added.

Special Agent Renee Halstead of ICE spoke up. "I'll take my people in from the south." She pointed on the route along Hwy 2 in Mexico.

"Let's move out." Tino climbed back in the pickup with Crow, Alfred, and Percy. Tank and Charlie headed south with the ICE faction.

The refuge Border Patrol led the way into the refuge. They found a hidden area to park the vehicles and spread out on foot, heading to the meet site.

~*~

Isabella couldn't sit still. By the darkness descending on the kiva, it was well past dusk. Why hadn't Rico come for her? Emilio had left several hours earlier, leaving Wes and Luis in charge of watching the women.

The two men played cards and told raunchy jokes.

"Wes, aren't you afraid your old man will find out what you do?" Luis asked, shuffling the cards.

"Naw. He knows what I do." Wes picked up his cards, one at a time arranging them in his hand.

Luis dropped his hands to the box with a thud, capturing Isabella's full attention. "But your old man is a sheriff. If people found out what you did, he'd be run out of a job."

Isabella stopped her pacing and listened closer. Could this nasty man be her half-brother? The thought soured her stomach. But his name was Wes and he had a sheriff for a father.

"Hell, he's more corrupt than I am. He's the one that got me running drugs when I was a teen-ager." Wes narrowed his eyes. "He's the one that taught me you take what you want. And I want more power than him."

The last statement swirled in Isabella's mind. "*He's the one that taught me to take what you want.*" That was the mentality she'd conjured up when Cody told her about how she was conceived.

"What are you staring at?" Wes growled and threw an empty water bottle at her.

Isabella ducked and sat down by Sky. She didn't want him thinking she had any motives about him. But she now wondered if Cody had known who he was and if so why he hadn't said anything.

Her curiosity ate at her like a kitten lapping up milk. She wanted to know his last name and more about his father…their father. Not because she wanted to know the man on a personal level but because she wanted to find a way to bring him down for dishonoring her family.

Revenge didn't settle well in her mind or her heart. It felt like a worm eating away at her good sense. Now she understood Tino's need. Revenge was a narcotic that had to be avenged.

"What are you thinking? You look as murderous as Wes."

Sky's words slapped Isabella in the conscience.

She didn't want to be like Wes or their father. Revenge couldn't consume her or she would become just like them. She wanted a Hopi life. Fulfilled with digging up knowledge of past lives and righting wrongs through proper means. Not taking matters into her own hands.

A light shone at the top of the ladder.

"Wes, bring Dr. Mumphrey up the ladder. She has a date with destiny."

Rico's voice sent ripples of dread creeping through her veins.

She hugged Sky. "Remember our plan," she whispered and walked to the door of the cage.

Wes pulled a key from his right pants pocket and unlocked the door. He grabbed her by the arm, pulling her to the ladder. "Move!"

Her hands grasped the rungs and she climbed to the surface. The fresh evening air filled her lungs like a sweet elixir. Having spent the last forty-eight hours in the stench down in the kiva, she breathed in deep.

A strong hand gripped her upper arm.

"We wouldn't want to keep Tino waiting." Rico pulled her away from the ladder and tied her hands behind her back. Wes and then Luis stepped off the ladder.

"Keep her moving. When I give the order, bring her to me." Rico headed down the opposite side of the ridge she and Cody had hiked.

Halfway down the ridge, she found her chance to get close to Wes. She tripped over a washed out root. She couldn't stop her fall into the back of him. Her body took him to the ground.

"Damn klutzy whore!" Wes swore.

Isabella rolled around on top of him until her fingers slipped into his right pocket and came out with the key to the cages. Her grip on the keys was tenuous. Luis yanked her to her feet and the key landed on the ground. She did a quick three-sixty mental photo of the area. It had been a while since she'd used her photographic memory skills, but she would find the key when she was sure Tino was safe.

Luis and Wes each grabbed one of her arms, pulling her along behind Rico. Her heart pumped like a galloping horse. What was

Rico's plan? She knew he wouldn't go to meet Tino with only the two men. He had to have others positioned around the meet area. And Tino wouldn't meet Rico without backup. But how many were on each side?

She or Tino could get caught in crossfire.

"Stay." Rico ordered and walked ahead ten feet. "Tino! I know you're out there. I have your Dr. Mumphrey."

"If she is harmed you will suffer greatly!" Tino's voice was strong and full of confidence.

"She is not harmed." Rico cackled. "Not yet anyway. Once I have rid myself of you, I will take my fill of your doctor, then send her to meet you."

"Don't let him antagonize. He'll do no such thing!" Isabella hollered.

"Shut her up!" Rico ordered.

Wes clamped his hand over her mouth.

A bush to her left moved. Luis crumpled to the ground.

Wes released her to save himself and ran through the bushes.

A Native American dressed in camouflage walked up and cut the ropes binding her hands.

"I got her," he said into a walkie-talkie.

"Thank you, but I have some place to be." She took off at a run as gunfire rang out behind her.

She expected the man to follow, but when she stopped at the spot where the key had dropped, she looked back. No one followed. The ravine echoed with gun reports and ATV motors. Lights from flashlights and vehicles bounced among the brush and cactus.

On her knees, she ran her hands through the sand at the base of the creosote bush she fell beside. Her fingers touched metal. She scooped up the key and hurried up the side of the ridge, digging in with her hands and feet. At the top, she spotted the ladder and headed down.

The woman all stood at the cage doors. Isabella drew in a deep breath, unlocked Sky's cage and handed the key to Judy.

"Help me pull the ladder down. We don't want anyone thinking they can hide from the patrol down here." Isabella and Sky pulled the log ladder down into the chamber.

The women were all free.

"Start pulling the rocks down, but be careful no one gets hurt."

Isabella found her camera in her pack and took photos of the carvings and drawings on the wall. The ones she'd stared at all the previous day. They were etched in her mind, but she needed proof of their existence to get a research crew back out here.

"We can go through," Sky said, motioning to the hole the women had made in the rock wall.

Isabella dumped out her backpack and Cody's. She repacked their weapons, his first aid kit, and grabbed several boxes of the granola bars and a water bottle for each of them into her backpack. Sky handed Isabella's survival tin to her.

"Thank you." She handed Judy Cody's flashlight and picked her flashlight up from the pile of items she'd dumped out of the backpacks. "I'll take the lead, Judy and Sky, you bring up the rear. The tunnel is about two miles long. It will take about an hour. Most of the way you can only walk single-file. Everyone be aware of who is in front and behind you, so we stay together."

She shouldered her backpack and stepped through the rock wall into the tunnel. Cody's flashlight was brighter and did a good job of lighting the way for the women behind her. She could walk faster, but the women had been cooped up in the cages with little food and no exercise. She couldn't have made them go faster if she'd wanted to.

Her mind raced back to the scene she'd left. The Shadow Eagle who set her free would have apprehended Rico. He was the threat to Tino. They would no doubt be looking for her, but as soon as they hit a Border Patrol, she'd have them radio Tino and let him know she was safe.

The floor became slick from the area under the spring.

"Be careful walking through here. The floor is slick from an underground spring." She informed the woman behind her. "Let the others know to watch their step."

If someone fell and injured themselves, it would slow them down and be hard to deal with in the small tunnel.

Everyone made it through the slick spot. A tap on her shoulder stopped her feet.

"Yes?"

"They ask that we rest," the woman behind her said.

"Okay, but only for a few minutes. I want to get you all to the Border Patrol before morning."

A collective sigh carried through the tunnel. Clothing rustled and bodies lowered to the floor.

She wanted to keep on pushing. Cody had to be coming their way by now. It couldn't be more than a few miles to the border. He had to of made it there. Perhaps he contacted Tino and was told to stay away until they had Rico.

The woman behind her pulled on Isabella's pant leg. She leaned down.

"Sky says she hears something behind us."

Shamutz! Did some of Rico's men drop down into the chamber to hide and see their escape hole?

"Tell everyone to get up and move faster. There is a chamber at the end of this tunnel, we'll have more space to navigate if we can get there."

And bats to deal with.

She started forward at the pace she would have preferred when they started. The sounds of the women struggling behind her kept her focused on getting to the chamber.

The tunnel widened and she pressed against the wall moving the others by her. "Keep going. When you get to the chamber keep walking until you can see the sky through two boulders." She pressed her light into the first woman's hands and said the same thing over and over until Sky.

"There is an opening between two boulders. Take the women out and turn right. Follow the ravine until you run into Cody or Border Patrol." Isabella gave the woman a nudge to get going.

"What about you?"

"I'll stop whoever is following and catch up." She didn't know now many were following them, but she'd set up a roadblock.

Sky hugged her. "Be careful."

"Don't worry, I'll be right behind you."

The sounds of the women faded. Isabella tipped her head and listened back the way they had come. There it was. A slow shuffle of someone unsure of the path.

Her mind whirred, selecting and ditching ideas. Most would make noise and give away she was here preparing a trap. The only course she could see would be to wait at the opening of the chamber and take the person by surprise.

Chapter Eighteen

Tino went into stalk mode after Crow announced he had Isabella. He dropped low to the ground and listened to the chaos of rifle fire, ATVs revving, and squawking coming from the walkie-talkie. He dropped the box even though it was his only communication with the patrol and Shadow Eagles.

One goal repeated in his head. *Take down Rico.* He didn't want to live with the threat of the rogue agent anymore. He and Isabella deserved a life where they weren't looking over their shoulders all the time.

He headed in the direction he'd heard Rico's voice. ATV lights lit up the area ahead of him. He saw someone running. Keeping low and moving quickly, he caught up to the man when he stopped to talk in a small radio.

Rico.

Tino tackled his enemy, taking him to the ground hard. He scrambled up Rico's body, wrenching his arms behind him. Tino held the traitor immobile with one hand and pulled out his cuffs. Rico squirmed but if he wrenched too much Tino's hold on his thumb would pop the digit out of the socket.

He had one cuff around Rico's wrist when something slammed

into his head and sent him sprawling. His ears rung and his vision blurred. He tried to push to his knees and a blow landed in his ribs, knocking him to his back and forcing the air out of his lungs.

"I knew you'd come in handy," Rico's voice sounded like he stood in a metal tube.

Tino tried again to stand. The butt of a rifle came into view moments before it collided with his head.

"Bring him."

He heard the command before darkness overtook him.

~*~

Isabella stood inside the cave ignoring the fluttering overhead and straining to hear the person moving down the tunnel toward her. From the sound of the women's voices they stopped outside to rest. She willed them to move on before the person following them caught up. If it was one of Rico's men, it was possible he would have a radio to give the location of the women.

She took her long-sleeved shirt off and stood ten feet back from the tunnel entrance. Her plan wasn't as foolproof as she'd like but would have to do.

Barely breathing, she listened. Footsteps grew closer. A dark shape entered the cave. She swung her shirt in the air, scattering bats.

Wings flapped past her head. Her heart jammed in her throat and her limbs paralyzed. This was what she'd hoped would not happen. She couldn't move, couldn't speak as the small creatures fluttered around her. The iron tang of fear stung her tongue and rooted her feet.

They're only three inches long. They can't hurt you, played over and over in her head, but the puffs of wind from their wings and the flapping sound raised her emotions to override her good sense.

The sound slowly died. She heard the other person breathing not far from where she stood.

A ribbon of light seeped between the two boulders.

Do I make a run for the boulders?

The person walked toward her. She could sense his movement. Her pack was at her feet from taking off her shirt. She quickly donned her shirt and shoved the pack at the pursuer's feet.

He tripped and went down.

Isabella jumped on his back, pulling a revolver from his side holster and pressing it to his back. "Who are you?"

132

"Lt. Jonny Crow. You better be Dr. Mumphrey. I'd hate to hurt a woman." The deep voice held a trace of humor.

"As in the Shadow Eagles?" She slowly stood.

The man on the ground rose and flicked on a flashlight. The beam of light made her blink and shield her eyes.

"What are you doing following me?" she asked, bending to pick up her pack.

"That was my job to locate you and bring you to Tino." He ran the light around the cave. "Is there a way out of here?"

"Yes." It dawned on her. His voice was the one she heard talking into the radio that he had her. He must have lit out after her when he had a chance to escape the shooting. She walked to the light between the boulders. "You did take care of Rico before you came after me?"

The silence sent a quiver between her shoulder blades.

"My target wasn't Rico. It was you."

Tino was still in trouble if this man didn't take out Rico. She slipped her arm between the boulders and started out.

A hand grasped hers on the cave side.

"I can't get through there and you aren't going anywhere without me." Lt. Crow's voice and grip on her hand was hard to deny.

"Cody made it through here twice so you should be able to." She wiggled her fingers and slid free. When her feet would have carried her away and back to the area of the shootout, her mind kept her planted. She stood to the side and waited as first Lt. Crow's hand holding his rifle appeared and then inch by inch his body slithered through the narrow opening.

The lieutenant stood beside her staring at the boulders. "How did you find this?"

She shrugged. "I have a knack for finding the truth about the Native American." Isabella headed down the ravine. "Come on, we should catch up to the women, and you can get them to Border Patrol."

"Women? The ones Cody said you stayed to help?" Crow's long strides covered the desert ravine quickly.

"Yes. Rico was planning to sell them. Some of the women have been in the kiva for several weeks."

"The smell told me there had been captives. I didn't realize it was a kiva."

"It's undocumented. But I'll get a research team out here, and we'll get it documented and keep the public away." The sacred place had seen enough depredation. She'd make sure it was renewed to its original state and used only for Hopi ceremonies.

They came around a bend and found the women sitting together chatting.

Sky leaped to her feet and hugged Isabella. "I was afraid something happened to you."

"I'm fine. This is Lt. Crow. He'll escort you to the border patrol."

"You're not going with us?" Sky asked.

"Yes, she is. I promised her fiancé she would not leave my sight once I found her." Lt. Crow planted his feet and crossed his arms.

"I'll stay with you if you can get on a radio and make sure Tino is safe." Isabella waited for the man to pull out a radio of some sort.

His hand went to his belt. He glanced down. "Damn. It must have fell off when you tripped me." He grabbed her arm. "You aren't going anywhere but to the border patrol with all of us."

"That will be farther away from Tino. I'm the reason he's out here. I need to find him and make sure Rico didn't kill him." She tugged her arm, but the man had a vise-like grip.

"You will stay with me until I can contact Tino." He turned his attention to the others, but kept his grip on her arm. "Up ladies, let's get moving."

The women all looked to Isabella. She smiled and nodded, reassuring them to get up and move along. She was pretty sure if she asked them to mutiny they would. She was seen as their savior and she wasn't male. Something most of them were probably going to steer clear of for a while.

They headed out with Isabella and the lieutenant in the lead. About ten minutes passed and they spotted several men moving toward them halfway up the ridge. Lt. Crow cupped his hand to his mouth and howled like a coyote. The men halted and a return call sang through the still desert air.

"That's Cody." He released her and huddled the women like a covey of quail.

Isabella recognized Cody's silhouette as they group grew near. He was with two Border Patrol. One man and one woman. She was happy to see the female officer. It would make the women feel better when she left to have another female present.

"I see you got them out." Cody said, putting an arm around her shoulders.

Lt. Crow raised an eyebrow but didn't say anything about the familiarity.

"Yes. We managed to get free and picked up a hitch hiker along the way." She nodded to Cody's superior.

"I thought you were with Tino?" Cody questioned.

Isabella was itching to head over the ridge and see what had happened.

"My job was to find and rescue Dr. Mumphrey. I had her, then she slipped away, so I tracked her." Lt. Crow's voice held disapproval. "Have you heard anything from the others?"

"No. We've had the radios turned off so the noise wouldn't give us away." Cody pulled his radio off his belt and turned it on. "What frequency were you using?"

Lt. Crow rattled off the frequency.

Cody messed with the dials. A garbled mass of voices clicked on and off.

Lt. Crow took the radio. "This is Lt. Crow. I have the dove. What's the status of the mission?"

Silence followed.

Isabella's heart pounded so loud she was sure everyone near her could hear it too. She prayed Tino's voice would ring out from the radio.

"We captured four traffickers and are missing three of our own. ICE and border are chasing ATVs that got away."

"Tank, do you know who is missing?" Lt. Crow asked.

"From what I can tell it's Tino, Percy, and a border agent."

Tino was missing! He was either hurt or after Rico.

Isabella grabbed the radio. "Is Rico Montoya still alive?"

"He isn't one of the bodies we've found so far."

She shoved the radio at the lieutenant and charged up the ridge. Voices shouted at her, but she kept going. When she reached the top, she didn't look back, just headed down the other side. Tino was out there somewhere and so was Rico.

A hand grabbed her pack, halting her forward motion. "Stop."

She pivoted to swing a round kick. But instead of connecting, her foot was grabbed and she started to fall backwards.

Cody steadied her. "You can't go running off alone. We'll find him together."

She glared at him. "This is better if I do it alone."

"Why?"

"If I go alone, I only have to worry about me and Tino. If you go with me then I have to worry about you and how Mother will feel if something happened to you while helping me." She pinched the bridge of her nose with her fingers to stop the tears threatening at the back of her eyes. Life was much easier when the only person she had to worry about letting down was herself.

"That's the same way I feel if something happens to you. I'll have let Mother down. She has loved you as strong as if you'd been growing up in her home. Don't make me go home to her and say, I walked away because Isabella asked me to." He let go of her foot. "I can't."

"Do you have any idea where we might find Tino or Rico?" she conceded.

"I know the coordinates where the showdown took place, and I figure Rico would be heading back to Mexico." He pulled out a compass, studied it, and turned to his left. "Let's head this way."

She started ahead of him.

"But keep your eyes and ears wary. We don't know if they are on foot or have a vehicle."

Chapter Nineteen

Tino's head throbbed. Each breath seared pain through his chest. His face pressed against pebbles. He tried to push up and realized his hands were tied behind his back.

"Put him on his knees," ordered Rico's voice.

¡Coño! Rico had him. But at least he didn't have Isabella. She was safe with Crow. If he must die at least it would be to save Isabella. Something warm trickled down his forehead and into his eye. The world took on a red tint.

Rough hands grasped his shoulders, righting him. His knees pressed into the gravel. He blinked and willed his eyes to focus. Slowly, the moonlight filtered through the red blur. Shapes took form.

"¡Coño! You dirty bastard!" Tino tried to rise to his feet but someone behind him held him down.

Percy raised a radio and turned the volume up.

"We captured four traffickers and are missing three of our own. ICE and border are chasing ATVs that got away." He heard Tank say.

Crow asked, "Tank, do you know who is missing?"

"From what I can tell it's Tino, Percy, and a border agent."

"Is Rico Montoya still alive?"

Hearing Isabella's voice and knowing she was safe with Crow

helped him regain his composure.

Tank offered. "He isn't one of the bodies we found so far."

The radio went dead.

Rico chuckled and walked toward Tino.

"That woman of yours has nine lives, just like a cat. I think we should dangle a mouse for her to come play with."

"Leave her alone. You have me." Tino's chest burned from forcing the words out.

"Yes, I do have you. And I think your little hellcat should know." He turned to the traitor Shadow Eagle. "Percy, call in a sighting of me." Rico stood in front of Tino, his arms crossed, legs spread acting as if he were invincible.

Tino growled and shoved to his feet, lunging at the man. It took all his effort and air to hurtle his body at his enemy. Rico tumbled to the ground, but two men jumped on Tino, pummeling him into unconsciousness.

~*~

Isabella walked stealthily through the desert bushes. The golden glow of dawn hovered to the east. She willed the sun to stay down for a while longer. The gray of the early morning was a better shield for their activities than the glaring hot sun.

Cody's radio crackled. He turned the volume down and placed it against his ear. She could tell by his stony expression it had to do with either Rico or Tino.

He clicked the radio off and stepped close. "Percy, one of the Shadow Eagles has spotted Rico on foot headed our direction."

She started to move out, but he grasped her arm.

"I don't trust Percy. He knew more about the bounty on Tino's head than anyone else. He may be like Montoya, playing both sides."

"You think this might be a trap?" She scanned the area ahead of them. "Do you think it's to lure Tino or me?"

"It could be both." He pulled out his night vision binoculars and scanned the area. "There is movement at two o'clock. Let's stay together and make decisions based on what we find."

She nodded and followed Cody. He had more experience with stalking and surveillance.

Twenty feet from a man obviously standing guard, Cody took off his rifle, handing it to her. He snuck up behind the man, putting him down quietly.

Isabella moved through the growing dawn and caught up to Cody. The man on the ground at his feet was Luis. They bound his hands and feet and sliced off the corner of his shirt, using it as a gag.

Cody put his mouth up to her ear. "We will circle searching for all the men on the perimeter. We'll take them out then move to the center and see what we find."

She nodded and followed. When she spotted the next man, she tossed a pebble at Cody's back and motioned. He saluted and crept up behind the man, taking him down. They encountered six more sentries, taking each one out and tying them up.

"Now, we'll go see what they were guarding." Cody gathered his rifle and started toward the center of the circle.

Isabella followed, walking as quietly as the man in front of her.

The sun cast beams of light down onto the arroyo when they stopped behind a bush large enough to hide both of them.

She peeked between the branches. A bloody body lay crumpled in a heap. Her heart raced with fear. "Please don't let that be Tino," she whispered, and stared, looking for something that would reveal who the man was. He wore the olive green border patrol shirt. But there was a border patrolman missing.

The man flinched and tried to sit up, but his hands and feet were bound. Blood oozed from two cuts. One in his hair and one on his forehead. Her breath stopped as she recognized Tino.

In all their escapades this was the bloodiest she'd seen him. Her heart ached for him. She wanted to run out and soothe his aches. But her feet stayed rooted behind the tree. Getting herself caught wouldn't get Tino help. Guilt gnawed on her conscience. This wasn't the first time Tino had been hurt due to her. Flashes of him being bound and sent afloat in the Usumacinta River in Guatemala and Tino's bloody beaten body in the underground room off the Mexico City sewer tunnels crossed her mind.

"We have to get him out of here," she whispered.

"We will," Cody whispered in her ear. "He's alive. He's strong."

She nodded and gulped to clear the knot in her throat. They had to get Tino free from Rico.

"Percy is the tall one. Is Rico the Hispanic beside him?" Cody asked.

Isabella nodded then drew in a sharp breath as she recognized the man standing behind Tino, keeping him on the ground. *Wes.*

Cody spun her and peered into her eyes. "You've figured out who Wes is?"

She nodded, not surprised he'd kept the knowledge from her and that he accepted her recognition.

"I can shoot Rico and Percy because they are together. But you'll have to take care of Wes." He held her shoulders and stared into her eyes. "Can you do this?"

Her heart hammered in her chest. Her whole life she'd wanted family and siblings. Wanted her life to be filled with family. She glanced at the vicious sneer on Wes' lips. Her gaze dropped to the bloody man on the ground. Tino was her family and future, not a half-brother who took pleasure in hurting others.

She nodded, slipping out of her pack and gripping her Guatemalan knife by the handle.

"I'll wait until you are behind him before I shoot."

Gripping the knife tight, she ran to the next bush, ducked behind it, and continued this pattern until she was ten feet behind Wes. She nodded to Cody.

Two shots rang out. She threw a jumping side kick at Wes. Her foot slammed into his back, dropping him to the ground at the same time she landed on both feet. She dropped onto her knees in the middle of his back, holding him on the ground and tossing his weapons away from him.

He struggled, pushing up with his hands, trying to dislodge her. Hot, hazed anger blurred her vision. She didn't see the young man under her, she saw the emptiness of her life, because of the man he was like. She raised the knife, the long, wide blade above the man's back.

"Don't. You'll regret it," Cody's firm voice said from above her.

She twisted her wrist and struck Wes alongside the head with the end of the knife handle, knocking him out. Scrambling off him, she crawled to Tino.

"Tino? Hey, come on. Look at me." Isabella rolled Tino over. Hot tears trickled down her face at the sight of his bloody and bruised face. "What did they do to you?" She ran her fingers gently over his cuts and bruises.

"We have traffickers for transport and need a medevac stat." Cody's strong confident voice pulled her attention to him.

"Did you kill them?" She didn't want to think her brother would kill even though the men were both traitors. Bile rose up her throat. She'd been seconds from thrusting a knife into Wes' back before rational thinking and Cody's voice pulled her out of her murderous haze.

"They might make it. I cuffed them in case they do." He crouched next to her and Tino. "How's he doing?"

"He's breathing, but struggling. They may have injured his ribs. And he hasn't come to." She stroked the hair off his forehead revealing a long gash with congealed blood that would require stitches.

"Why would anyone do this to another person?" She said it more to herself than for a real answer.

"Because some people don't value life." Cody stood.

The sound of a helicopter grew near.

"Your ride's coming. I'll clean up the mess here." Cody waved the helicopter down.

Paramedics leaped out and started for Rico and Percy.

"No! Over here!" Cody waved and pointed to Tino.

One of the paramedics fell to his knees and started evaluating Tino.

"What about those two?" the other paramedic asked.

"They'll get treatment after we take them in and book them. They'll stay alive that long." Cody's radio crackled. He walked away to talk.

"Can I ride with him? He's my fiancé." Isabella stood, giving the paramedics room to work.

"We can take you. Are you hurt anywhere?" The paramedic did a slow perusal down her body.

"No, I'm fine." Her stomach rumbled. "Just hungry."

They loaded Tino on a gurney. The paramedics carried the gurney to the helicopter with Isabella following close behind. At the helicopter she turned back, waved at Cody, and climbed into the loud machine.

Chapter Twenty

At the hospital, Isabella was ushered to a waiting room. From the expressions and people moving away from her, she knew she must look and smell like a transient after her captivity.

Her stomach growled. The paramedic on the flight had given her a candy bar, but her stomach was in need of real food. Now that the sterile environment had time to settle around her, she could smell herself and didn't want to walk into a cafeteria or any restaurant with the cloud of stench.

Finally, she couldn't ignore her stomach. She walked over to the nurse's station. A fiftyish woman in blue scrubs and a name tag that read Sylvia Cooper, RN, looked up.

"Is there someone who could go to the cafeteria and bring me back a tray of food?" Isabella asked.

The nurse smiled. "You could go yourself, and we'd let you know of any changes."

"It's not that I'm worried about missing information. I've been held captive in a small area with half a dozen other captives."

The woman's eyes widened at her mention of being a captive. "Do we need to call the police?"

"No, I'm fine. The authorities know the story. It's just, I reek and wouldn't want others in the cafeteria to lose their appetites. But my stomach is aching I'm so hungry." At that moment her stomach made a pitiful sound.

"Margie, go get this woman a tray." Nurse Cooper then moved from behind the counter. "Come with me." She led Isabella down the hall to a lounge. "Through there is a shower and you'll see clean scrubs folded in a cupboard. Find a pair that fit."

"Thank you!" Isabella would have hugged the woman but she hurried out of the room. No doubt from being in the confined space with the odor.

She stripped off the nasty clothes, tossing them in the shiny stainless-steel wastebasket. Under the strong spray of the shower, she used the medical soap and scrubbed every inch of her body and her hair, preferring the sanitized scent to the stench of captivity. Using a rough, white towel she dried, squeezed water out of her hair, and put on a dark blue pair of scrub bottoms and a top with geometric designs. She even found a pair of rubber booties and slid her feet in. Her hiking boots would look awkward with her scrubs. Tying the laces together she carried the boots out to the nurse's station and found a tray of food waiting.

"Thank you, again!" she said to both nurses. "When my belongings catch up to me, I'll pay you back." She started to turn away to find a place to eat, but stopped. "Have you heard anything about Tino Konstantine?"

He had remained unconscious through the helicopter ride and the landing. She'd heard bits and pieces of his vital signs and what the paramedics told the staff that was waiting on the helipad when they arrived.

"Because he's unconscious and can't tell us where he's in pain, they are running him through tests and a cat scan. Once he's been evaluated and treated he'll go to ICU. Then you'll be able to sit with him."

"Thank you." She scanned the waiting area. Half a dozen adults and two children huddled in two small groups close to the emergency room doors. She walked over to a chair in a corner by itself and sat, holding the tray on her lap. As hungry as she was, it took several attempts to take a bite. Her mind flashed over the events that happened before the helicopter lifted them out of the refuge. She'd bludgeoned her half-brother. Her stomach turned.

Closing her eyes, she saw Tino's bloody, beaten body and Wes standing over it full of himself. She knew he was the one to have inflicted all the blows to Tino. The rage she'd felt wasn't just for Tino but at the kind of person who would use his power to hurt others.

The snap of the spork shot her eyes open. The pointy end lay in the mashed potatoes. She couldn't let herself become like the man that forced himself on her mother or his legitimate child, Wes.

She forced her thoughts to the pure side of her family. To Cody. Her last sight of him, he stood guard over the nine apprehended men. All drug and human traffickers. She'd witnessed several vehicles heading his way as the helicopter buzzed out of the refuge and over to Tucson.

Isabella flexed her hand. The one that held the knife as she knocked Wes unconscious. Her mind whirled trying to conjure up emotions she should have felt for her half-sibling. But she couldn't muster up any sympathy. Not having witnessed Tino and the way Wes had treated Sky.

Sky. Where were the women? Being taken care of she hoped. So much had happened. And she had no one she could call. Her phone was with her backpack. Would Cody have the presence to pick it up for her or would it bake and fall apart over time like all the other belongings left in the desert by UDAs?

She picked up the broken spork and using the wide end, slowly, bite by bite swallowed food. Her stomach ached less with each spoonful. The tray held only crumbs and gravy when commotion behind her surprised not only her but the other people sitting about the waiting area.

"I want to see my daughter. She came in on a helicopter with Border Patrol." Daddy's voice boomed through the building.

She smiled, stood, and let the happiness of seeing him sweep through her.

"There's my girl." Three long strides brought him to stand in front of her. He picked her up in one of his signature bear hugs.

He may not be her biological father, but he would always be her daddy. She hugged him back.

"How did you know I was here?" she asked, when he set her back on the floor.

"I have my contacts." He tweaked her nose. "How's that man of yours?"

Her smile faded. "I don't know. They wheeled him away two hours ago, and I still haven't heard if he's in surgery or what."

He held her at arm's length. "Looks like you could use some clothes and a shoulder." Daddy pulled out his phone and hit a number. "Ana, yes, I'm with her. No, she's fine." He rolled his eyes. "Your mother would like to talk to you."

Isabella smiled. Her mother was only a third the size of her husband but he did what she wished.

"Hello."

"Isabella. Were you hurt? I heard you were held captive." Her mother's clipped and to-the-point conversations at times had annoyed her, but now she understood the woman she called mother had had that title forced on her out of loyalty.

"I'm fine. Just hungry. I could use some clothes. I'm wearing hospital scrubs right now."

"I'll have one of our operatives in Tucson bring some over right away. Give my regards to Tino."

Isabella swallowed a lump. "I will when he regains consciousness."

The line clicked and her mother was gone.

Wiping at a tear, she handed the phone back to Daddy.

His arm looped around her for support. He was always there for support.

"Thank you," she whispered and leaned against his broad chest.

"Miss? Miss, your fiancé has been treated and will be in ICU in about twenty minutes. You can go sit with him then, and the doctor will discuss what they've found," Nurse Cooper said, replacing a telephone receiver.

"Thank you. I'll be right here when I can go back." Isabella grasped her father's hand and led him to a section of chairs in the corner with no one sitting close, and sat facing him.

She touched her knees to Daddy's and leaned forward. "I need you to use your connections and find out some things for me. First, please make sure Cody returned safely. Then if you could find out how the women who were in the kiva are doing. Especially Sky."

Daddy patted her knee. "Always worrying about everyone but

yourself."

She smiled, she did seem to always be championing the underdog. "Then make sure Rico Montoya won't get out and that a henchman of his named Wes is still locked up."

Daddy's eyes stared into hers. "Why do you want to know about this Wes?"

"He was the one beating on Tino, and I-I bashed his head to apprehend him."

Large arms scooped her into a much needed hug.

"You know, this is the reason I didn't want you to become an agent. You have too tender a heart to have to use force against anyone."

She pushed out of his embrace and stood. "I'm not a little girl, and you can't shield me from all the vile things in this world."

His eyes narrowed and his face became an expressionless mask. He knew she knew.

"What did Cody tell you?" He ground the words out.

"The truth. Something I should have been told long before now." She sat and grasped Daddy's hand. "I love you and mother, but now, knowing the truth, so many things are making sense."

"You can't tell anyone." His stern tone would have garnered him a faithful yes just two years earlier.

Now, she'd grown stronger in so many ways. She owed it all to the mentor who lured her to the Guatemalan jungle and Tino.

"Tino has a right to know. He will be my husband." She put up a hand when he started to protest. "But I'll not tell anyone else. It's wonderful to know that the connection I've felt for Aunt Una was based on the purest of connections—mother and daughter." Her smile faded. "I will stay away from the paternal side of my heritage. I had a glimpse of it and don't care to see any more."

"That's good. I've tried for years to get that man locked up, but he's slippery as they come."

She'd wondered after Cody told her, why the man was still loose when Daddy had so much clout in the sphere of law agencies.

A woman dressed in navy slacks, a pale blue cotton shirt, and loafers walked up to them with a shopping bag. "Mr. Mumphrey, your wife sent me with these." She handed the bag to Daddy.

He smiled and handed the bag to Isabella. "I believe these are for you."

She opened the bag and inside were two pair of underwear, jeans, t-shirt, socks, sneakers, and a sweatshirt all in her size. "Thank you!" she said to the woman.

The woman smiled, spun around, and left.

"She wasn't very talkative. Don't you get tired of working with such by-the-book people?" Isabella stood.

"I like people who do what they're told and mind their own business." Daddy stood. "If you're going to be okay alone, I'll take off and check into those items for you."

"I'll be fine. Thank you for coming." She stood on her tiptoes and kissed his cheek.

"I'll always be here for you." He touched her nose and strode to the exit.

Isabella walked over to the nurse's desk. "Could I use the same shower room to change into my clothes?" she asked Nurse Cooper.

The woman nodded. "When you get back I can take you to ICU."

"Thank you, I'd appreciate that."

She walked down the hall to the shower room. At the bottom of the bag, she found a small shoulder purse with a hair brush, tooth brush, and a hundred dollars. "Mother, you think of everything." She shoved the extra pair of underpants in the purse, put the scrubs she wore in a clothes hamper, and headed back to the waiting area.

The nurse who brought her the food stood at the counter. Isabella handed her a twenty.

"This is too much," the woman insisted.

"It was worth it to get something in my stomach." Isabella turned to Nurse Cooper. "I'm ready now."

She followed the nurse through the doors, down a hall, past a chapel, then a left and through the ICU doors. At the end of the hall, Nurse Cooper motioned to the last door.

Isabella took a moment to steel her emotions. Tino didn't need her falling apart when he would need strength to mend.

She stepped through the threshold with a smile on her face. The smile instantly dissolved at the sight of Tino's head wrapped in gauze where the largest gash had been. A tube stuck out of a shaved spot on his head. He had a tube in his mouth and wires and IVs spread across the white blanket like roads and rivers on a map. A machine to one side of the bed beeped and on the wall at the head of the bed a monitor had moving colored lines.

The shock of seeing her virile fiancé looking vulnerable caused a lump to bob in her throat. She held back the tears welling behind her eyes and studied his bruised, puffy face. If not for his dark eyebrows and the shape of his ears, she would have thought they brought her to the wrong room.

And his hands.

She drifted over to the side of the bed and gathered his right hand in both her hands. This hand had taught her the touch of a man and the restrained strength of Tino. She leaned down, kissing the back of his hand. Any doubts she had about the depth of her love for him vanished. She loved him because of who he was and what he stood for. Blinking back the tears, she studied the slow up-down rhythm of his chest.

She'd never seen him so helpless. Her heart ached. She wanted to curl up beside him on the bed and give him her strength.

A sound from the doorway, drew her gaze from Tino. A man of Asian descent walked in and stood at the end of the bed with an electronic tablet. He looked up and smiled. "You must be the fiancée." He held out a hand. "I'm Dr. Tsao."

She clasped his hand. "I'm Isabella Mumphrey. Thank you for taking good care of him."

"Don't thank me yet. He's strong, but took a lot of hits to his head and body. As you can see he's unconscious. We had to put a stint through his skull to release pressure on his brain. He also has four cracked ribs and bruised kidneys and spleen." The doctor moved to the opposite side of the bed and messed with dials on the machine. "His head trauma and the bruised organs are what we are watching closely. Being unconscious will keep his body at rest and he's more likely to heal faster. But if he doesn't wake up by tomorrow and the swelling hasn't gone down on his brain, we may have to operate."

Isabella pulled her gaze from the doctor. "What happens if you operate?"

"We'll do what we can to see what is causing the swelling and do what is necessary to save him."

"But digging around in a brain can be dangerous."

Dr. Tsao came around the foot of the bed and placed a hand on her arm. "It can be dangerous. But this patient is healthy other than his injuries. We won't do anything invasive unless there is nothing else to save his life."

She nodded and returned her gaze to Tino. "Tino. I'm here."

Something bumped the back of her legs. She glanced back.

Dr. Tsao held a chair behind her. "The best thing is to talk to him and hold his hand. Let him know there is someone out here who wants him to wake up." The doctor left the room.

Isabella sat in the chair and laced her fingers with Tino's. "You probably thought you were being gallant taking that beating." She raised his hand to her lips and kissed the back. Rubbing her lips across the dark hairs, she couldn't hold the tears. He was her heart and her life. He had to pull through. They had no one else to fear from his past. The future could be lived without wondering when an enemy would show up in their lives.

Chapter Twenty-one

Isabella gradually woke. Her neck hurt and someone shook her
shoulder. Blinking at the sunlight streaming through a window, she
moved her head from side to side, popping the stiffness from her neck.

"You should go find something to eat while we tend to the
patient." A woman ten years older than Isabella and dressed in scrubs,
raised her arms to change the I.V. bottle at the head of Tino's bed.

"I'm not leaving him." Isabella wiggled her bottom snugger into
the chair.

Dr. Tsao entered the room and separated her fingers from Tino's.
"We'll call you if he wakes before you get back." He led her to the
door and waved to someone down the hall.

"Come on, honey, Dr. Tsao knows what he's doing. Let's get
breakfast." Daddy took her arm, leading her away from Tino's room.
"And I have news for you."

She leaned against Daddy. Letting him lead her to the cafeteria.
She followed him down the line, picking out food at random. Her mind
was still numb from lack of sufficient sleep since leaving Walpi.

"Have you talked to Aunt Una?" She sat at the table Daddy picked
at the far side of the room away from the other occupants.

"Yes. She called asking about you and Tino. Cody briefed her on

150

what happened." He drank from a cup of coffee and watched her over the rim.

"I don't want her thinking this was all her fault." She spread butter on a piece of toast.

"Why would she think that?" His voice was noncommittal, but his intense gaze revealed he was waiting for something.

"She called and asked me to come check out a cave the youth of First Mesa found. And while I was there she mentioned a girl had gone missing and the rumor was she had been kidnapped by a couple of young Hopi men." She bit the toast, chewed, and swallowed. "I hadn't planned to stumble onto the human trafficking ring. I gave all the information about the missing girl to Tino to pass along to law enforcement. But I *was* determined to find the ceremonial kiva that happened to be where Rico Montoya held the women he'd planned to sell."

She pushed the tray away. Thinking of the disgrace he'd brought to the kiva and the human race in general turned her stomach.

"Did Una send Cody with you?" Again, he asked like he didn't care but his tense body and intense gaze proved otherwise.

Why was he so interested? She'd told him yesterday she knew the truth about her parentage.

"In a roundabout way. I told Tino where I was headed. He didn't want me to go—"

"With good reason!"

She smiled benevolently. "Yes, he did have a good reason, but I knew I'd never get funding for an expedition to hunt for the kiva."

"You could have waited until Montoya was apprehended." Daddy's tone reminded her of when she was small and he recounted one of her rash decisions.

"Who knew when that would happen? I had the information and wanted to move while I had taken days off." She pulled the tray closer and tried another bite, then a drink of her orange juice. "Aunt Una called Cody and told him where I was headed and what I was looking for. He took vacation days, and after consulting with Tino, came after me."

She waved the toast. "And I'm glad he did. If I'd have been alone when we stumbled onto the traffickers and the cave, I wouldn't have been able to get those women out. And quite possibly ended up in some foreign country trying to make them understand I shouldn't be there."

"They wouldn't have cared. Once a man pays money for a white slave, the woman will either conform or be killed."

His matter-of-fact tone made her study him closer. He had seen many bad things and it appeared he took it all for granted. He believed the worst in his fellow man, yet he always had a smile and caring nature for her.

"Then I'm glad I acted brash and stormed down to that area of Arizona. Will capturing the traffickers help them find the missing girl from the reservation?"

"It might. It depends on if they took her or if she was bought by someone else."

The idea more people might be at the border trafficking women enraged her. "You mean there are more places on the border where women are being held?" Her palms pressed on the table and her body rose.

Daddy put a hand on her shoulder, forcing her back into her chair. "Sit. You can't go traipsing all over the state looking for white-slave dens."

"Did you find out about Sky and the others?" She tucked a forkful of scrambled eggs into her mouth. They had little flavor but filled the emptiness she couldn't seem to shake in her stomach.

"They are all at the ICE detention center in Eloy waiting to be debriefed and then sent home." Daddy took a bite of the eggs and shoved his tray to the middle of the table.

"Would you take me there this morning? I really would like to speak with Sky and get her information so we can stay in touch." She also wanted to talk to the other women and see if any of them might have been held other places.

"It's an hour away. What about Tino?" Daddy's eyebrow raised as he peered at her with parental concern.

"I'll see what the doctor says after he checks Tino. From what he told me last night, I don't think Tino will wake any time soon. He wouldn't want me sitting beside him worrying." She smiled. "And if he wakes when I'm not there, they'll call me, and I'll be there before he knows it."

"How will they call you?" Daddy's gaze fell on the visibly half-empty purse on the table beside her plate.

Shamutz! Her phone was with her pack. "Have you spoken to Cody? Did he happen to pick up my pack?"

"He said he'd drop by this morning." Daddy glanced over her shoulder. "And it must be morning."

She half turned and spotted Cody walking through the cafeteria door. Isabella shot out of her chair and rushed across the room, wrapping her arms around her brother. They'd been through a lot together the last few days and the genetic bond was now also an emotional bond.

Cody hugged her back. He looked up and his body stiffened.

"Ignore Daddy. I told him I know how I came into this world." She let go of him and led the way to the table.

"Cody." Daddy said in an accusatory tone.

"Mr. Mumphrey," replied Cody in a wary voice.

"Listen you two. I love you both and you better get along." She sat between the two but turned her attention to Cody. "How'd you find me?"

"I stopped at Tino's room. They said you were down here." He ran a hand over his face. "He doesn't look so good."

Her effervescence slowly popped. "No. He hasn't regained consciousness. They may have to do surgery if the swelling in his brain doesn't go down."

"He knows you love him. He'll come around, if for no other reason than to kick my butt for leaving you alone in that kiva." Cody tugged on her braid.

She giggled. "Yeah, he probably wasn't too happy when you called and told him you left me behind." She picked up another piece of toast and bit into it. "Did you happen to bring my pack? I need a phone number to give the hospital, so they can call me."

"Yeah, I did. But why would they need to call you. You're right here."

Daddy's phone buzzed. He checked the number, frowned, and stood. "I'll be right back."

Isabella watched him walk into the hall and stand where she could see him. The conversation wasn't making him happy.

"Hey, I asked why you need a phone when you're right here." Cody tapped her on the shoulder.

She continued to watch Daddy, but said over her shoulder. "I want to go see Sky and the other women before they get sent home, Daddy says they're at the Eloy ICE detention center."

Whoever Daddy was talking to had him spitting mad. It had been a long time since she'd seen him so angry.

"I can take you if you want." Cody's offer sounded like a plea.

She turned her attention to him. "I'd like that. I asked Daddy, but I didn't really want him along. He would pry too much."

"Damn it!" Daddy returned to the table. The fire in his eyes told her he wasn't happy with someone. He set his gaze on Cody. "Don't let Isabella out of your sight. I'm calling in police protection for Tino."

Isabella and Cody both stood and said at the same time, "What's going on?"

"That was the state police. Wes Warren escaped when they took him to a hospital for treatment."

Isabella gasped. She was the one that put him in need of medical attention. She never dreamed he'd get loose.

Cody swore. "Come on, I'll take you to check on Tino then we'll go to my rig to get your stuff."

Daddy was already on the phone calling for security for Tino.

Her legs wobbled like a new foal as Cody escorted her down the halls to the ICU. The nurses were finishing up, and she didn't see the doctor.

"Where would I find Dr. Tsao?" she asked the closest nurse.

"He was called away for surgery." The woman finished checking the monitors.

"I'd like to leave my cell number with you to call when Tino wakes." She glanced at Cody standing in the doorway his arms crossed, looking as formidable as a large boulder.

The nurse went over to a white board on the wall. The day nurses and Dr. Tsao were listed. She wrote fiancée's number and waited.

Isabella rattled off her cell number. "Is there a number I can call and check in?" she asked.

"You won't be gone that long," Cody interjected.

She smiled. If she found a solid lead about Wes from the women she was visiting, she would find him and bring him in. It was the least she could do to keep Tino safe.

The nurse handed her a business card for the hospital. "Ask for the

ICU nurses station and then ask the nurse on duty for an update."

"Thank you." Isabella approached the bed. She picked up Tino's hand and squeezed. Leaning over him, she kissed his cheek, "I'll be back soon. When I am, you better have those eyes open and looking at me." She kissed him, again, and gently placed his hand at his side.

Without looking back, she walked out of the room. Cody's presence behind her was comforting. He wasn't going to like her plan, but she knew he'd help. She was safer following leads on Wes than she was sitting in the hospital room next to Tino.

At Cody's pickup, she stopped and took deep breaths of the mid-morning desert heat. Sitting in the sterile, air-conditioned hospital was almost as hard on the lungs as the urine and unwashed body odor of the kiva.

He unlocked the doors, and they climbed in. Her pack was on the passenger side floorboards. The handle of her Guatemalan knife reminded her of clobbering Wes.

"He's going to come after me." She stated flat and truthful.

"Who? Wes? He doesn't know it was you who snuck up behind him and whacked him. It's most likely he's after Tino. I can see a degenerate like Wes believing his arrest and getting whacked on the head was Tino's fault. Which makes Tino the target." He started the pickup and pulled out of the parking lot. "That's why I don't mind taking you on this little trip. Keeping you away from Tino and letting the police do their jobs will catch Wes."

She swallowed at the guilt slowly building in her chest and creeping up her throat. He had a right to know her plans, but she wanted to make sure she had concrete leads before enlightening Cody.

Chapter Twenty-two

They entered the ICE detention center in Eloy an hour later. Cody
showed his ICE identification and vouched for Isabella.

"We'd like to talk with the women brought in from the op that
happened yesterday morning in the Cabeza Preita refuge," Cody said
when they were asked why they were there.

A female officer handed him several forms to fill out and sign
before they were taken to a wing in another building.

"I don't understand why they are being held in a place that looks
like a jail." Isabella walked beside Cody, noting the groups that
appeared to be Hispanic families clustered about the grounds
surrounded with a tall wire fence.

"It's a safe place to debrief them before letting them go," said the
woman, leading them through the area.

"But it doesn't give them the sense they are free after being kept
in cages." Isabella shuddered, remembering her short stay in the kiva.
Her thoughts went to Suri who had been in that hole for two weeks or
longer.

"Here you are. Just tell the attendant who you wish to see." The
woman held the door and closed it behind them.

The inside resembled scenes from movies set in prisons. Only the rows of beds didn't have bars separating them.

"Can I help you? Men aren't allowed any farther than this area." A woman close to retiring with short gray hair stepped in front of Cody. The tag on her uniform pocket read Officer Jane Worthy. She was tall and large boned. Even at her age, she looked able to take care of any scuffles.

"We're looking for the women who were brought in yesterday when a human trafficking ring was busted up." Cody's gaze scanned the area.

"Sky, Suri, Judy, and Marie were half of them," Isabella said, hoping by supplying names it would help the woman's memory.

"That bunch is over at the psych center." She motioned for them to follow her out the door. Once on the stoop, she pointed to a building thirty feet from where they'd started. "That building there is the medical facilities. They're being debriefed and seeing what damage may have occurred."

"Thank you." Isabella set out for the building. She heard Cody's footsteps hurrying along behind.

At the medical building, she walked in and scanned the area for a receptionist. One was stuck in a small cubby to the right.

"I'm here to speak with the women who were brought in from a human trafficking ring bust." She watched the woman's dull eyes scan her computer screen. "They're in Dr. Vaughn's waiting room. It's down the hall and to the left."

"Thank you," Cody said, as Isabella charged down the hall.

She stepped through a door with a sign that read: Dr. Vaughn.

Sky flew off a chair and flung her arms around Isabella. "We thought we wouldn't see our guardian angel again."

Emotion clogged Isabella's throat. She swallowed, forcing it down, and patted Sky's back. Until this moment she hadn't fully realized what her small act had meant to the women all crowding around and hugging her.

She'd given them their freedom back.

It was humbling to have all seven women trying to talk and thank her at once. She raised her arms, quieting the group.

"I'm so glad I was able to help you. Now, I need a favor from you." They all agreed without hearing what she wanted.

She smiled and wiped at a tear trickling down her cheek. "You have all been through so much. First, I would like you to each write down your name and contact information so I can keep in touch with you."

They all agreed and cheerfully wrote in the journal she'd pulled from her backpack and brought along for taking notes. While each one wrote down their information, Isabella pulled Sky aside.

"You won't have the information I'm asking for because you arrived straight from your kidnapping to the kiva. But I do want you to keep in touch."

"I will keep in touch. Your bravery and ingenuity gave me hope to continue my education in law enforcement."

Isabella smiled. "I thought you might have had some kind of training."

Suri brought the journal over. "Thank you for getting us out. I had lost hope until you arrived."

Isabella took Suri's hand. "Life is too precious to every give up. Would you mind answering some questions?" She scanned the group. "I don't want to frighten you, but Wes is no longer in custody. He slipped away when they took him to a hospital for treatment."

A gasp went up.

"I don't believe you have to worry. But I'd like to know if any of you were hidden anywhere other than where I found you." She watched the faces. Many shook their heads, but two, Suri and another woman exchanged glances.

"Suri were you and, I'm sorry, I didn't learn your name…" she smiled at the other young woman.

"Rae, my name is Rae." The petite blonde girl chewed on her non-existent nails.

"Suri and Rae, were you two kept together at another place?" She opened her journal to a fresh page and waited.

The two glanced at one another again, and Suri cleared her throat, but Rae started.

"We met at a party in Nogales, Mexico. A group of us went down there to let off steam after exams. Suri and I woke up in a small room in an adobe house. We banged on the door and that was the first time we laid eyes on Wes."

Both women shivered.

"He said if we didn't keep quiet he'd hit us or worse," Suri added.

"When he'd bring in food, he wouldn't give it to us until…" Rae's face reddened and her hands started to shake.

"I told him I'd rather starve." Suri wrapped her arms around her small body. "He laughed and said then I better sample the goods before you die."

Isabella wanted to hug the younger woman but restrained.

"He hit us for no reason and when he—he—His hands hurt and his eyes were hard." Rae shuddered and held her arms around her body, a replica of Suri.

"I'm sorry." Bile rose in Isabella's throat thinking half her genes came from the same place as the vile man.

"It's not your fault," Suri was quick to say.

Cody moved from where he was standing away from the group and squeezed Isabella's shoulder. "She's right," he said softly in her ear.

He knew what she was thinking. Because he was the only other person in this room that knew her connection to Wes.

"Were you able to see anything when they moved you to the hole in the ground? How long was the trip?" She needed a way to figure out where Wes might be hiding.

"They gagged us and tied our hands. Then put a burlap sack over our heads." Rae rubbed her wrists. "The carried us over their shoulders down a ladder, I think. It was dark. We walked for a long way."

"It was cool and our steps sounded hollow," added Suri.

"It felt like we'd walked several blocks, before we stopped. They put me over a shoulder again and carried me upwards into a house," Rae said.

"How do you know it was a house?" Cody asked.

"You could smell food cooking and the sounds. You know, people talking, dishes, a television." Rae's face lit up. "This information is helpful, isn't it?"

"Yes, it's very helpful." Isabella had a feeling the girls were transported through a tunnel from Nogales, Mexico to Nogales, Arizona. "What happened next?"

"They picked me up, and I felt like I was put in a coffin." Rae shivered.

"They put us in the trunk of a car," added Suri. "The trunk closed, an engine started, and we were moving."

"Could you tell how long they drove?" Isabella knew this wasn't a solid way to get information but it might help.

"We were transferred to ATVs just before daybreak," Rae said. "And I'm sure we didn't drive all night. They probably waited until after midnight to take us out of where we were. I think we may have driven about three hours."

"Did you hear any conversations while you were in the house?"

"No. Nothing that was understandable." Suri looked at her feet. "I'm sorry we couldn't help more."

Isabella took her hand. "You helped us a lot. Thank you all for your addresses. I promise I'll keep in touch." Isabella hugged each woman, then left the building with Cody.

"Do you think they'll be able to put this behind them?" she asked.

"It will be a lot easier since you found them before they were broken completely." Cody put an arm around her shoulders. "The courage it took for you to stay with those women when you could have left with me tells me a lot about you."

She shook her head. "It had nothing to do with courage. I couldn't walk away from them. They needed help and I had to help them."

"You are a true Hopi. You think of others before yourself and always look for a way to make the future brighter." He hugged her tight. "I'm proud of you, sis."

Her chest expanded to allow for the love pouring into her heart. "I'm pretty proud of you too, brother."

She playfully punched his side, something she'd wanted to do with a sibling her whole childhood, and ducked out of his embrace.

They left the detention center and headed south, back to Tucson.

"I wish I could ask for information on Wes and his family through WIA, but then Daddy would get wind and put an end to my finding Wes." She glanced sideways at Cody. "He wasn't too pleased to hear you told me about my biological father."

He studied her a second then returned his attention to the road. "I didn't expect he would be. But you had a right to know. You're intelligent. You would have figured it out sooner or later. Our mother has dreamed of the day you'd walk into her house, and her arms, and know she was your mother."

Isabella thought of her recent trip to Walpi. Aunt Una had been beaming when she'd shown her off to the cousins. "And the only people who knows this truth are you, mother, and my mother and Daddy?"

"Yes." He glanced over. "Why?"

"I just want to make sure. Everyone she introduced me to at First Mesa were so welcoming, that I was wondering if they knew the truth."

"No one. Father never told his side of the family and mother would never say a thing. Both never spoke of it to one another." Cody's tone held finality.

A question that had been plaguing her since seeing the psychotic nature of Wes had to be asked. "How is she so sure that my father is Wes' father? Very few couples know to the day when a child is conceived."

"My father did not see my mother's sacrifice with the full heart she had given it." Cody's forehead wrinkled into a scowl.

"Your father blamed your mother for doing what she thought would keep the family together and safe?" Remorse rippled through her. Now she felt even more responsible for the actions of a man she didn't know but planned on learning everything about.

"He went to his creator knowing he'd been a fool for treating mother so, but his vanity wouldn't let him see her sacrifice until it was too late." Cody's neutral tone showed he loved both his parents.

"Oh, if I'd known all this sooner I would have visited and given mother a bit of solace." Her heart ached once more for the mother she'd missed as a youngster. When this ordeal was over she planned to make up for all the lost years and spend time sifting through her emotions and the events that led to her being raised unaware of her full heritage.

Cody slowed as they entered the Tucson traffic. "I'll drop you off at the hospital."

"What are you going to do?" She watched him closely. They may have just had a quiet family discussion, but she could see his mind had also been on their mission.

"While you check in on Tino, I'll go visit some friends. See what I can find out about the Warren family and if anyone has had eyes on Wes for his illegal activities." Cody pulled up to the front of the hospital.

"I'll leave my backpack with you. Come get me when you have

information. I don't want to be left out of the loop." She opened the door, grabbed the purse, and hopped out.

Cody drove away. She watched the pickup disappear into the traffic, squared her shoulders, and walked into the hospital, heading straight for ICU.

A bulky man stood at the door of Tino's room. His long-sleeved shirt clung to muscular arms and the athletic pants on his lower half strained across his thighs. He nodded when she approached but didn't ask to see her ID or question her.

"Aren't you even going to ask who I am?" She stopped in the doorway, staring up at the man.

"I don't need to. I memorized your photo. You're the fiancée." His voice was deep and condescending.

"How did you get a photo of me?" She scanned the length of him one more time. "When did the police allow street clothes for security duty?"

"I'm not the local P.D. I'm with global security group." He peered over her head, watching something down the hall.

Global security group. That would be WIA. Daddy must not have had any luck getting the police to take threats on Tino serious.

"Thank you for looking out for Tino." She ducked into the room and stopped.

The machines, monitors, and tubes were all still attached and making noise. She'd hoped when she came back he'd be awake and she could tell him she was ready to set a wedding date. Of all the near death experiences they'd had, this one had knocked her to her senses. She wanted to spend the rest of her life with the man fighting for his life in the hospital bed.

She sat on the chair still pulled up to the bed and captured his hand in hers.

"Tino, you have to wake up. We've got our whole lives ahead of us. There are so many places I want to go, and I want you there by my side." She kissed his hand and held it to her cheek.

Beeping on the heart monitor accelerated.

He knows I'm here!

She kissed his hand again and started discussing wedding plans. There was no sense in telling him about Wes and what she and Cody had planned. She didn't want him becoming stressed when he should be focusing on getting well.

An hour had passed with her talking non-stop about all their wedding options when her phone rang. She pulled the phone out of her purse, but didn't recognize the number.

Hesitantly, she pushed the answer button. "Hello?"

"It's Cody. Be down stairs at the entrance in fifteen. I know where to look." He hung up.

Isabella clutched the phone. As much as she wanted to capture Wes and know Tino and young women were safe from him, she didn't want to be the one to take him down. He was family even if in an odd convoluted way. All her life she'd believed in the power of one's heritage and roots. She drew in a deep breath of air and slowly released it. But she and Cody were the only people who had witnessed the depth of the man's depravity, and they were the ones who wanted him apprehended the most.

She stood, leaned over the bed, and kissed Tino on the cheek. "I'll be back soon. You better have made up your mind about where and when we're getting married. I gave you all the options." She kissed him, again, and backed away from the bed.

At the door, she turned, blew him a kiss, and stepped out of the room. The same hulking man stood by the door.

"Do you get a break?" she asked, being congenial.

He stared at her and nodded. "There's no set time for breaks. It keeps everyone on their toes."

"That's a good idea. See you later. That is if you're still here." She swung her purse over her shoulder and took two steps.

"Where are you going?" the guard asked.

"Shopping." She had a feeling he'd been told to keep tabs on her as well.

He looked skeptical, but she didn't care. Daddy didn't need to know her plans.

She stepped out into the hot summer day and thought about waiting in the air-conditioned lobby. But the sun and clean air was worth the blast of heat.

Shading her eyes with her hand, she scanned the street and the cars moving by. Could Wes be lurking here while they ran all over looking for him?

She pulled out her phone and googled Sheriff Warren in Arizona.

Up popped Sherriff Douglas Warren of Coconino County. The photo of him in his uniform showed a tall, thin man with an angular edged face and hard dark eyes. She shivered. It was almost like looking at an older version of Wes.

The sticky crackle of tires driving on hot asphalt drew her gaze away from the image. Cody's pickup pulled up beside her. She clicked her phone off and climbed into the passenger side.

"Where are we headed?" She shoved her purse into her backpack and studied Cody.

"Wes has relatives in Nogales, Arizona. Drug officials say when Wes is a suspect in a crime he visits the Nogales relatives. Then pops up on the other side of the border where we can't touch him until there conveniently becomes a new suspect for his crimes."

The idea a law official would put an innocent person behind bars to keep his own flesh and blood safe shouldn't have appalled her, but it did. "You mean his father finds someone else and pins Wes' crimes on them?"

"Yep. The Feds have had several family members of the people incarcerated for his crimes send them letters. They've been looking in on the allegations, but the people who land in jail don't end up living for very long, making it the family's word against all the evidence that Sheriff Warren amasses."

The more she heard about her biological father and half-brother the more she wanted to bring them to justice. "It's time Wes paid for his crimes." She stared ahead. "In time, Sheriff Warren will also be brought to justice." She couldn't bring herself to call him her father. He was too despicable a person to even want to be linked with the man in any form.

She would feel no remorse seeing that both the Warren men got what they deserved.

Chapter Twenty-three

An hour after leaving the hospital they arrived at the outskirts of Nogales, Arizona. The city spread out over rolling hills. The border fence was a rippling brown line between Nogales, Arizona and Nogales, Mexico.

"Do you have a plan?" Now that they were here, Isabella wasn't feeling as sure of herself. What if her need to capture Wes ended up with Cody getting hurt?

"I've contacted a couple of ICE agents in the area. They have been keeping tabs on Wes. They had an idea he was part of a human trafficking ring but were having trouble pinning anything on him." Cody navigated past the chain stores and housing tracts to the heart of the city.

Two blocks from the fence separating Arizona from Mexico, he turned left down an old part of town.

"I told my contacts we'd meet them and discuss what they know and what we want to do." Cody pulled into a parking lot beside an adobe building. The sign read Rooster's Bar.

"We're meeting them in a bar?" She was thinking something more along the lines of an office or restaurant.

"They've been down here undercover for six months. We're

supposed to go in an act like tourists. Sam is the bartender and Willa is the cocktail waitress." Cody took off his ball cap and ruffled his hair.

"You don't look like a tourist," she said, taking in his tight T-shirt under an unbuttoned long-sleeved shirt, canvas cargo pants, and boots. She plopped her floppy hat on her head. Reaching into her backpack, she wrapped her fingers around her survival tin and slid it into her purse. Who knew if they would make it back to the vehicle to grab packs or anything else?

Cody put a hand on her elbow and escorted her into the bar. She stopped three steps in and took off her sunglasses. The interior was dark. Stale, musty air circulated from what sounded like an ancient air cooler. The hum of the cooler was background for a Marty Robbins lilting acoustical ballad pulsating from a vintage jukebox.

When her eyes adjusted, she spotted a tall, broad-shoulder man standing behind the bar. He had silver hair, crow's feet at the outside of his eyes, a prominent nose, and broad smile.

"Welcome to Rooster's!" he said, waving them forward.

Isabella noted the three men, two Hispanic and one Caucasian, in their mid-twenties sitting at a table to the right, and four older gentlemen in a discussion at a table to the left. She walked toward the bar, plopped her purse on the counter, and sat on a stool, using her hat as a fan.

"I don't think I've ever been in so much heat before in my life. Do you have an iced tea?" She smiled at the bartender and immediately liked him as the smile he bestowed on her lit up his eyes.

"We do indeed. Would you like that straight or half lemonade and half tea?"

"That sounds even better," she said, smiling at him but watching the other occupants' reflections in the mirror behind the bar.

"I'll have a beer." Cody sat down on the stool beside her.

She didn't say anything but raised an eyebrow when Cody glanced her way.

"Dark or light?" the bartender asked.

"Dark."

Isabella started to say something then noticed Sam, the bartender, poured her glass half full of tea and filled a beer glass with tea. He topped her glass off with lemonade and handed it to her. He winked, poured a glass of dark beer and then switched the beer for the tea he poured when he wiped the glass with a rag. *Sneaky*!

"Haven't seen you two around here. Are you tourists or settling here?" Sam wiped at the counter with his right hand and poured the beer in the glass out with his left.

"Tourists. My girlfriend wanted to see the Mexico border." Cody rolled his eyes.

Now she knew their roles.

"I figured this would be the closest you'd ever take me out of the country." She braced her forearms on the counter and leaned forward. "I bet you take your significant other to wonderful exotic places."

Sam laughed. "From your lips to Willa's ears. My wife doesn't realize how good she has it. We make a monthly trip over the border to buy liquor. It's a whole lot cheaper over there."

"You're not helping me, buddy," Cody said, picking up a menu. He nudged Isabella. "Since we're here we might as well eat."

"Okay by me, but can we sit at a table?" She wanted to pick one where they had a good spot to see the whole establishment.

Cody shrugged. "I don't care, it's your exotic vacation."

She knew the table she wanted without making a spectacle. She plopped down on the bench seat and when Cody started to sit across from her she pouted and grabbed his hand. "You could be a little more romantic and sit with me. Or else I'll go back to the bar and flirt with the bartender."

He raised his eyebrow, but slid in next to her.

She opened her menu and held it up to cover her mouth. "This way we can both see the whole room and talk in low tones and it will look like we're being romantic."

"You are quick." Cody smiled and raised his menu.

"So does Wes come in here or is this a place to make contact with Sam and Willa?" She dropped her gaze to the menu as her stomach rumbled.

"I don't know. I didn't get in that much detail with the people I talked to."

"So you didn't talk to Sam?" She was having a hard time deciding what to pick on the menu.

"Shit!" Cody bumped her menu up higher, to cover her face. "Wes just walked in."

She could think of a lot stronger word to use. Wes would know it wasn't a coincidence that they were hanging out in a bar he frequented.

"We can't hide behind these menus the whole time." She peered around the menu with one eye. He was on the opposite side of the room from the restrooms. If they could make it to the restrooms, they could duck out a back door and not be seen.

Willa sauntered up to the table. She stood directly in front of them, blocking Wes' view.

"The special today is toasted tuna on sourdough." In a whisper she added, peering at Isabella, "Walk alongside me to the restroom sign. Then go straight out the backdoor. You'll come out in the alley. You'll have to go to the right and behind two businesses before you'll find the alley to the road out front."

"We can't both hide beside you." Isabella stared at Cody.

"Once you're outside, I'll distract Wes and your boyfriend can follow you." Willa tapped her pencil on the pad and turned to walk away.

Isabella slid to the side of the booth and walked slowly, keeping the waitress between her and Wes. Once in the hallway, she picked up speed and stepped out in the alley. She stood to the right of the door and waited. Not three minutes passed and Cody exited.

"Come on." He grasped her elbow, and they hurried down the alley and turned right.

A group of Hispanic young men stood between them and the road.

"So you think they know who we are?" Isabella said under her breath to Cody.

"I think they're just a group of thugs who hang out in the alley." Cody started forward.

A young man with several pale scars on his face stepped forward. "Whoa amigos. You can't use our alley without paying a tax."

"This is public property, we don't have to pay you a tax." Cody was taller and broader than every one of the young men. His size didn't seem to bother them.

She could see they had a pack mentality. They would all dive on him and inflict pain. She looped the strap of her bag over her head. With the strap across her chest, her hands were free.

Cody took a step forward and the group of six lunged at him.

Isabella stepped into the melee. She threw a round kick, catching a young man off guard. He went down and another came at her. She couldn't keep track of the damage Cody did and stay focused on her attackers.

She stood her ground ready to take on the next young man, but no one moved.

Taking her gaze off the group she found Cody. He stood over the leader. Blood trickled from the corner of his mouth, and he had a knot forming on his forehead.

"You should get a job. Or go back to school," Cody said, pointing a finger at the young man on the ground holding his head. "Beating people up isn't a good long-term investment in your future."

He motioned to Isabella. They left the alley, hurrying down the street to the pickup.

Once they were in the vehicle and driving away from the bar, she let out a huge sigh. "That was close. What are the odds Wes would walk into the bar when we were there to get information?"

Cody's hands gripped the steering wheel. "I don't like it. Sam said Wes only comes in the bar at night. Why did he show up this afternoon right after we'd arrived?"

"Someone in ICE is giving him information," Isabella said, glancing at Cody.

Cody slammed his palm on the steering wheel and pulled over into a parking lot. "Grab your stuff. He could have put a locator on my pickup before coming in the bar."

Isabella hopped out and slung her pack on her back. "They know we're looking for Wes. Did they know we are also looking for the tunnel?"

Cody started off to the north. She followed. "I only asked about the whereabouts of Wes. I didn't mention we know about a tunnel."

"Do you have the address of this place he stays with family?" They had traveled several blocks from the vehicle.

"I was hoping to get it from Sam. But now, I'm not sure who we can trust anyone in ICE. I don't think it's Sam or Willa. They did get us out of the bar. But it could have been a ruse to get us to confide in them." Cody motioned to a small café and ducked inside.

Isabella followed. Her stomach rumbled. "Let's eat and come up with a plan." She shoved her pack into the bench seat and sat at the end. Cody took the side opposite. They ordered sandwiches, and Cody pulled out his phone.

"I'll see where the nearest car rental place is." He studied his phone. "Two miles north is a rental place. We'll eat and head there. Then I'll call Jonny Crow and have him get on the computer and find out the relatives address."

"I think at this point the more agencies we can keep out of this and stay with people we trust the better our likelihood of catching Wes and not the other way around." Isabella leaned back as the waitress placed her sandwich on the table in front or her.

"Eat, we've got a hike to make when we're done." Cody bit into his sandwich and they ate in silence.

~*~

They picked out a nondescript sedan with tinted windows at the car rental agency. Driving off the lot, Cody pointed to a modest-looking motel.

"Let's get a room and I'll call Crow. Then we can get together maps and make a plan."

"I like the idea of a plan."

Isabella paid for a motel room with two queen beds. Once inside, she dropped her pack and took out her phone. She called the hospital while Cody stood outside the room on his phone talking to the Shadow Eagles.

"ICU please." She listened to the new-age music. It stopped abruptly.

"This is Reena Newcomb, R.N., how can I help you?"

"Hi, this is Isabella Mumphrey. Tino Konstantine, my fiancé, is a patient in the ICU. I'm calling to check on his status."

"Mr. Konstantine has shown some improvement. He wiggled his fingers about two hours ago."

"Is he awake?" Her heart raced. *Tino would be fine*. He was waking up. Her desire to be with him battled with her need to catch Wes and know Tino was safe. They were so close to catching Wes that she didn't want to leave until he was apprehended.

"No. But I believe he will be by tomorrow."

"The minute he does wake, call me." Tears burned the back of her eyes. She wanted to be by Tino's side, but she also had to get Wes behind bars where he belonged.

"We will. Is this the number on the white board in his room?" the nurse asked.

"Yes."

"Will you be in to see him tonight?"

"No. I'm working. But call if he wakes. I'll get there as quick as I can." Isabella chewed on the cuticle of her index finger. She was torn. Tino needed her to help nudge him out of his unconsciousness, but getting Wes behind bars would help Tino and many others.

"He's in good care," the nurse said.

"I know. Thank you."

The phone clicked, and she listened to the dial tone.

Cody entered the room. "You okay?"

"Yeah, just torn. I want to be with Tino, but getting Wes behind bars will help so many as well as Tino." She unzipped her backpack. "I'm going to take a shower."

"Do you want to know what Crow found out?" Cody sat on the bed closest to the door.

"He's found information all ready? I thought you were just asking him to start looking." She sat on the bed by the window.

"As soon as he heard Wes got loose, he started digging for information. Crow knows who Wes is related to and wants nothing more than to dethrone his father." Cody pulled a bottle of water out of his pack. He took a swig. "I guess no one really lives in the house here. It belongs to Wes' aunt. He supposedly has permission to stay there when he's in the area. It has been raided, and they didn't find anything incriminating. Crow's texting me the address and the name of the aunt. He also said Luis is turning evidence. If he stays alive this might be what we need to put Wes and his dad in prison."

Isabella stood. "This is all good news. Did you want to check the house out tonight? If we give him time to clean up or hide the tunnel we may not get another chance to find it."

"Take your shower. I'll get a map of the town and we can plan our attack." Cody stood and headed for the door. "Throw the lock and safety bar. I'll come back in an hour."

She followed behind him, putting all the safely locks on the door.

Stepping into the shower, she tried to forget all the reasons she shouldn't be in Nogales.

Chapter Twenty-four

Isabella sat in the sedan eating potato chips and watching a crumbling adobe building sitting all alone in the bottom of a ravine.

"I don't think that building is in any shape for a person to walk through let alone dig a tunnel under."

"That could be what they want everyone to think." Cody pulled out his night vision binoculars.

"See any movement?" She brushed the salt from her fingers and leaned forward studying the smaller outbuildings to see if anyone was watching them. The house sat in a gully east of town down a deserted road. There was no way to get here without being seen. If this was an entrance to a tunnel, there had to be sentries somewhere watching activity around it.

"I've scanned the area and the hills on either side and don't see a thing." He lowered the binoculars and stared at the house. "This could be what it looks like. A derelict house. But why would people say Wes stayed here when it doesn't look like anyone could live here?"

Isabella patted her vest. "Let's go see if the place is livable." She opened the door and stepped out.

Cody was right behind her when she stepped on the stoop. She tried the door knob. Locked.

"Damn! I don't want to break the door down. That would tip Wes off that someone had been here." Cody ran a hand across the back of his neck.

She smiled. "We don't have to break the door down." Digging in her vest pocket, she pulled out her pick set and crouched in front of the door.

"That's also illegal," Cody said, over his shoulder as he watched the driveway.

"But if we find what we think we'll find, we can say the door was already unlocked. Our word against a slave trafficker."

Click.

She turned the knob and walked into a deteriorating house. Holes in the roof allowed the moonlight to beam down into the rooms. Tiny feet scurrying across the stone floor proved no one but wildlife lived here.

"I don't think there's a tunnel under this house." Cody walked by her, kicking debris out of his way.

"We should check each room. This could be a ruse." She flicked on her LED flashlight. "You take the room on the left, I'll take the one on the right."

The room she entered was the kitchen. Ancient appliances had gaping doors. Mouse and larger vermin had left feces piled in the corners of the stove and refrigerator. She covered her nose with her arm. The stench was enough to convince her no one had been here for a long time, but she diligently flashed her light all around the floor looking for a sign there might be a trap door.

"Shit!"

Cody's terrified cry started her feet in motion. She leaped the debris and landed in the other room. Cody clutched the wrist of his right hand with his left. The sound registered the second the echo of her footsteps faded.

Rattlesnake.

"Where's the snake?" She flashed her light on the floor at Cody's feet.

"Under that board. I reached to pick it up. That's when it got me."

"Back this way. We need to see what kind it was." Isabella pulled on the back of Cody's shirt, drawing him out of the room.

"How are you feeling?" She grasped his wrist, lowering his hand.

"It shocked me at first, but I'm slowing my heart rate."

His hand was starting to swell. She scrounged up two short pieces of wood, ripped his shirt tail and immobilized his hand.

"Keep that hanging at your side to slow the movement of the blood to your heart."

"I know. This isn't the first time I've been bit. Go find out what kind of rattler it is." He grimaced.

That he could remain calm helped his chances of minimal damage from the bite.

"I can do that. Wait here." She walked over to a small side table and broke the leg off.

Back in the bedroom, she used the stick to lift up the board. The chirr of the snake's rattles started low, but grew in volume as the board moved higher and higher. She only needed it high enough to get a good look, but that meant putting her body within striking distance. She dropped the board and the rattle shaking became more vigorous.

Scanning the room, she found a five-foot-long two-by-four leaning up in a corner. She grabbed the longer board and pried the panel up, again. This time she could see the snake. It was tan with darker brown spots. A sidewinder.

She dropped the board and hurried back to Cody.

"Come on. We need to get you to a doctor for an anti-venom shot. It was a sidewinder."

They turned to the door.

BOOM!

The blast knocked them backwards as the walls crumbled and the roof toppled down.

The dust and debris drifted down around Isabella. She remained on her back, one by one assessing her limbs and body. Everything appeared to move. No broken bones. Her chest hurt. The moon shone down on the rubble like a twenty-watt bulb. A roof beam had her pinned. The pressure didn't squish her, only held her in place. She wiggled and felt things shift under her.

"Cody? Cody?" she called and tried to look the direction he'd been before the blast. One thing was certain, this house had been blown up for one reason. Wes or whoever was keeping an eye on the place wanted them dead.

A groan and a board flying through the air proved Cody was alive.

"Don't move. I think I can get out. If you strain to get loose you'll rush the venom to your heart. Just lie still. I'll come to you." She wiggled again, feeling things under her shift. Using her hands, she shoved at the boards, chunks of adobe, and debris until she could scoot out from under the beam.

She stood and surveyed the area. Some of the walls remained standing like jagged teeth.

"Say something so I can find you without stepping on you."

"I'm over here." His voice was weak.

Following his voice, she found him. A large chunk of the wall had landed on one of his legs. A beam held his chest down.

"Which one is causing the most pain?' she asked, examining his leg.

"The leg."

"Then I'll get that off you first."

"You can't lift it." He coughed. "Call for help."

She pulled her cell phone out of her pocket and dialed 9-1-1. "I have a male with a snake bite and a crushed leg on a dirt road two miles past the end of east Hudgins Rd. Please hurry."

Leaving her phone open, she slipped it into her pocket and began studying her options. There were two piles of debris on either side of his leg. If she could get a beam across them...

She uncovered the ends of the beam on Cody's chest. Once the board was loose, she lifted the beam one end, and then the other, setting the heavy board to rest on the debris on either side of Cody's body and above the chunk of adobe on his leg. She opened her survival tin and took out the ten feet of four-gauge snare wire.

The wire wrapped around the beam and the chunk of wall twice. She used the broken table leg and slipped it between the doubled wire and slowly turned it, tightening the wire and lifting the chunk of adobe off Cody's leg. When she had several inches between his leg and the piece of wall, she grasped Cody under his arms and pulled him out. Once he was free, she started clearing a path to the outside. She didn't want him straining to stand, and she could only drag him to safety.

The sound of sirens screamed through the night as she dragged Cody the last few feet out of the rubble. She collapsed next to him.

"How you doing?" she asked, using the moonlight to study his face.

"I don't know how you got me out, but I owe you, sis."

"You don't owe me anything. We're family."

A county car slid to a stop by the sedan.

An ambulance followed close behind.

Shamutz! She hadn't figured on the police. How connected was Wes' father to law enforcement across the state?

"What happened?" the deputy asked as soon as he stood over them.

"We were inside when someone tried to blow us up." Isabella patted Cody on the chest and stood.

He grabbed her ankle and squeezed. She took the gesture as a warning to not say too much.

The EMT's arrived with a gurney.

"He was bit by a sidewinder before the house crumpled." Isabella informed the crew.

"Who are you and what were you doing in that house?" the deputy asked in a tone that proved he wasn't used to people stonewalling him.

"I'll answer your questions as soon as I know my friend is going to be okay."

She followed the gurney carrying Cody to the ambulance. Taking his hand, she squeezed. "I'll be right behind the ambulance."

"Now you have two men to worry about in the hospital," Cody said.

"Yeah, what's with the men I hang out with?" She joked and released his hand as they lifted him into the ambulance.

When the doors closed, she turned to the deputy. "Cody is with ICE, and we had reason to believe there was a drug tunnel in this house. We staked it out, didn't see any activity, and decided to take a look. We hadn't found anything when Cody was bit and an explosion lowered the building on top of us."

The deputy studied her a minute. "Let me see your identification."

"It's in the car." She led him over to the rental car.

"Why are ICE agents using a rental car?" he asked.

"Our car was compromised when the person we were following spotted us." She opened the car door and reached in for her purse. It and their backpacks were missing.

"Shamutz!"

"What?" the deputy put his hand on his revolver. She glanced at his name badge. Morales.

"They took my purse and both our packs." She looked in the ignition. "And the car keys."

She slammed the door and started pacing. There was only one thing to do. She pulled her phone out of her pocket and hit the number of the only person who could get her out of this. As much as she hated to pull him in, there wasn't any choice.

"How's my girl?" Daddy's voice was comforting and filled her with guilt.

"Not so good. Cody and I were checking out a hunch. He was bit by a snake and the house was blown up while we were still in it."

She held the phone away from her ear as Daddy let loose with profanity.

"Are you in the hospital? Where? I'll come get you."

"I'm not in the hospital, but I need you to vouch for me. While the traffickers were blowing up the house, they also took my purse and both our belongings." She knew he understood the ramifications by the silence. "There's a deputy here. Would you talk to him so he will take me to the hospital to check on Cody?"

"Hand him your phone."

She dutifully handed her phone over to the deputy who eyed it skeptically.

"Yes, sir."

She half listened to the one-sided conversation as she scanned the hills on either side of the house. There had to be someone up there watching them. That was the only thing that made sense. They knew she and Cody were coming to this house to have had the bombs already set.

It was time to stop using the agencies and go it alone. That was the only way to stay ahead of these people who appeared to have snitches in every law enforcement agency.

Deputy Morales handed the phone to her. "I'll take you to the hospital."

"Thank you." She slipped her phone in her pocket and slid into the passenger seat of the county cruiser. This had officially become a WIA Op. She wasn't going to rely on the agencies that Sheriff Douglas Warren could manipulate.

Chapter Twenty-five

Deputy Morales delivered Isabella to the hospital. On the drive in, he tried to wrangle more information out of her. She only gave him enough information to help him fill out an incident report. She left out names and what they were looking for.

He was reluctant to leave her, following her into the hospital and hanging around as she asked about Cody.

"I don't know what Mr. Mumphrey said to you, but I'll be fine on my own now. Thank you for the ride." She shook the deputy's hand and motioned for him to leave. He moved away from her but stayed by the hospital exit.

"Miss," The nurse at the emergency desk caught her attention. "They just finished x-rays on your friend. He doesn't have any broken bones. They'll finish patching him up and he'll be ready to leave."

"Thank you. I'll be here in the waiting room when he's ready." *With no vehicle.*

She took a seat in a corner as far away from the deputy as she could get and dialed the Tucson hospital.

"ICU please." She waited, listening to soothing harp music. *If only my life was a serene as the music.*

"ICU," said a clipped female voice.

"Hi, this is Isabella Mumprey, Tino Konstantine's fiancée. I'm checking in to see how he's doing. Is he awake?"

She didn't want him to wake without her by his side, but she also knew the longer he remained unconscious the more complications he'd have.

"He has been stirring, awake for brief moments."

Happiness he was waking stamped down her guilt of not being by his side. "Please tell him I'll be there to see him soon. And as soon as he is well enough would you help him call me. Any time, I don't care."

The nurse agreed she'd help Tino call her. *He's getting better*. Her happiness for his well-being filled her chest. Keeping him well and on the mend meant getting Wes behind bars. If she didn't, Tino would try before he was well enough. She knew her stubborn Latin lover. He would single-handedly try to take down the man.

Isn't that what you are doing?

She ignored her conscience and dialed Daddy.

"We're at the hospital and in need of a vehicle. Is there a chance you have connections in Nogales and can get a car to us?"

"A car is ready for you to use. I'll have Agent Hernandez bring it over. She also has intel on Warren. I want you to keep her in the loop on your activities. She has been undercover down there for a while and knows people who are willing to help."

This was the best news she'd heard since Suri and Rae described the tunnel.

"Thank you. I called the hospital. Tino is slowly waking up. I want to get Warren locked up so I can help Tino recuperate."

"I know. I have the guard on his room reporting to me." Daddy cleared his throat. "You should be at Tino's bedside not out chasing a slave trafficker."

"If I don't get Warren locked up, Tino will wake up and try to go after him before he's ready. I'm doing this for our future."

"Be careful. I don't have a lot of agents in that area, and I don't know whose pockets the Warren's are lining."

"I'll be careful."

The doors to the emergency room opened. Cody, looking a bit woozy and disgruntled, emerged in a wheelchair.

"Cody's ready. I have to go. Thank you for all your help."

"Call if you need anything." Daddy's choked words brought tears to her eyes.

"I will." She turned off the phone and hurried to Cody's side.

"Wow, do I have to lug you around in this?" she joked and slugged Cody's arm.

"No. They said it's policy. I have to be wheeled out of here."

"We don't want to release him yet. He should stay in the hospital overnight for observation. Snake bites and the anti-venom can cause adverse reactions." The nurse said, scowling down at Cody.

"I told you, this isn't the first time I've been bit. I know what my reactions are. I'll be fine." Cody wiggled the fingers on his bandaged right hand.

The dark scowl on his face told Isabella he was ready to kick butt, and she knew who the recipient was.

"Can you leave him here by the door? Our ride isn't here yet." Isabella nudged the nurse away and pushed Cody over by the door where the deputy had stood until his radio crackled and he hurried away.

"What ride? Where's the car?" Cody started to raise out of the chair.

Isabella pushed him back down and studied the slit in his left pant leg and white gauze wrapped from his ankle to his knee. Her gaze wandered to his right hand. "What is the extent of your injuries?"

"My leg has some scratches and bruises. And you know about my hand." He peered into her eyes. "I don't like hospitals. A good night's sleep in a motel and I'll be ready to roll tomorrow. I promise."

She wanted to believe him but his color was paler than usual and his eyes dilated.

"What about that ride? Where's the car?"

"While they were blowing up the house with us in it, the suspects stole our packs, my purse and the car keys." She didn't like the anger she saw flash in his eyes. "The deputy gave me a ride."

"How did that go? Did you have to tell him everything?"

"I told him enough to make our presence there reasonable then I handed him over to Daddy. Who is sending us a vehicle and an agent who has been undercover down here and is willing to help us. That way the Warren's won't know what we're up to."

The emergency doors opened. A tall, stout Hispanic woman

wearing high-heel boots that stopped at her knees, skinny jeans, and a cropped top that barely covered her full breasts strode through the door.

She walked over and hugged Isabella.

"I was worried when you didn't arrive on time," she said loudly. And whispered in Isabella's ear. "I am Angel Hernandez, your father sent me."

"Angel, I'm sorry we worried you." Isabella hugged her back and smiled wide, when the woman released her.

She glanced down at Cody. His eyeballs nearly popped out of his head and his mouth hung open, salivating.

"Angel, let me introduce my friend, Cody." She stifled a giggle as the woman leaned down and hugged Cody, smashing her breasts against his neck.

"It's a pleasure to meet such a fine specimen of a man." Angel winked at Cody and took control of his wheelchair.

Once they were all loaded into her car, her whole posture and demeanor changed.

"I was told to house you and give you all the intel I have on Wes Warren and his group." Angel glanced over at Isabella. "But I need to know why you are after him and what you want exactly."

"We, Cody and I, stumbled onto where he was holding women to sell. His boss, Rico Montoya, has a vendetta with my fiancé and me. Wes nearly beat my fiancé to death. Wes was in custody and slipped away. We don't know if he plans to carry out Montoya's vendetta against Tino and me or if he's out to kill us for his own revenge." Isabella glanced back at Cody. "He tried killing Cody and me tonight by blowing up a house we were in."

Angel whistled. "Montoya and Warrens are out for your blood. It's no wonder you had to call in help from WIA."

Cody spoke up. "You said Warrens. We thought there must have been someone reporting to the sheriff. They seem to know every step we take."

"My sources say the old man is very interested in the outcome of this. He was the one who helped Wes get away at the hospital." Contempt tinged Angel's words.

"Can that be proven?" Isabella wanted to take down both Warren men.

"No. We know it was a drug trafficker who arranged it all, and he had a visit from the sheriff as soon as Wes was arrested. But without the trafficker turning on the sheriff, it's his word against the good sheriff of Coconino County."

As many years as he'd been covering up his illegal activities it would stand to reason he'd have himself bulletproof for any convictions. Isabella relaxed into the leather car seat. The car was a new expensive model.

"What is your cover?" she asked, almost afraid to know after piecing together Angel's appearance and the car.

"I own a strip joint." Angel smiled.

Cody leaned forward. "Are you one of the dancers?"

Isabella laughed and exchanged a glance with Angel.

"I only do private dances with people I need to ply for information." Angel glanced in the review mirror. "Are you in need of a private dance?"

The color blasted back into Cody's face. Isabella laughed as Angel pulled the car into a driveway on the north side of Nogales. The house was large, ornate stucco. The area was a newer, upscale neighborhood. The garage door went up and they pulled in.

"Don't get out until the garage door closes," Angel ordered.

The door closed and lights came on in the garage. "It's my precaution. Once the garage door is down the security system comes back on."

"Has your cover been blown?" Isabella didn't want to bring one more person problems.

Angel laughed. "No, you would think being a WIA agent would require the security, but it's my cover, strip club owner, that requires all the security measures. There are weirdoes that think if they follow me home, they'll get what I don't give out at the club. And then there are the religious zealots that have labeled me a whore and try to take my life to stop the club." She sighed. "I can only say this cover down here will be my last of this sort. It gets old being on the alert all the time."

She got out of the car. The door to the house opened and a middle-aged Hispanic woman stood in the threshold.

Isabella helped Cody out of the car.

"Isabella and Cody, this is my mother Adelina, but when we are around others, she is my housekeeper." Angel draped an arm about her mother's shoulders. "Sí, Mama?"

"Yes, I am helping my daughter with her job." Adelina turned and headed into the house.

"I have plenty of room for you to use my home as a base." Angel dropped her purse and keys on the hallway table. She glanced at the clock on the wall. "I have to leave for the club in two hours. I can brief you once you have settled in and had something to eat." Angel strolled through a large living room. "Mama, please fix us some lunch. I'll show them the guest rooms."

Isabella studied the paintings on the walls and the sculptures on the tables and shelves. She whispered to Cody, "Either they set her up well or she is making good money at the strip club."

He didn't respond. She glanced at him and noticed his gaze was following Angel's swaying backside.

She slugged him in the arm.

"Ow!" He glared at her.

"If you can't keep your mind off her curves, I'll take you back to the hospital because you're going to be of no use to me." She said this under her breath.

Angel had stopped by a room. She narrowed her eyes and watched them approach. "This will be your room, Isabella. There's a shared bathroom and this door," she moved down to the door in the hallway, "will be for you, Cody."

"I see you don't have clean clothes to change into. Lucky for you I keep a full array of sizes in both men and women. The women's clothes are in the room you have, Isabella. Cody, there are men's clothes in the closet in your room." She waved Cody forward and opened the door for him. "We'll have lunch in thirty minutes, and then I'll brief you."

Isabella ducked into her room, took off her vest, and draped it over the chair. The room rivaled any she'd stayed in at five-star hotels. A fluffy, inviting, sky-blue comforter covered a king-size bed. The art on the wall was a beautiful Arizona landscape. The chair, side table, and bed were made of massive dark wood.

Sniffing, she caught a whiff of herself. A quick shower and clean clothes would not only clean her up but refresh her mind. Laughing in the hallway trickled through the walls. She snorted. It didn't matter if

Cody and Angel got on as long as it didn't interfere with getting Wes.

She opened the closet and selected underwear, socks, a shirt, and pants in her size and wandered into the bathroom. Crossing the expanse between her bedroom door and Cody's, she noted the double showerheads, brass fixtures, and well-lit mirror. The lock clicked on Cody's side. She stripped and stepped into the shower. The two showerheads wet her down quickly. Shampoo, conditioner, and body wash hung on dispensers in the shower. She cleaned up and stepped out, grabbing a large fluffy towel from the open shelves next to the shower.

How did a WIA agent live this well? If the strip club was a cover, she wasn't making any money working there. It would really be owned by someone else. Was WIA paying for all the extravagance?

Something wasn't adding up. Her parents didn't even live this lavish and both of them were on the WIA payroll a lot higher up the chain of command than Angel. She towel dried her hair, wrapped the towel around her and unlocked Cody's door. She knocked on the door.

"Yeah." Cody sounded tired.

She opened the door and walked through. "You sure you should have left the hospital?"

He reclined on the bed, his bad leg on the mattress, the other dangling over the side.

"I'll be fine tomorrow. You through in there?"

"Yeah." She sat on the end of the bed. "Doesn't it strike you as odd this house is so opulent?"

"I don't know. I don't work for a worldwide agency like you and Angel."

She was relieved to see he didn't take up sides. "Well, Mom and Dad have worked for WIA since my birth and both have high status, but they couldn't afford something like this. And I can't see the organization paying for this as a cover."

"When she goes to work, give Mumphrey a call and ask." He pushed off the bed. "Get back in your room, I'm going to take a shower."

"What about your leg and your hand?" She glanced at the gauze on his leg.

"The leg isn't as bad as the bandage they put on it. I'll keep my hand up. I know better than to get a bite infected." He limped as he walked to the door.

"You're sure the leg isn't bad? You're limping." She hurried through the door but stood in the bathroom.

"I'm limping because my leg and my hand hurt like a son-of-a-bitch." He waved her to keep on going.

"Did they give you anything for pain?" She refused to budge until he had allayed her fears.

"I have a pain pill I didn't take. I'll take it after we eat and I can sleep all night." He walked over and pushed her out of the bathroom.

The lock clicked behind her. She dressed and hurried to the kitchen. After Angel briefed them and left, she'd put that call into Daddy. There was something about this place that didn't feel right.

Chapter Twenty-six

The lunch Adelina put together was filling and delicious. Both Isabella and Cody thanked her several times before Angel led them into a small office, complete with monitors keeping tabs on the perimeter of the house.

"This is high-tech gear," Cody said, studying the equipment.

Isabella noted the admiration in Cody's voice. She hoped he kept a level head when it came to Angel. If the WIA agent happened to be on the take, Isabella didn't want Cody to go down in the fallout.

"When I saw the potential for people breaking in, I took two month's pay and had this all installed. I've gathered information that if it fell into the wrong hands could cause trouble for not only WIA but a couple of other organizations." Angel clicked a button and a large screen came to life. "No offense. Even though you look like your photos, I need to make sure you are who you say you are before I brief you."

Angel tapped on the keyboard. Several seconds later, Daddy's face appeared.

"Mr. Mumphrey, I have Isabella and Cody with me. But to make sure, I'd like you to verify they are who they say they are." Angel moved a camera on the top of the screen, pointing it at the two of them.

Isabella was at a loss. Did she address Daddy in that informal manner in front of Angel? Angel would know her last name was the same as the man on the screen.

"Isabella. I'm happy to see you and Angel connected. Cody, you look a little worse for wear. Are you sure you should have left the hospital?" Daddy had his all-business persona on.

She'd do the same. "Yes, Angel came to our rescue and is getting ready to brief us. As for Cody. What would you like to say?" She turned to her brother.

"There was no way I'd stay in a bed when there's some SOB out there trying to kill us. A good night's sleep and I'll be ready to roll." Cody remained standing.

Isabella could see he was in more pain than he let one. Hopefully a good night's rest would help.

"I've sent everything we have on the Warrens to Angel. She'll add what she's gathered since her last report. You're in good hands." Daddy's expression turned more serious. "Angel, Cody, would you step outside the room while I discuss something with Isabella."

Angel gave her a questioning glance. She took hold of Cody's arm and the two left the room drawing the door closed behind them.

"What did you want to talk to me about?" Isabella pulled up a chair and pointed the camera down to her face.

"Have you checked in on Tino?"

"Not since we left the Nogales Hospital. Why? Has something happened?" Her chest constricted as fear for Tino raced her heart.

"When our sentries were changing, they caught a man trying to sneak into Tino's room. He didn't get a chance to do anything and refuses to talk. I've had Tino transferred to a private hospital in Phoenix. I didn't want you calling the hospital and have the nurse tell you he was no longer there."

"Thank you. That would have terrified me to think he was either kidnapped or ..." she couldn't say the word dead.

"I figured as much. He'll be well taken care of. He's under the name Gus Kosta."

Isabella giggled. "Wait till I tell him you made him Greek."

Daddy chuckled. "They say he's slowly coming around. You need to catch Wesley and get back to your fiancé."

"That has been my goal all along." She stared at her father.

"What is it, Pumpkin?"

"How well do you know Angel?"

His brow furrowed. "She's been a good agent. Why?"

"This house, the things in it. They're all very expensive. Is the agency paying for all of this?" She hoped Angel wasn't playing too many sides.

"You don't have to worry. Angel is a very rich woman. Her family owns several oils wells. She works for us because her brother and a cousin were killed by the factions we fight." He narrowed his eyes. "Specifically, Sheriff Douglas Warren."

The knowledge landed a large knot in her stomach. "Thank you. Now I know why she has so much information about them." Isabella pressed a hand to her belly. "I better go or they are going to wonder what all we're talking about."

"Listen to Angel and you'll accomplish your mission." Daddy disappeared.

Isabella took a moment to pull herself together then went to the door. She opened it and found Angel and Cody talking together quietly.

"Sorry to take up your time with family business." She backed into the room and took a seat in one of the chairs at a small table.

Cody watched her closely as he took a seat beside her. "Is everything okay?"

"Yeah. I'll tell you later." She placed her trembling hands in her lap. How many people's lives had her biological father ruined? Her stomach churned with shame. It wasn't rational to take on the guilt of a person she'd never met and didn't care to meet, but knowing his genes were part of her makeup made her nauseous.

"Are you sure, you're okay?" Cody put a hand on her shoulder.

She gazed into his eyes. Half of her genes also flowed in this man. A good man. She nodded. This was the side she had to think about and use to get her through this mission.

Angel cleared her throat.

Isabella peered into the woman's eyes. Was that a flicker of comprehension?

"This is the information I received from the agency when I started here and this," she pulled out a folder twice the size of the agency file.

"This is the information I've been skimming from my sources."

Cody took the thick file and opened it. Wes' photo was stapled to the inside of the cover.

"You can read through those after I leave. What I'm going to tell you now, will be what you'll want to move on." Angel picked up a cell phone. She turned the apparatus for them to see. "This is the outside of the building where there is a tunnel that Warren uses for moving drugs and humans from Mexico to the U.S." She enlarged the photo. "The man there owns the restaurant."

Isabella inhaled and nearly choked. Emilio stood beside the door. "He's part of the trafficking."

Angel shook her head. "He's ICE. He's been working the last two years to become acquainted with Warren and Montoya."

Isabella shook her head. "No, I could tell, he wants to take over. He was alone with the women after Cody got free. He crushed my face into the bars and told me I would pay."

Cody's face reddened and his jaw twitched. "I told you to come with me."

"I couldn't leave the women behind. They'd all be sold now if I hadn't stayed and helped them get away." She turned to Angel. "Emilio is not helping you. He is helping himself."

Angel frowned. "Then we'll allow him to help us and then arrest him along with Warren."

"Do you know if Montoya is rolling on any of his underlings?" Isabella had a thought. "If we could get him to think Warren is the one who leaked information that helped to lure him out, he might turn on Warren."

Angel's face brightened. "That's a clever idea." She punched numbers in her phone and asked to speak with an ICE agent.

Isabella studied Cody as he watched Angel discuss the possibility of leaking false information to Montoya about Warren. Cody seemed mesmerized by the woman. She didn't know if this was good or bad.

Before saying good-bye, Angel did a lot of cajoling and fast talking. She turned to them a scowl marring her pretty face. "I don't think they will do that. Something about Montoya's lawyers will use the 'coercion' in the courtroom and he could walk."

Cody slammed his fist on the table, making Isabella and Angel jump. "I despise the fact the crooks get all the breaks in court." He stared at Isabella. "What about the victims' rights?"

He was thinking about their mother. She reached over and squeezed his hand.

Angel watched the exchange but said nothing.

"Why did you show us Emilio?" Isabella asked to get back on course.

"I was hoping you could go to his restaurant and watch the people he talks to and have him give you a signal. But if he knows you, that won't work." Angel clicked her fake fingernails on the table top.

"You go to work. Cody and I will rest up and that will give us tonight to read these files and maybe come up with another plan." Isabella nodded toward the digital clock readout on the monitor screen.

Angel nodded. "You're safe here. No one knows you're here, and Mama won't let anyone in. Rest. We'll make our move tomorrow."

Isabella stood, picked up the folders, and watched Cody slowly get to his feet. They exited the room and Angel drew the door closed behind them.

"What time will you get back?' Isabella asked.

"Four in the morning. Don't worry. I won't wake you. We'll strategize when you are both ready in the morning." Angel picked up her purse and car keys. "Sleep well. We'll carry out justice tomorrow."

Isabella watched Angel leave through the garage door. "She's an interesting woman," she muttered.

"Yeah." Cody continued down the hall to his room. At the door he nodded for her to follow him. He stretched out on the bed. "Bring me a glass of water and the pill sitting on the counter, please."

She filled a glass with water and brought it and the pill to him.

He downed the full glass of water and the pill. Setting the glass on the bedside table, he patted the mattress next to his leg. "What did Mumphrey have to say to you alone?"

She smiled. "He didn't want a subordinate to see him playing daddy." If he was here right now she'd give him a big hug. "Someone tried to get to Tino at the hospital. Daddy's agents stopped him and Daddy moved Tino to a private facility. He wanted me to know before I called the hospital."

Cody's expression softened. "Good. Then he's safe. I wondered if it was something like that. Angel and I were discussing the conditions we found those women in. She is very determined to take down the

Warrens. And I mean that in plural."

Isabella nodded. "I asked Daddy about Angel. You know my impression she was playing sides…"

Cody nodded. His eyelids were drooping already.

"She's had two family members killed by the Warrens, as in plural. And the affluence…her family has money. She joined WIA to take down the Warrens and people like them." Knowing this about the woman, added another level of respect for her.

Cody's lips barely moved.

He was asleep. She hoped the pill eased his pain till morning, but it was early evening and it was possible the pill would wear off. Tiptoeing out of the room, she picked up the file folders she left on the bathroom counter and entered her own room leaving the adjoining doors open so she could keep an eye on Cody.

She sat cross-legged on the bed and picked up the file from WIA. How much about the Warrens would she learn? Did she want to know to help the mission or to fill a gap in her own existence?

A deep breath and she opened the file.

This was the second time since learning of her birth that she stared into the face of Douglas Warren. This picture was much the same as the one she'd studied on the phone. The cruelness in his eyes and the set of his mouth made her shudder. She flipped the photo over and started reading. Most of the allegations against him only went back the last ten years. The more she read, the more she distanced herself from the idea he had anything to do with her existence. He was a monster and that was how she would view him from here on out. He was a predator and she would find a way to put him in a cage where he belonged.

Chapter Twenty-seven

Wood bumping wood woke Isabella. She flipped on the light beside her bed and saw the cause of the commotion. Cody stood in the bathroom opening and closing the cupboards.

"Are you looking for something?" She glanced at the clock by the bed. 3:20.

"My leg is hurting. I'm looking for some pain relievers." He shut the cupboard door. "But I don't see any."

Isabella walked into the bathroom. Cody had stripped down to his boxers. He had a wide muscled chest and a six pack. She dropped her gaze to his leg.

"You said you had cuts and bruises. Those are stitches." She shoved on his shoulder turning him. "Get back in bed. I'll find a first-aid kit and get that wrapped back up and find some pain relievers."

"You're bossy." Cody sat on the bed.

"Lean back and relax." She gave him a gentle nudge, and he laid back on the pillows.

She wore a tank and underwear; her usual sleeping attire. She walked out of Cody's room and headed down the hall. Angel's mother came out of the first room along the hallway.

"Can I help you?"

"I'm looking for a first-aid kit and some pain relievers. Cody's cut needs bandaged, and he's in pain." She wondered if there were sensors on the doors as quickly as the woman popped out of the room.

"We have a first-aid kit in the kitchen, and I will get the pills." Adelina headed down the hall and turned into the kitchen.

She dug in the pantry and came out with a doctor's bag. "This should have anything you need. I will get the pills."

Isabella headed back to Cody's room. "Why didn't you tell me you had stitches?' She dabbed antiseptic on the row of eight stitches, then antibiotic ointment and a sterile gauze. The case had several ace bandages and even a roll of self-sticking wrap. She did a double wrap of gauze, then used the self-sticking wrap to go around his leg four times.

"There that should hold until tomorrow night when we need to let it air and change the bandage."

Adelina knocked and entered. She had two bottles in her hands.

Isabella picked up the bottles, reading the contents. "There's a four hundred milligram Ibuprofen or a pain pill with codeine."

"No codeine. That stuff knocks me out. I want to ease the pain but still function." Cody held his hand out.

She grabbed the glass on the night stand, filled it with water, and handed the glass and two Ibuprofen to him. "That should hold you till morning, big guy."

Handing the bottles back to Adelina, Isabella noticed the woman hesitated as if she wanted to say something.

When Adelina walked to the door, Isabella followed and stepped into the hallway with her.

"Is something wrong?" she asked, stopping Adelina with a hand on her arm.

"Angel hasn't called to say she is on the way home." Adelina looked close to tears.

"She said she gets home at four. It's only three-thirty."

"She arrives home at four and calls before she leaves the business at three-thirty." She dabbed at her eye with a white hankie. "She usually calls by now."

"Maybe something happened at work that has her running late tonight." She tried to console the woman, but she was inconsolable. "Is there someone from her work you can call?"

"I could try the bartender. I have his number." Adelina hurried to the phone in the kitchen.

"Before you call him, why don't you try Angel's cell phone first?" Isabella didn't like the fact Angel wasn't following her routine after picking them up at the hospital.

The older woman dialed and listened. "It went to voice message." She replaced the receiver and flipped open a small book on the counter by the phone. With one finger on a number, she dialed and waited.

"Richard? This is Adelina Hernandez, Angel's mother." She listened and smiled faintly. "Sí, it has been a while since I talked to you. I'm calling because I have not heard from Angel. She usually calls before she leaves. Is she still at the business?" The woman listened, again. This time her brow furrowed. "She left early? Where did she go?" She listened and shook her head.

Isabella eased the phone out of Adelina's hand.

"Hi Richard. I'm a friend of Angel's. Did she leave with anyone?"

"Yeah. The guy with the restaurant. I think his name's Emilio," said a male voice.

Fear for Angel made Isabella's knuckles ache from squeezing the phone. She willed her emotions to ease up. "What time did they leave together?"

"About one. I haven't seen her take an interest in any man since she's been here. They could just be hanging out together, you know." The implication in his voice was laughable considering what Angel knew about Emilio.

"Yeah, I know. Did she do anything different tonight?" There had to be something that would indicate why Angel would go off with Emilio after the information Isabella had told her.

"She gave a personal party for that Emilio and a blond guy about thirty. I didn't like the wild look in his eyes. Angel was a bit off after that and left shortly with Emilio."

Isabella had a hard time sounding natural when she hung up the phone. "I need to head over to Emilio's restaurant." She grasped Adelina by the shoulders. "Cody is going to be worthless until those pain killers wear off some. If I'm not back in three hours, wake him and tell him where I went and why."

"You should get help." Adelina reached for the phone.

"No, the people we're dealing with have moles in law

enforcement. The only people I can trust are Cody and Angel. Cody knows who to call if I'm not back. The people who aren't under the thumb of a corrupt sheriff."

Isabella hurried to her room. She pulled on the jeans and shirt she wore earlier, sneakers, her vest, and a light, long-sleeved shirt over the top.

After reading the files earlier, she'd looked up the restaurant on her phone and had its location mapped out. When she popped out of her room, Adelina stood in the hallway, car keys dangled from her fingers.

"Behind the house off the kitchen is a small garage where I keep my little car I use for errands."

Isabella hugged the woman. "Thank you. I'll get your daughter back." She took the keys and headed to the kitchen and into the small garage. An older model, dark blue compact car gleamed under the light.

She slid in, started the car, and hit the garage door opener. Once on the street, she oriented herself and headed to the south end of town. She wasn't going to let another person fall victim to the Warrens. Why had Angel gone with Emilio when they'd come to the conclusion he was in as deep as the rest?

Driving this early in the morning there was limited traffic. She drove past the restaurant, staring at the building. She couldn't see any lights upstairs or downstairs. Keeping her speed at a pace that wouldn't draw suspicions, she drove around the block, checking down alleys and trying to get a feel for the building and all the entrances.

The only way to truly see what she was up against was to get as close as she could and try to find a way in. She parked the car a block away, set her phone on vibrate, locked the doors, and pocketed the keys.

If she turned her phone off Daddy wouldn't be able to follow her with GPS. When Cody called him in three hours that would be the first thing Daddy would do. Turn on her tracking device.

She stayed to the shadows of the buildings, moving at a snail's pace toward the back of the restaurant. Her movements were slow and methodical creeping up on the building. If a toe stubbed and knocked something over or if she moved fast someone on watch would notice the movement of the shadow.

Finally, she stood at the corner of the building next door. She drew in a deep breath and let it out slowly. The trick would be walking across the moonlit space from this building to the next.

Scratching on metal behind her, spun her on her heels. A large dog stood on its hind legs trying to get something out of a dumpster. Cautiously, she walked toward the dog.

"Good dog. Is there something in there you want?" she whispered, keeping her body close to the building.

The dog dropped to all four feet and watched her approach.

She peeked into the dumpster and saw an open gallon can that had held chili. Lifting the can from the dumpster, she allowed the dog to smell it. His big tongue came out and licked the inside. She moved back along the building and at the corner, allowed the dog to sniff the can before she sent it rolling up the alley opposite to the direction she needed to go.

The dog took off after the can barking and making noise. Isabella ran for the corner of the restaurant in shadow.

Pressed against the wall of the building, she scanned the side she stood against. There were two vehicles parked on the shady side of the building. Leading her to believe there were at least two people in the building. Neither vehicle belonged to Angel.

She sent a text of the two license plates to WIA to find out who she might be dealing with. Wall sitting, she waited for the reply and continued to assess the area and how she planned to get in. Her phone vibrated. One belonged to Emilio and the other was stolen. It was a good bet the stolen car either brought Wes or a few thugs here. As a fugitive, Wes wouldn't be driving around in a vehicle that he owned.

Sliding along the wall, she moved to the front and looked around. The street was still clear. She didn't find any doorways on this side. The only access to the building was through the front or back. She stopped at the corner of the building and studied the back door, wall, and dumpster.

How long would it take me to pick that lock? I'll be in the open the whole time. She pulled the pick set out of her pocket. The tension pick slipped through her fingers. She crouched and moved her fingers along the ground feeling for the pick. A glint of light blinked in her peripheral vision. She turned her head and noticed a thin light on the ground under the dumpster.

There was an opening under the dumpster. That had to be the entrance to the tunnel. Moving the dumpster would require muscle and would be noisy. She remained crouched, staring at the slit of light and ran possible scenarios over and over in her mind.

The only way she could see getting in there and finding Angel was to get caught. But she didn't want them to know she knew about the tunnel. She sent a text to Cody telling him where the tunnel entrance was located, and then stepped out of the shadow and walked straight up to the back door and started picking the lock.

In less than a minute the knob turned and she stepped into the building. Closing the door wrapped her in complete darkness. She slipped the pick-set back in her pocket and listened.

The whirr of appliances, perhaps freezers or refrigerators, vibrated the air to her left. In slow motion she raised her arms, feeling for walls. Her right hand bumped into a solid wall.

Running her hand along the wall, she took cautious steps forward, listening between each step. Her hand touched a doorframe, then a recessed door. She found the door knob and tried turning.

It spun and the door moved.

A dim light seeped through the gap in the door.

With one eye, she peeked through the gap. A trap door stood open and the light came from the hole in the floor. With measured slowness, she inched the door open far enough for her to slip through. The area behind the door was filled with stacked sacks of dirt. That was how they kept the digging a secret.

She crept over to the opening and peered over the edge. A ladder was attached to the bottom of the floor by hinges. Isabella sat down beside the hole and pulled out her survival tin. Opening the tin, she plucked the mirror from the bottom.

Lying on her side next to the opening, she held the mirror above the hole where the ladder attached and tipped it to see down under the floor. A man sat with his back against a wall. She slowly moved to angle the mirror the other direction. The tunnel went under the alley behind the building. It was lit with low-watt bulbs and electrical wire. She tipped the mirror more and saw the edge of the outside opening.

If she could take out the one guard she could follow the tunnel.

But what if Angel and Emilio are just upstairs? Her gut told her they weren't lovers. If Emilio and Wes took her, it was to extract information. The best place to do that without threat of retaliation would be out of the United States—in Mexico. They must have taken her under the border.

Chapter Twenty-eight

The only way to remove the guard would be by surprise and force. The dug out area under the floor was only six feet deep. She could swing down without fear of injury.

Isabella put her hand over the lens end of her LED flashlight and scanned the room for something to use to gag and tie the man. She found an empty cloth sack identical to the ones storing the dirt and tucked a corner of a bag into her back pocket.

With her legs folded under her, she positioned herself at the end of the hole above the ladder. Everything would have to be timed just right. She squeezed her eyes shut and mentally went through the motions she had planned. After one last vision of Tino awake and smiling at her she opened her eyes.

A deep inhale, slow breath out, and…

She sprang forward, grasped the other side of the floor, swung down, and thrust her feet into the man's chest as he stood. The force slammed him back against the wall.

He shook his head, gathered his feet under him, and lunged. She threw a round kick at his head, knocking him out. Isabella pulled a Swiss army knife out of her vest pocket, slicing strips of the bag to bind his feet and hands and putting the remainder in his mouth.

With the man immobilized, she scanned the area. Burlap sacks like the kind used to carry drugs on backs, were piled in a corner. She didn't see any sign of the illegal substances.

She walked around the ladder and into the tunnel. The tunnel was six-feet high and four-feet wide. Beams were installed every five feet with overhead beams holding the earth from falling into the opening. When she'd mapped the restaurant's location from Angel's house, she'd also noted the distance from the restaurant to the closest building on the other side of the border. It was a distance of two-hundred-and-fifty yards.

The low-wattage bulbs dangling from the single electrical wire every twenty feet gave enough light to travel with ease. But that also allowed anyone who might be heading her direction to see her at the same time she'd see them. For that reason, she moved cautiously keeping her gaze trained as far ahead as she could see.

At what she believed to be the halfway point, a narrow iron track started. A small flatcar sat at the end of the track. The idea was ingenious. It saved wear and tear on the people lugging the substances through the tunnel. Steel track was piled to one side. It appeared they planned to expand the rails.

This was a good place to set a precaution for the return trip. Using her shirt tail as a hot pad, she unscrewed a light bulb, placing the bulb on the ground to allow it to cool. She dug her survival tin out of a vest pocket and ripped a corner off the three foot sheet of aluminum foil folded in the tin.

The piece of aluminum molded perfectly over the socket end of the bulb. Holding the socket, dangling from the wire, she carefully screwed the bulb in far enough to keep it from falling out but not turn on.

With the tin back in her vest pocket, Isabella slipped around the flatcar and continued through the tunnel, hugging the wall and straining to see far ahead.

Five minutes deeper into the tunnel she noticed a brighter light ahead. Hearing alert, her footsteps became lighter as she listened for activity at the light. The closer she moved to the light, the slower her steps. She would be of no use to Angel if she was caught. And getting caught could mean she would never see Tino and he would never rest until he found out what had happened to her. Fear of his need for revenge kept her alert and careful. She wanted him to live a long life and if all the deities listened to her silent prayers she'd be alongside of him.

Close enough to see the brighter light was the end of the tunnel and the space was unoccupied, she hastened forward. Three flatcars sat at this end of the track. It would be good to disable them. But did she want to do all three? Yes. It would be faster and easier to run rather than rely on the conveyance.

She retrieved her survival tin, taking note of the items that were used. Without the snare wire used to lift the chunk of wall off Cody, she would have to use the sewing bobbin holding fifty feet of braided fishing line.

She tied the end of the line to the front axle of the first flatcar. Then wound the line around each axle on each car to the back, looped the line around the end braces of the track, and back around each axle going forward, and then returning to the back braces. The bobbin held enough line to string it across from the track brace to a wooden beam bracing the wall and overhead boards. A good solid knot and that was set.

Isabella moved to the ladder and listened. All appeared quiet. She extracted her mirror from the tin and climbed the ladder far enough to use the mirror to take a look at the room above. Sacks of dirt were along one edge, stacks of what appeared to be blocks of marijuana sat along another wall.

She eased on up the ladder moving the mirror in different directions. The only reflection was of an unoccupied room. Still cautious, she crept up two more rungs and peeked over the floor.

Empty.

Crossing to the only door in the room, she put her ear to the crack and listened.

Voices.

The more she listened she knew who was on the other side. Wes, Emilio, and Angel. The men were interrogating Angel. Isabella smiled as Angel zinged a retort. The sound of a palm hitting flesh, made her cringe. How badly injured would Angel be when they made their escape?

Emilio's voice rose. "She cannot tell us anything if you kill her."

Rage burned in Isabella's stomach. Wes had to be stopped. His violence had caused grief to too many good people.

Did she dare open the door a crack to get a view of what she was up against? Her heart raced in her chest as she listened a few more minutes. She wiped her sweaty palm on her shirt and slowly grasped the door knob, turning it a millimeter at a time. The quiet snick of the mechanism moving happened at the same time as Wes shouted at Emilio for being too soft.

The memory of Emilio slamming her face into the bars of the cage, didn't mesh with how Wes saw the man.

Millimeter by millimeter, she drew the door toward her. The second she had a slit wide enough to get a visual she stopped.

Angel was tied to a chair in the middle of the room. Blood trickled from a crack in her lip. She had a large bruise on the side of her face. But her head was up and she glared at Wes.

He stood directly in front of her. His hair stuck out from his head in wild disarray as though he'd been running his hands through it. Was he on the verge of cracking? Emilio stood with his back to the door, just to the side and slightly ahead of Wes. He spoke in soft, soothing tones.

Isabella watched the scene. She didn't have a gun. But it didn't appear Wes or Emilio did either. She could take them out one at a time, but she didn't have enough confidence in her taekwondo to be able to take down both without being caught. This would require a diversion. But that would be hard to do stuck in this room.

Leaving the door ajar, she spun to the room and scanned the contents. Much like the other end of the tunnel this room had no windows, the one door, stacks of dirt, a few timbers, and little else. Her gaze lit on the fuse box. If she cut power to an area of the building would they fumble around looking for the fuse box, or did they know it was here and this would be the first place they looked? Possibility, but not a good one.

Commotion in the other room, drew her back to the door.

"The order is here," said a man, cradling an automatic rifle.

"Good. I need to speak with the driver." Wes headed for the door.

Emilio started to follow.

"You stay here." Wes ordered.

Emilio's face grew dark and stormy. "You do not order me." He stormed out of the room behind Wes.

She heard them arguing as she opened the door, crossed the room, and sliced through the zip ties tethering Angel to the chair.

"How did you know I was here?" whispered Angel.

"Your bartender said you left with Emilio." Isabella ushered the woman through the door and closed it quietly. She stacked bags of dirt against the door.

Angel helped until they heard voices returning.

"Quick down the ladder." Isabella followed Angel.

"Stop!" She grabbed Angel's arm, keeping her from tripping over the line she'd stretched. "Step over that."

Angel smiled. "You've been busy." She stepped over. "Are there any more?"

"Not that will injure you. Go."

Men were shouting and banging against the door above.

They took off at a run down the tunnel.

Shouting echoed down the shaft, covering the sound of their footsteps.

The sound of metal scraping and more cursing followed in their wake.

At the end of the track, Isabella stopped to screw in the unlit light bulb. The tunnel disappeared into inky blackness.

She smacked into Angel's back. The darkness had stopped her.

"We can't see, either," Angel whispered.

"Just keep moving forward. Put a hand on the wall and walk as fast as you can. They have to deal with the track." She wanted to reserve her flashlight to use when she felt they were far enough ahead their assailants couldn't use the light to follow.

As Angel became accustom to the darkness her pace picked up.

Isabella stayed right behind her. Judging they should be close enough to the end, she stuck her hand in her pocket to grab her flashlight.

The sound of two bodies colliding and two in sync exclamations, "Oh!" happened in front of her.

She whipped the flashlight out of her pocket, flipping it on in the same instant.

Cody squinted. "Hey, get that out of my face."

"Go!" Isabella spun him around and pushed the two ahead of her. "I take it if you are down here, there isn't a threat waiting for us when we get to the ladder?"

"No, I took out the delivery driver backed up to the tunnel opening." He glanced over his shoulder. "I see you found Angel."

"Yeah, Wes and Emilio had her. Wish we could have apprehended them, but I wanted to get Angel out first. With both our testimonies we should be able to get them locked up."

Cody stopped. "You sure you want to do that? Testify?"

She knew what he meant. "We'll discuss it later. Keep moving."

They arrived at the bottom of the ladder. Cody ascended first. Gave the all clear, and Isabella sent Angel up the ladder.

She put her hand on the ladder rung. A shiver traveled through her body. She glanced back down the tunnel. The darkness felt palpable, the eeriness that crept through her body told her someone watched from the darkness and he had murder in mind.

Chapter Twenty-nine

More people than Cody and Angel greeted Isabella when she climbed out of the tunnel. The building was wall-to-wall agents of WIA and ICE. Some milled about while others photographed the room and the entrance to the tunnel.

Cody turned to her. "I called Mumphrey as soon as Adelina woke me up. He turned on the GPS in your phone. When you popped out on the other side, they pinpointed the house. There should be WIA and Mexican authorities taking care of things on that end."

The relief she felt knowing officials were dealing with the Mexico end of the operation didn't quite shake the feeling she'd had in the tunnel. Someone didn't get caught south of the border, and she had a notion who.

One WIA and one ICE agent pulled Isabella and Angel into separate rooms and took down their statements. An hour later, tired, hungry, and wanting to get to Tino's side, Isabella walked out of the small room where she'd been interviewed.

Cody draped his arms over Isabella and Angel's shoulders. "I'm taking you two back to Angel's for a shower, breakfast, and some R and R."

~*~

She didn't say anything until they were all seated at the table eating a huge breakfast prepared by Adelina.

"Cody, I know you've been working when this should have been a vacation, so if you want to hang out here for a day or two..." She glanced at Angel. "That is if Angel wants to put up with you." She could tell by the way the two were eyeing one another that they both liked the idea of Cody staying. "But I need to head to Phoenix and Tino."

"I figured you'd say that. So did Mumphrey. He had a car delivered while you were in the shower." Cody grabbed her hand. "Be careful. Mumphrey also said Wes wasn't rounded up over the border."

She nodded her head. That was why she wanted to get back to Tino as soon as possible. Wes knew she had now thwarted his operation twice. He would be out for blood. Hers and Tino's.

After the meal, she said her good-byes to Angel and Adelina. Cody walked her out to the SUV parked at the curb.

"You think Wes is going after Tino?" Cody leaned against the side of the vehicle taking weight off his injured leg.

"Yes. I felt him in the tunnel watching me after you and Angel climbed up the ladder. He has a vicious streak in him. He won't be happy until we pay." She opened the driver's side door. A packet lay on the seat.

"You think he knows?" Cody studied her.

She shook her head. "If I've been kept a secret this long by the people who know, I really don't see how he could learn of any connection." Opening the envelope, she found a new driver's license, a credit card, and cash. Her mother thought of everything. She was the detail person. A trait she'd inherited.

Cody pulled her into a hug. "Be careful, sis. I want to have family gatherings at Walpi."

Isabella hugged him back. "Me too. I have so much I want to know and learn about our people. Mother would never talk about her heritage."

He released her. "We will be honored to teach you." He held the door as she slid behind the steering wheel. "And bring Tino. We'd like to get to know him."

"I will. Thank you for all your help." Isabella closed the door.

"We're family." Cody backed away.

She started the vehicle and headed out of Nogales. Her nerves fizzed. She glanced in the rearview mirror every five miles. She couldn't shake the feeling someone watched her.

The two-and-a-half hour drive to Phoenix, while uneventful, gave her lots of time to think about Wes and the comment Angel's bartender made. "He had crazy eyes." She'd noticed his instability early-on as well. It was that instability that scared her.

She drove straight to the private-care facility where Daddy had transported Tino. Walking through the doors, she was immediately impressed with the security she saw in place. Men in blue and green scrubs might have been holding charts and talking with staff, but she could tell by the way they studied her and their stances they were security.

One nodded to her as she walked by. Daddy must have showed her photo to them so they knew to expect her. The nurse's station had several bouquets of flowers sitting on the counter. She separated two vases and peered down at the woman in scrubs typing into a computer.

"Excuse me."

The woman started and glanced up. "Yes?"

"What room is T-Gus Kostas in?"

The woman's face lit up. "Oh, you're his first visitor. He's been asking for Isabella. Is that you?"

Her heart started racing. "He's awake?"

"Yes, about three this morning the nurse on duty said he woke up and wouldn't quiet down until he made a phone call."

"Please, what room?" Isabella couldn't wait to see him and fill him in on everything she'd been doing and learned.

"One-thirty-two." The nurse pointed. "Down that hall and to the right."

"Thank you!" She headed down the hall at a jog. Her feet didn't touch the ground. At the door she stopped, patted her hair, and entered.

"Ezzabella!" Tino's shining eyes and bright smile matched her own exuberance.

She hurried to the bed, happy to see he wasn't connected to any monitors or IVs, and wrapped her arms around his neck, pressing her lips to his.

Tino folded his arms around his little dove and kissed her. His chest ached with happiness and relief. He'd awakened and she wasn't by his side. He'd feared she'd gone after the traffickers on her own. He'd heard bits and pieces of what she'd told him while he'd struggled to gain consciousness. Even talking with her father hadn't taken away the anxiety.

Now, he held her in his arms. He tasted salty tears seeping into their kiss.

He held her face away from his. "Mi pichon, what is wrong?"

"I'm so happy. I thought…I thought…"

"Shhh. You should know by now I am hard to kill." He held her to his chest. Her body was the perfect fit for his. "Climb onto this bed and tell me where you have been."

She slid her body onto the bed next to him and rested her head on his chest. "Can I just lie here a minute and soak you in?"

The need in her voice tugged at his heart. She had been through an ordeal it was clear.

"You may take as long as you wish. They will not allow me out of here until this time tomorrow. Something about watching for adverse reactions to the unconsciousness."

She snuggled closer to him, making his body hum. He stroked her hair and played with the fingers on her left hand. The ring he gave her at Christmas wasn't on her finger. They'd agreed it would only be worn when she wasn't working. In their lines of work, the enemy knowing they had a significant other was leverage.

Isabella cleared her throat. "I told you about Cody and our true connection."

"Sí. He is a good man."

"You don't know the half of it. He helped me rescue the women from the human traffickers, then together we found you. And he helped me discover where the trafficking ring brought their goods in from Mexico. We found a tunnel that ran under the border." Her voice trailed off.

Her body shivered. He pulled her tighter against him. "What are you not telling, querida?"

She leaned up on an elbow. The torment in her green eyes made his gut twist.

He traced her lips with his finger. "Nothing you say will make me love you less."

"I know. It's…what I found out makes me nauseous."

"What makes you nauseous?" He'd never witnessed Isabella looking or sounding so desolate.

"Cody isn't my cousin." She stared into his eyes. "He's my half-brother."

Tino shook his head and studied her impassioned expression.

"How is he your half-brother?" He listened intently to her tale of Cody's mother's rape and giving her daughter to her sister to raise. His heart went out to Isabella. She'd been searching her whole life to feel a part of a family and it was there the whole time. Tino kissed her forehead. "You have been blessed with two mothers."

"Now I understand so much more about my childhood. I can't wait to learn more about my real mother and Cody." The love she had for the two emanated from her eyes and her words.

"I do not understand how this makes you nauseous when you look so happy?"

Her eyes flashed to an emotion he'd not witnessed in her eyes before. Hatred.

"It's the half of me that came from the vile man who raped my mother that has me nauseous." She scooted up, sitting against his side. Her eyes held his. "I know who the man is who raped my mother. I know how vile he is, and his son—my half-brother—is the person who nearly beat you to death and who I believe is out to kill us both."

He knew how strongly she believed in family. How knowing this about her own blood would eat at her. Tino sat up and embraced her to him. "You have me and your Hopi roots. Do not let this other side eat you up."

She clung to him. "I'm scared. This is the first time since meeting you that I feel I have no control, no knowledge that will save us."

"We have been through tough situations before. We came out stronger. This will be the same."

The door opened. Tino peered over Isabella's head.

"Oh, sorry! I didn't know you had a visitor." The nurse stood in the threshold. "I need to take your vital signs."

Tino smiled at her and gave Isabella a squeeze. "The sooner they give me the all clear the sooner we can go home."

She wiped her nose on his hospital gown and smiled weakly before slipping out of his embrace and off the bed.

Isabella had known Tino would be her anchor. He knew how to act and what to say to keep her grounded and not allow her to wallow or get swept away by errant emotions. She watched the nurse take Tino's vitals. His gaze remained on her, his smile never wavering. Her trip into the Guatemalan jungle had netted her the best thing in her life—Tino.

"Everything is showing normal." The nurse wound the blood pressure cuff up and placed it on the monitor.

"Any chance I could get out of here tonight instead of tomorrow?" Tino asked the nurse.

"That is up to your doctor. He'll be making rounds in about two hours. You have to convince him." She glanced at Isabella. "Would you like me to order two dinners for this room?"

"Please." Her stomach took that moment to growl.

"I'll bring in some granola bars and fruit." The nurse said, stopping at the door.

"Thank you. My appetite has come back with a flourish now that I know T-Gus is safe." She almost slipped, again. Tino sent her a curious gaze.

The nurse left.

"Why did you call me Gus?"

"Daddy has you listed as Gus Kostas. Wes—my evil half-brother—vowed to kill you and the person who knocked him in the head—me—when he escaped. And now that my discoveries brought the Mexican and American law enforcement down on his drug and human trafficking tunnel, I'm positive he won't stop until he's wrought his vengeance." A tremor slithered through her body.

"Come here, let me hold you." Tino patted the bed.

She sat on the bed and lay back into his arms. "I've missed your arms," she said, relaxing into his embrace.

"I've missed you." He kissed the side of her face.

She turned, and fell into his welcoming kiss. His tongue, lips, and hands always made her feel special and wanted. Now, they drove a need so tangible it made her whole being ache.

Her hands easily found his warm skin, she untied the hospital gown and pulled it down his arms so she could run her hands over his pecs and sift her fingers through the sprinkling of curls on his chest. Their tongues tangled, and his hands slid under her shirt, kneading her back muscles.

"Oh!"

The exclamation was like cold water splashing on her ardor. Isabella buried her head in Tino's neck to hide her embarrassment.

"I'll just leave these snacks here on the table, and I'll pull the curtains closed."

The giggle in her voice made Isabella chuckle.

"I think we embarrassed her," Tino said, nuzzling her neck and nibbling her ear.

"I'm sure if she tells your doctor you're fully functional, he'll allow you to go home." She giggled as he raised her shirt and dropped wet kissed on her pert nipples.

She stood, slipped her jeans and underwear off, and slid under the sheet with Tino. When their bodies touched skin to skin every nerve tingled. His wonderful hands knew where to apply pressure to bring her the most pleasure. Her lower back, nipples, behind her knees.

His touch had her weak.

"I want to bring you pleasure but you're making me…" She quivered from his touch. Her genitals throbbed.

"Shh, querida, watching you is my pleasure." Tino drew her up his torso and expertly slid her down over his erect penis.

Sliding over him, his fullness pressing deeper, she wanted to weep with happiness. He was her sanctuary and light. The bed squeaked as he powered into her. Her body clenched, her mind buzzed, and he captured her mouth with his, kissing her senseless and carrying the aftershocks of the climax to a new high.

Her mind drifted back to earth. He gave one deep thrust and erupted, clenching her to him and singing her praises in Venezuelan with his lips buried against her neck.

Tangled together they fell asleep.

~*~

"What is going on?" A male voice boomed into Isabella's conscience. She inhaled Tino's masculine scent and an antiseptic overtone. A naked male body was under her.

Tino's.

Her hands moved to the sides. They were on a small bed.

The hospital!

Her mind jerked awake with such speed it made her dizzy.

"Could you wait outside a minute, please?" Tino's scratchy voice asked from somewhere above her head.

The door slammed.

Isabella quickly scrambled off Tino and the bed, picking up her clothes and diving into the lavatory off the room. She didn't regret making love with Tino. They both needed it after being so worried about one another. What she worried about was Daddy finding out what she'd done. Not that he was a prude, but it didn't reflect well on the agency.

She washed, dressed, and finger-combed her hair. Braiding the long strands, she then wound it into a bun and stuffed the end into the bun. One last glimpse in the mirror showed a put-together person.

Stepping into the room, she was surprised to see Tino alone.

"Did the doctor come back?" she asked, sitting in the chair.

"Yes. He said if I could cavort in a hospital bed I was ready to be released. The nurse will be back with the paperwork and the clothes I arrived in." He swung his legs over the side of the bed. He hadn't replaced the hospital gown. The only thing covering him was the sheet across his lap.

Staring at his naked body made her hands itch and her body heat remembering the enjoyment he could conjure.

The nurse knocked, peeked in, saw her sitting on the chair and entered. She stopped short when she noticed Tino sitting in his birthday suit. Holding a large plastic bag at arm's length she walked up to the bed.

"I think you're waiting for these."

Tino grabbed the bag and peered inside. His nose wrinkled. "Sí, it is my dirty clothing."

"And these are the discharge papers." She went over the legalities of leaving, gave him a list of complications to watch for, and had Tino sign two papers. "Ring for a nurse when you're ready for us to bring the wheelchair."

"We will," Isabella said, getting antsy to get to their apartment. She missed her cockatoo, Alabaster, and being in her own surroundings.

The nurse left and Tino stood. He was a bit wobbly.

Isabella moved to his side. "Is this the first time you've stood since waking?"

"No, I walked to the lavatory twice before you showed up." His face was set with determination. "I had to prove I could get up and move around to get all the machines unhooked from me."

"When we get home, you're going straight to bed."

The devilish grin on his lips said she'd be with him.

She cringed when he pulled the bloody, dirty clothes from the bag. "I should have ran home and brought you clean clothes."

"I can manage until we get home. You can help me take a shower, and then we can go to bed early." The heat in his eyes matched the desire blossoming in her body.

Their love making in the hospital bed only heightened their desire. She'd learned it took several hot passionate bouts before they were both sated and could behave like a normal couple.

Once Tino was dressed and sitting in the chair, she pushed the call button. They waited another fifteen minutes. Isabella opened the door and stuck her head out three times before an orderly arrived with the wheelchair.

Isabella left Tino sitting in the wheelchair with the orderly while she jogged out to the parking lot and brought the SUV around to the doors.

The hospital was twenty minutes from their apartment. She pulled into the parking lot and spotted her Jeep. Someone from WIA must have delivered it. She'd call to have the SUV picked up when Tino was settled.

His complexion had paled considerably by the time they walked in from the parking lot, up the elevator, and to the door of their second-floor apartment.

Isabella turned to Tino, "Do you have the key? I lost mine in Nogales." As she said it a shiver ran down her spine. Who had her key? Was it Wes?

Tino dug in his pocket and brought out the key. She slid it in the lock and swung the door open.

White feathers were everywhere.

Chapter Thirty

"No!" Isabella screamed, jumping the toppled and broken furniture to get to Alabaster's cage. The cage was on the floor, the door wide open.

"Ally, Ally?" she called, throwing pillows and moving the debris of the tossed apartment.

"I don't know where the bird is, but I have an even better way to make you suffer."

The voice sent chills up her spine. She whipped around and found Wes holding a knife to Tino's throat. A healthy Tino would have the upper hand. She saw the agony and knowledge he was no match for the vindictive man in Tino's eyes.

"There's no need to do this Wes," she said, reaching into her vest pocket and clutching her phone.

"Bring your hand out of your pocket and toss whatever you got this way." Wes wrenched on Tino's arms.

She tossed her phone on the floor at the men's feet.

"Grab that scarf on the floor by your feet and bring it over here," ordered Wes.

Isabella plucked the Mayan print scarf Tino gave her from the carpet and navigated around the disaster in her living room. Each measured step she ran scenarios through her head of how to get Tino away from Wes.

The man was smarter than she'd given him credit for. As she walked closer, he slid his body, putting Tino between them, but holding the knife to Tino's throat in a way that one movement would slice it open.

"Tie his wrists. Tight."

She wrapped the scarf to look tight and allow Tino to get loose at some point. Squeezing one of Tino's hands, she stepped back.

Wes checked the knot and motioned to the door. "Come on we're going for a ride."

"I need to get my keys." She started for the bedroom.

"You have the keys in your pocket." He pointed to her bulging jean pocket.

"Those keys are to the agency vehicle."

He thought a moment then asked, "They got GPS on their rigs?"

She pretended to lie. "No."

"You're lying! Get your keys. I'm watching from the door and if you do anything stupid, lover boy here is dead." Wes shoved Tino toward the bedroom.

She stopped at the doorway. It was a mess. He'd torn this room apart too. A quick scan noted the keys and the reason she wanted in the room.

"Great your interior decorating is going to make finding the keys fun." She kicked at the bigger items going around the room.

At the side of the bed away from Wes, she dropped to her knees. "Must have slid under the bed."

She shoved her electronic tablet under the bed and with one hand turned it on and opened her email, while using the other hand to shove things out from under the bed. She sent an email to WIA. urgent. wes has us. using jeep.

"Come here you little buggers." She grabbed the keys from in front of the night stand and stood, dangling them from her finger. "Found them."

"Get over here."

"Where's my cockatoo?" she asked, exiting the bedroom.

"That's one for you to think about. Move." He jerked on Tino nearly pulling him off his feet.

"Hey." Isabella tried to grab for Tino. Wes's arm flew out, connecting his hand, fisted around the knife handle, with her cheek.

The blow knocked her back, jarred her jaw, and brought stars.

"Don't help him or you'll get more of that." Wes shoved her in the back. "Get in the elevator."

Her head was ringing, her mind spitting and sputtering. She stayed on her feet, and he propelled them to the elevator.

The contraption bounced at the first floor causing her stomach to heave. She bent over and vomited.

Wes grabbed her by the arm, pulling her and shoving Tino. At the parking lot he grabbed a fist full of her hair, holding her head up. "Where's your Jeep?"

"The silver one. Over there." Her arm was lethargic as she raised it to point.

"Come on. You two are making a spectacle."

Us two? "You're the maniac wielding a knife and threatening us."

"Shut up and open the doors." Wes shoved her to the driver's side.

She pulled out the keys, unlocked the door and the other doors.

"Get in you're driving." She slid into the driver's seat, willing her grogginess to ease.

"Don't do anything smart. I'll slice open your lover's throat and then I'll slice yours." Wes opened the back door, slid in, pulling Tino in behind him. "Get out and shut the door," he ordered.

She slid out, shut the back door, and returned to the driver's seat. "Where are we going?"

"Head toward Ajo."

He wasn't headed to the border. That was a good thing. She left the parking lot and headed to Hwy 85. The first hour of the drive she was still woozy from the hit she took. Focusing to stay on the road required all of her attention. By the second hour her mind was working overtime. Where are we going? When will WIA intercept? Daddy should have activated the GPS on the Jeep.

Her gaze locked on Tino's pale face in the rearview mirror every ten minutes. She saw the fight in his eyes, but knew he was physically in no shape to take on the crazy man who'd kidnapped them.

Ten miles from Ajo, Wes spoke up. "Take that road to the right."

She turned onto a dirt road and had to slow to a near crawl. "This isn't much of a road."

"Shut up and drive. This is a Jeep, you can go faster than this."

Peering at Wes's wild eyes in the rearview mirror, she cringed. He was getting worked up over killing them.

The front tire fell into a trench. She fought with the steering wheel to get the tire out. Sweat beaded her forehead as she worked to keep the vehicle from jarring too much. Tino hadn't opened his eyes the last hour. She didn't know if he was sleeping, gaining energy or wiped out.

They traveled another twenty minutes. The Agua Dolce Mountains rising before them, was a good inclination of where they were headed. He was taking them to the kiva.

"There, go off the road toward that ravine." He pointed to her left.

The ravine was the one where Cody caught up to her when this whole ordeal started over her need to find the ceremonial kiva. She continued on dodging mesquite and creosote bushes until the Jeep tires sunk in the sand.

"We'll walk from here." Wes opened the door on his side and pulled Tino out.

As if in slow motion, Isabella watched as Tino dropped his body into Wes, causing their kidnapper to lose balance and fall backwards. She heard the two struggling.

Before she could get around the vehicle to help, Wes had recovered. Tino cried out as Wes sliced his thigh.

"See what happens when you go against me. I will slice you up into pieces for the coyotes to fight over." Wes grabbed Tino's unbound hands.

He held the lengths of the scarf in the air and glared at her. "You caused this. You tricked me with the knot you tied in this." An evil smile distorted his face. "Because of your trickery, I'm going to take my time killing your lover and you will watch it all."

"I'm sorry. I'm not good with knots. I should have told you." She grabbed the scarf from Wes and dropped to her knees at Tino's feet. She did her best to stop the bleeding.

"Get up and get going. It will be dark soon. It's harder to find in the dark."

Isabella draped Tino's arm over her shoulder and started up the ravine. She knew exactly where the kiva was. The whole time she and Cody were hiking around, she'd set all the images in her mind.

She continued on a direct course for the kiva. The less walking

Tino had to do the better. His already dirty pants had an added dark red stain from his latest wound.

The hot summer sun beat down on them. She licked her dry lips and wished she had her hat. But it was with her backpack. The way her apartment was tossed, she knew who had her backpack and her apartment key. The maniac breathing heavily behind them.

An hour walking in the hot sun wasn't helping Tino. She felt his legs giving out. He became heavier and she became more lightheaded. She stopped.

"Keep going, we're almost there." Wes shoved on her back.

"I need water." She glanced at his red face, and the sweat pouring down the sides. "*We* need water."

He watched her a moment. "We'll have water at the hole in the ground." He smiled. "Yeah, that's where I'm taking you. Put you in a cage and let you watch me cut up your lover."

"If I don't get water, you won't have an audience." She lowered Tino to the ground and studied where they were. "If we drop down, we'll come to the spring."

"No. The hole in the ground isn't that much farther. Pick him up. Let's go." Wes kicked the foot on Tino's injured leg.

"Don't! He needs to rest." She pointed to Wes's red face. "You even need to rest." She scanned the area. "There's a saguaro cactus. There should be fruit on it. That will give us some liquid."

Isabella helped Tino into the shade of a bush. Then she scoured the desert floor for a hard, long skeleton of a saguaro cactus. She found one about four feet long. With the length of dead saguaro, she poked at the red fruit up high on the cactus. Four fruit eventually fell. She scooped them up in the hem of her shirt and deposited them beside Wes.

"Use that knife you're so fond of to slice these open."

He stared at her a moment before cutting them in half.

She carried two halves over to Tino. "Here eat this, it will help."

Handing one half to Tino, she bit into the red, seedy middle of the fruit. The mild sweetness was welcome to her parched mouth and the nutty, crunchy seeds welcome filler to her hungry stomach. Once she'd eaten all the inside of the fruit, she watched Tino finish his then glanced over at Wes.

She should have known. He'd eaten the rest of the halves.

"Get up. It's going to be dark soon. We have to get to the hole." He prodded them with the toe of his boot.

Isabella helped Tino to his feet and once again took her place under his arm. By her calculations they would reach the kiva in about ten minutes. If Tino wasn't injured, she'd lead them around for hours. The thought of having more violence in the kiva made her heart ache.

She had to hope that before they got to the kiva help would arrive. She'd expected to hear a helicopter by now. Some sort of surveillance in this area after what had happened here days earlier.

She spotted the ladder sticking out of the hole. Surely after what had gone on here they'd notified the Hopi and had things cleaned up.

"There! Go to the ladder." Wes gave her a shove on the back.

Any familial connection that she might have hoped for was lost. She didn't condone a single one of his actions. She wanted to blame it on his upbringing, but she knew deep down it was his genes. Genes that weren't as strong in her as her Hopi genes.

At the hole she stopped. "How do you know there isn't law enforcement down there waiting for you?" She'd try any stall tactic to keep him out of the sacred place.

His eyes widened a moment. He laughed. "You think you can scare me. I know you're just trying to make me not take you down there. But I want to finish this where it started." He pointed to the ladder and then Tino. "You. Get down there."

Isabella helped Tino start down the ladder. The dullness in his eyes, tore at her heart. He was pulled into this because of her. She had to save them both. And keep Tino from being injured farther.

"Now you." Wes waved his knife. "And don't get any ideas. I'm going to be right behind you."

She started down the ladder. If I can pull hard enough on his leg, can I get him to fall? It was only ten feet. Not that bad of a fall. She'd probably make him mad. She saw his quick reflexes when Tino tried to take him off guard getting out of the Jeep.

Taking the last two rungs on the ladder, she scanned the area. The cages were still there, and the gaping hole leading into the cave. Tino sat with his back against the wall where they'd tied Cody up.

She dropped to the floor. Not a weapon to be seen. Everything but the ladder and cages had been cleaned out, including the buckets the women had used as toilets and the blankets they'd slept on. Why weren't the cages gone? She didn't want to be locked in one. It would make helping Tino harder.

But the door on one was open…

She stood to the offside of the ladder.

Wes looked her way, a nasty smile on his lips. The minute his foot touched the ground and he released his hold on the ladder, she shoved with all her might, toppling him toward the open door. He brought the knife around slicing her upper arm, before she could knock the weapon out of his hand.

He grasped at the bars and the knife fell to the floor.

She threw a side kick, knocking him into the cage. Shoving the door closed, she quickly unhooked the lock and snapped it shut.

Steeling herself to not look at her arm, she picked up the knife.

Movement in the cage caught her attention.

Wes pulled a small stiletto from his boot. His arm drew back to throw the thin blade.

She lobbed the larger knife through the bars, impaling him in the belly.

Isabella dropped to the ground beside Tino, holding the hand that threw the knife over her sliced, bleeding arm, and hiding her face in his shoulder. She could hide the sight but not the sounds of curses and gurgling as Wes, her brother, died from her hands.

The sound was muffled by people in camouflage bursting through the rock wall and down through the hole in the ceiling.

Epilogue

Isabella spent the first three weeks after killing Wes reliving the scene of him dying every night when she shut her eyes. She'd wake shaking, scared to acknowledge what she'd done and fearful of her unemotional reaction in her dreams. She'd spent her days staring into space, listless. She couldn't work, couldn't eat. Couldn't reconcile what she'd done.

Even the return of Alabaster by a neighbor who found him hiding behind a large planter in the hallway couldn't shake the feeling she'd brought dishonor to herself and her family.

"Querida, you cannot remain this way. You will blow away in a winter storm." Tino pulled her into his arms, after another nightmare. He offered her his strength and love, but she couldn't shake the feeling she had somehow altered her existence.

"Tomorrow we will go to Walpi and see your family. Perhaps you should talk with Una and see if she can help you with your troubles." Tino kissed her eyelids and lips. "Tomorrow, talk with Una, please."

She nodded and buried her face into his chest, waiting for morning to come and the shadows of night to leave her be.

~*~

The sun glowed an autumnal gold as Isabella and Tino drove up to

Walpi. Just seeing the village brought a renewed sense of life. She stepped out of the Jeep and drew in a deep breath. The clean air and cool nip to the breeze rejuvenated.

"You're here early. Good. I have a surprise," Aunt Una walked up to them. She hugged Isabella. "Introduce me to this man I've heard about, but have not met."

Isabella introduced Tino to Una. They hugged and Una turned to her.

"I see why your heart is taken by this man. He is good." Una took her by the chin, turning her face this way and that. "You have dark circles under your eyes. Why?"

She wanted to spill it all to Una but didn't want her mother thinking bad of her. She was Hopi, a peaceful people. How could she tell Una that she'd killed her brother?

Una grasped her hand. "Tino, do you mind if I have a talk with Isabella?"

"He'll be fine." Cody walked up, gave her a hug, and clasped Tino's hand.

"You're sure you don't mind?" Isabella asked, searching Tino's gaze for a way out of talking with her mother.

"Go ahead. Cody and I have some catching up to do." Tino released her hand he'd been holding.

"See, your man knows what you need. Come." Una led her away from the parking area, through the houses, and into her house. "I have tea ready. Sit."

Isabella sat but kept her hands tightly folded together in her lap. She couldn't tell her, but Una deserves to know. She didn't want her mother hatting her and just when she'd found her.

"Now tell me what has put the dark circles under your eyes." Una sat across the table from her, placing a cup of tea in front of both of them.

"I don't know why I came today. I don't deserve to be a part of this celebration." Tears burned behind her eyes. She'd finally found her place, her family, and she'd thrown it all away. She crossed her arms, holding herself together and keeping her distance from the one person whose love she desired most. Her fingers touched the still tender scar on her arm. A constant reminder of what she'd done.

"Shhh. You deserve to be here more than anyone. You have

fulfilled the Blue Star Prophecy."

Isabella stared at the woman across the table. She was crazy to think such a thing. "No, I've shamed you and the Hopi."

Una reached across the table, taking her hand. "You have brought a new light to the people. Your efforts returned more than one young woman to her family, put the ones behaving against our code in jail, and you found a lost ceremonial kiva."

She shook her head. "I don't deserve any praise. I killed my brother. I used violence against my own family."

"No." Una slapped the table with her free hand. The sound resonated in the house like a clap of thunder. "The man you killed would have killed you and Tino if you hadn't chosen survival. He was not your family. You didn't even know he existed until days before you had to defend yourself against him." She rose, came around the table, and pulled Isabella into an embrace.

"We are your family. Feel our hearts beating as one. Feel the positive energy of the people and the good harvest we are dancing for today. Use this ceremony to cleanse your heart and mind." Una drew out of the hug. "You are Hopi in heart and mind. Never forget that."

She eased Isabella back into her chair.

"Now tell me about your wedding plans." Una grinned and sipped her tea.

She smiled back at Una, "Tino and I would like to get married here and honeymoon in Venezuela."

Isabella took a sip of tea and stared into the sparkling eyes of her mother. The love she saw shining in their depths drew out all the negative energy she'd been battling. She was Hopi, she was resilient. Her people had withstood the coming of the Spaniards, the colonists, and now the encroachment of illegal activities.

She scanned the primitive adobe building. This was home. Her gaze caught and held her mother's. And this was her family, her people, her heritage.

~*~*~

Because *Secret of a Christmas Box* is a short story, making it impossible to put it in print, I have added it to the end of this book. Enjoy!

Secret of a Christmas Box
An Isabella Mumphrey Adventure
sequel

Chapter One

Isabella Mumphrey, anthropologist and World Intelligence Agency operative, stood in her kitchen making sugar cookies and singing Christmas carols. She hadn't been this excited about the holiday since her sixth birthday. She would be spending Christmas with her Venezuelan lover, DEA agent Tino Constantine.

Faint Native American drumming and Alabaster, her cockatoo, shouting "Who's there! Who's there!" interrupted Isabella's cookie making and sent her scrambling to find her cell phone.

Daddy!

She hit the respond button. "Hi Daddy! Merry Christmas!"

"You sound happy. I'm glad you have someone in your life you can spend the holidays with. But this isn't a personal call. I wouldn't ask you to take on a job right now, but it's in Phoenix and it needs a person who has knowledge of Maya artifacts."

Her happiness was squashed by his immediate business-like tone and the fact he was putting her to work on her first Christmas in twenty years that she could spend with someone she cared about.

"There are other agents in the area you could contact." She didn't want to sound like a whining, spoiled child; however, she wasn't about to miss this important first holiday with Tino.

"That's true. But none have your expertise. I promise, this won't interfere with any Christmas plans." He cleared his throat. "It's not classified. If you want to drag Tino along, I give my permission."

While she wasn't excited to even do the mission, having Tino along might make it go faster.

"Ok, what's the mission?" She strolled over to Alabaster's cage and handed him a brazil nut to chomp on and keep him quiet so she could hear Daddy's instructions.

"A package will arrive by messenger in an hour. There shouldn't be any problems, but keep in touch."

The connection clicked.

She wandered back into the kitchen and pulled the last pan of cookies out of the oven. Staring at the ingredients simmering on the stove, her chest tightened. She wanted to make this a Christmas Tino would never forget. He'd told her of a Venezuelan tradition he missed since the deaths of his family. She'd scoured the internet and found a recipe for *Hallaca*, a plantain-leaf-wrapped food that required days to prepare. A pot of chopped vegetables and meat simmered on the stove.

Should I keep making *hallaca* or am I going to have to go right out and get started on this mission? Watching the ingredients bubble, tears burned behind her eyes. I finally have a chance at a normal life and Daddy has to call.

This was the first time in over twenty years she would have a real Christmas. She'd purchased a fresh, well, fresh for Arizona, evergreen tree. The five-foot noble fir stood in the small living room waiting for she and Tino to decorate it with the ornaments they purchased during the Thanksgiving shopping crush. She couldn't wait for tonight. They'd decorate the tree, sip wine, and enjoy the first family Christmas either of them had had in years.

Once she'd discovered there wasn't a real Santa Claus, her parents had stopped making Christmas a magical time. Her seventh Christmas she'd come home from the boarding school and found only the housekeeper at the apartment. They'd watched Christmas specials on TV and the next morning there were two packages under the tree; a bright colored scarf from the housekeeper and a new coat from her parents. Once she became a teenager, her Christmas presents from her parents were their voices in a phone call.

Christmas wasn't about material things. It never had been, but the more her parents drifted away, the more she mourned the way her family had celebrated those first six Christmases. The three of them putting out cookies for Santa and on Christmas morning gathering around a Christmas tree her mother had delivered from a department store to see what Santa had brought.

And the Christmas day brunch. One of the few occasions throughout the year when they all sat down together as a family and had a meal. She had to lose these melancholy feelings and look toward the future.

Strong arms wrapped around her middle and Tino placed his chin on her head. "You're making hallaca for me?"

The warmth and excitement in his voice swept her misery away. She spun in his arms.

"Yes. You mentioned how you missed this dish. I only hope I can make it as well as your mother and grandmother." She placed her head on his chest and listened to the rhythm of his beating heart. She didn't have a doubt in her mind, she loved his man. Had from the moment he teased her about the howler monkeys in the Guatemala jungle.

"You already have the main ingredient, love." He kissed the top of her head.

Isabella tipped her face upwards and was rewarded with a knee-buckling kiss. If he kept this up, she'd be nothing but a puddle of needy woman by dinner time.

He drew out of the kiss, dropping soft kisses over her face. When he no longer kissed her, she peered into his eyes.

"Did I hear Alabaster yelling 'Who is there'?" Tino asked, picking up a cooled cookie.

"Yes. Daddy called. I have an assignment."

Tino swallowed the bite of cookie. "But it's only three days until Christmas. Our first Christmas together." His brow furrowed.

"He said it was local, and it wouldn't interfere with Christmas." She rubbed a hand up and down his arm. "And he said you could help me."

Tino's hand raising the cookie to his mouth stopped halfway. "I can help? Your father doesn't like anyone but WIA to work your cases."

"He said it wasn't classified." She bit the cookie waving around in front of her nose.

"What is the assignment?" Tino popped the rest of the sweet into his mouth and picked up another one.

"I'll find out when the package is delivered." She stepped out of his one-armed embrace. "While we wait, how about helping me with the hallaca."

Chapter Two

An hour later the doorbell rang. Isabella held one of the box of ornaments she and Tino had purchased. She stood by the tree scrutinizing the decorations while waiting for Tino to come out of the shower. This would be their first Christmas memory together. Decorating the tree.

"Door! Door!" shouted Ally moving back and forth from foot to foot and bobbing his white- plumed head.

"I have it, Ally, pipe down." Isabella opened the door.

A man in his mid-twenties wore a baseball cap with the insignia of a local delivery service. "Isabella Mumphrey?" he asked.

"Yes."

"Sign for a package." He held out an electronic clipboard.

She signed her name, and he handed her a carved wooden block the size of a softball.

"This is it? No envelope?" she asked, running her fingertips over the intricate carvings on every side of the cube.

"That's it." The man pivoted and left.

Isabella slowly closed the door, staring at the box. Why would Daddy only send her a small box? What was the assignment? To open the box? To discover where it came from? Questions bounced around in her head. She stared at the block of wood.

"Did you get the assignment?" Tino walked out of the bedroom, a towel draped around his lower body. He'd headed for a shower when the first batch of ingredients for the hallaca were in the pot simmering.

Isabella pulled her gaze from the wood to the half-naked man in her living room. Seeing Tino in only a towel, Isabella's thoughts dove straight to the bedroom and how she and Tino could celebrate his return home.

Tino snapped his fingers in front of her.

She shook off the steamy ideas swirling in her head and turned the block over and around.

"Where did you get that piece of wood?" Tino asked.

"It was delivered without a note or anything." Her fingers continued to trace the carvings on the cube. Her mind hummed, going through the photographic files in her brain trying to remember where she'd seen this type of symbol before. They had a classic square shape.

"It's Maya. Pre-Classic period." Her finger dipped into each crevice and over the swells. Some of the symbols were still used today, others… "I need to go to the university library."

"It is closed for the holiday," Tino said.

"I have keys."

"To the library?"

"No, but I'm good at picking locks."

"I'll get dressed. You might need someone along in case you get put in jail." Tino ducked into the bedroom.

Isabella slid the cube into her backpack, covered the cookies, and turned the burner off under the simmering mixture of meat, spices, and vegetables. She strode into the bedroom and grabbed her survival vest. What had started out as a security blanket of sorts at the age of ten, was now an essential piece of clothing when exploring and on missions.

"Why do you wear your vest?" Tino grabbed a pocket and pulled her against his now clothed body.

"This is a mission. I wear it on all missions." She pulled a lightweight jacket over the vest and picked up her backpack. "Are you coming?"

"I came home to be with you, so yes, I am coming." Tino slipped his feet into loafers and shoved his arms into a windbreaker. "Do you wish me to drive?" he asked, grabbing the keys to her Jeep Compass out of the tray by the front door.

"Please. I want to keep studying the symbols on the cube."

Isabella followed Tino down to the parking garage and slid into the passenger seat. "Park in my usual place at the university. We can go in through the anthropology department door."

On the drive, Isabella pulled out the block and continued to trace and decipher the symbols. This reminded her of the first time she and Tino worked together. She wasn't a WIA agent at the time and hadn't known that her parents were part of the organization. She'd been called to the dig in Guatemala to help her mentor. While there she'd uncovered a Mayan ritual and nearly lost her life.

Exhilaration raced through her as the story on the box became clearer.

"I don't know what I'm supposed to do with this cube other than decipher the images on the sides." She glanced over at Tino and smiled. "And I just about have the saying on this side figured out. I'm still missing several important symbol meanings though."

Tino pulled into her parking slot at the university and turned to her. "What do you think this is about? You weren't given any instructions what to do with that chunk of wood."

"The instructions are on the box." She kissed him quickly and dug in her backpack for the Anthropology Department door keys.

Once inside, Tino touched her arm. "Does the library have security?"

"Only in the archive section. We shouldn't need to go in there." She walked down the hall to the library and knelt in front of the doors. Plucking her pick tools from a vest pocket, she inserted the small metal picks and went to work on the lock tumbler.

"Wouldn't it have been easier to call someone to let us in?" Tino asked.

"I wouldn't have been able to stand the waiting. No one would get the message I wanted in until they checked their work messages and with the holiday that could be a week or more. I want this solved before Christmas."

She'd worked less than a minute when the clicks verified she was in. Smiling up at Tino, she turned the latch and pushed the door open.

Budget cuts had not only taken a toll on her department, it also had cut out man power to watch security cameras. Only the areas of the campus that housed important artifacts had working security cameras.

Due to the hours she spent in this part of the building, Isabella knew exactly where to find the book she needed. Using a small flashlight from a vest pocket, she made her way through the rows of books straight to the section that housed all the universities books on the Maya.

One by one she read the titles until she found the large tomb that would help her decipher the cube.

She set the book on a table and stared at Tino. "I don't understand what this block of wood has to do with WIA. I understand that Daddy knew I could handle the job here because the cube is clearly a Maya artifact. But why do I have to decipher it before Christmas?"

Tino shrugged and sat down in the chair next to hers. "That looks like a one-person job."

Isabella nodded. "I know which section to look at. You must be bored."

He leaned over and kissed her briefly. "I missed you and would rather be bored with you than miss our first Christmas together."

Her heart swelled with happiness. "I feel the same way."

He kissed her again, then tapped the book. "Figure this out so we can go back to the apartment and celebrate." His heated gaze and slightly raised eyebrow clearly expressed how he planned to celebrate.

Isabella opened the book to the section she needed. Within minutes she found the symbols she didn't recognize. "Hold the light, please." She dug into the inside vest pocket for her journal and a pencil, placed them on the table, and picked up the cube. Turning the block in the light of the flashlight, she determined the beginning of the message.

She matched each symbol with a word or phrase as she spun the box counterclockwise. Writing the words and phrases down her heart raced. This was a box made for a lover. The symbols told of binding their hearts with what lay hidden inside the box.

"What did you find? Your eyes are shining and you glow as if we have just made love."

Tino's voice reminded her she wasn't alone.

"This is a box given from one lover to another." She gazed into his eyes. "The message on the outside says there is something inside. This isn't just a carved piece of wood, it's a box." Her mind spun, flipping through her photographic memory, trying to remember where she'd read about such a box. "I have to figure out how to open this box."

Isabella turned the cube over and over in her hands, feeling the corners, edges, and top. It appeared a solid carved block.

"Have you figured it out?" Tino asked softly, rubbing her shoulder closest to him.

"No, not yet." Isabella shifted her attention from the cube to Tino. "Let's take it back home. I have some books on ancient puzzles. I might be able to come up with an idea skimming through those."

"I am getting hungry." Tino stood and extended his hand toward her.

"Oh, I planned a wonderful dinner for us!" Guilt ate at her conscience. "I'll work on this after dinner."

"Are you sure you will not burn dinner with your mind on the box?"

Isabella understood Tino's valid question. Once she latched onto a project her mind wouldn't let it go. Grimacing, she kissed Tino's cheek. "Dinner will probably end up burnt."

He laughed and pulled her into a one-arm hug as they walked out of the library. "Then I will make dinner while you study the box."

"Thank you!" She still couldn't believe how lucky she was to have found such an understanding man.

"You know that fascinating mind of yours is what adds to your appeal." He kissed her temple and motioned for her to leave the building ahead of him.

Isabella slipped into her car and waited for Tino to start the vehicle and pull out of the parking lot before she once again tumbled and rotated the box, all the while pressing the symbols.

When they pulled into the apartment parking lot, she wasn't any closer to knowing how to open the box.

"Maybe it isn't a box. Can you hear anything when you shake it?" Tino suggested as they walked to their second floor apartment.

She shook the box. There wasn't a sound or a vibration of anything moving inside.

Isabella shook her head. "It has to open. It would be a cruel trick for a lover to play. Giving his love a solid block with a message saying to open it."

Tino unlocked their door.

Isabella crossed the room straight to her extensive collection of research books on nearly every Native American Culture.

The first time Tino had seen her apartment, he'd strolled along her wall-to-ceiling bookcase reading the titles out loud. "You were not kidding when you said you take your career seriously," he'd said, then surprised her by asking if she let others read her collection.

"I will start dinner," Tino called from the kitchen.

"Mm-hum," she uttered, scanning the titles of books on the fourth shelf. There it was. Her section on puzzles in history. She'd found more than one culture who enjoyed making up puzzles for entertainment and then asked family and friends to find the answers.

She leafed through the section on stone works of art that could continue standing even when most of the base was removed. There were others that crumbled to ruin by the snatching of one specific stone. These were used against enemies.

Here it was. A section on ancient puzzles. She scanned the pages, locking them in her photographic memory. An account of a box similar to the one sitting on the table above her book caught her attention. The one in the book was made of stone. A much harder substance to carve and manipulate into a puzzle.

Reading the analysis of the construction, Isabella picked up the wooden box and once again ran her hands over all the sides and corners. The pad of her thumb found the slight notch on a corner. Still wearing her vest, she pulled out her survival tin, opened the lid on the Altoid-sized metal box, and plucked the x-acto blade from the bottom. With care, Isabella slipped the tip of the blade into the notch and gently pried until a crack wide enough to slip her fingernail in appeared. Using her nails and fingers, millimeter by excruciating millimeter, the gap widened and one puzzle piece came off the corner of the box.

"Dinner is—"

Tino's voice penetrated her concentration.

"Have you found a way to open the box?" He knelt on the floor beside her desk chair.

"Yes, the construction is tight, and I don't want to ruin anything on the box." She glanced at Tino. His gaze was fixed on the object in her hand.

"Do you know if the contents are safe?" he asked, placing a hand on her arm.

"The inscriptions on the outside cite this to be a box between lovers. I doubt there is anything harmful." But his question did spark a thought. What if the box had a Romeo and Juliet misfortune?

She peered into Tino's dark brown eyes. "I don't know if I'm supposed to open this or just decipher the message on the outside. Daddy didn't send any instructions." She tapped her finger against the top of the box.

"Call him and ask for more details." Tino grasped her hands. "But first come enjoy a meal with me."

Isabella's gaze lingered one last time on the slightly askew box. When her mind was preoccupied with a project such as this, she had a hard time concentrating on anything else. However, her longing to have a normal Christmas with someone she loved, drew her gaze back to the man who loved her unconditionally.

"How about I call him tomorrow morning. Tonight is our night. You've been gone three weeks, and I want to show you how much I've missed you."

Chapter Three

Isabella woke thinking of the box sitting on her desk. She peeked at Tino still deep in sleep. A smile formed on her lips. They'd enjoyed the dinner Tino made and then spent the remainder of the night naked, watching an Indiana Jones movie and then making love.

She slipped out of bed, pulled on her robe, and padded on bare feet to her desk in the other room. The box remained as she'd left it.

Daddy was in Washington D.C., two hours ahead of Phoenix. Retrieving her phone from the table by the sofa, she dialed his number.

"Did you finish the mission?" Daddy said with a lighthearted tone she hadn't heard in years.

"No. I'm calling to find out exactly what I'm supposed to do with the box." She pushed her hair out of her face and stared down at the puzzle.

"Have you cracked the symbols on the side?" His tone was once again professional, not cold, but distant.

"Yes. The box appears to be a gift from one lover to another. I started to open the box and a comment Tino made had me wondering if I was supposed to open it."

"Yes, the client wants to know what is inside."

"And what do I do with whatever I find?" She spun the box, once again making sure she'd deciphered the symbols correctly.

"The client has faith you'll know what to do with the contents."

The line went dead.

This whole mission was odd from the start. What did he mean the client has faith in me?

She placed the phone on the desk and picked up the box. Tracing the symbols and spinning the box, she once again fell under the spell of needing to know what was hidden inside. Small victories were being made on the box, when Tino's cologne filtered through her concentration.

"I see you are still obsessed with the box."

His husky early-morning voice swirled heat through her body and drew her attention. He stood an arm's length away in low riding camo-colored pajama pants.

Drool started to slip out the corner of her mouth at the sight of his tanned torso, flat stomach, sprinkling of dark curls, wide shoulders, and muscular arms that were crossed as he stared down at her. She noticed his gaze on her leg, bare from her foot up to where the robe hung open at her hip.

"Querida, no matter how many times we make love, I will never stop wanting you. You are a drug I cannot live without." Tino leaned down, capturing her lips in an incendiary kiss.

Never had she dared dream of having a lover, let alone one who craved her as much as she craved him. Growing up with a genius IQ and years younger than her fellow students, she'd been ridiculed and the butt of many jokes. It hadn't helped she had a metabolism that allowed her to eat like a lumber jack yet have little curves or womanly attributes. And to think, Tino loved her for her mind as much as her stick-figure.

The kiss stole her breath and heart all over again.

She wrapped her arms around his neck and Tino picked her up, carrying her back to the bedroom. The box could wait. It hadn't been opened in centuries, what did a few more hours matter?

Chapter Four

Isabella believed she could easily say no other woman had been as thoroughly loved as she. Tino never put himself first and her body hummed from all his attentions. Their stomachs both grumbled at the same time.

"I think that's my cue to make breakfast." She threw the covers back, but an arm snaked around her middle, drawing her back under the covers.

"Are you making breakfast or getting lost in opening that box?"

She cringed. It was a legitimate question given her obsession with any puzzle.

"I promise to make breakfast and not look at the box until we have the next part of the hallaca made."

Tino kissed her long and deep. He released her body and lips at the same time. "Then you may leave the bed."

Isabella laughed as she dressed. She could see herself living a long and wonderful life with this man. Her merriment subsided. She would also be happy with what they have right now. He had a deep desire to avenge his family's deaths. His mission in Mexico City would have vanquished his demons if she hadn't stumbled onto his undercover operation and nearly gotten them both killed. It was a twist of fate that the man Tino had set out to avenge for his family's lives was the same man who saved them.

Isabella made scrambled eggs and bacon for breakfast. They ate in comfortable silence. Tino tickled her leg with his bare feet as they ate. Yes. She could easily spend the rest of her life with this man. In the event he ever asked her.

After breakfast, Tino cut the plantain leaves into squares while she made the dough. They placed the dough in the leaves and added the mixture from the day before. Wrapping and tying the plantain leaves into small bundles, Tino placed them on a platter.

"Are you going to cook these today?" Tino asked.

Isabella glanced at the recipe. The bundles boiled for three hours. She smiled. "Yes. They take three hours to boil." She handed Tino a hand towel. "Thank you for your help."

Tino kissed her. "You're welcome." He sauntered into the living room and settled onto the couch to watch the news.

She set the bundles to boiling and sat at the desk.

Slipping the x-acto blade in another crack, she cautiously peeled a puzzle piece at a time off the outside layer of the box and discovered a box inside of the box. The inner cube was slick and unadorned. This time she found the notched corner right away and began the slow process of discovering the lines and pieces to open the object.

"Ezzabella," Tino's voice penetrated her concentration.

"Yes?"

"I read there will be a version of the Charles Dickens *A Christmas Carol* being performed tonight. Would you like to go?"

Isabella glanced up. Tino had never suggested they go to a play together. "Do you like 'A Christmas Carol'?"

"Sí, it has always been one of my favorite Christmas stories since my family moved to the United States." Tino folded the paper he was reading. "If you get changed we can have a nice dinner before the play."

She studied him. He wore his dress khakis and nice button-up, long-sleeved shirt. He had already dressed to go out.

"Did you ask me about this earlier?" She searched the recesses of her brain to see if she'd missed a conversation earlier today.

"No. I want to go with or without you." He stepped close to the chair. "But I would prefer with you." He placed a kiss on her lips and stepped back.

Isabella opened her eyes, shoved the box to the center of the desk, and stood. "Then I guess I better get dressed." She'd dreamed of them spending their first Christmas together. She wasn't going to be like her parents. Her loved ones came first, not work.

Chapter Five

All through dinner and the play, little bits and pieces of the past couple of days played in her head. Lots of things about the box weren't adding up. Tino was sticking to her closer than he had since moving in. Granted it was going to be their first Christmas together and the first Christmas they were both looking forward to in years, but there was something else. Something she couldn't quite grasp.

Back at the apartment, Tino danced her into the bedroom. Under his wonderfully heated ministrations, she lost herself in the ecstasy of being thoroughly loved. She dozed off and woke after midnight. The box was on her mind. She had to discover what was inside before any more distractions drew her away.

A quick peek revealed Tino was sound asleep. She slid out from under the covers, donned her robe, and headed to her desk. The desk lamp cast a soft, warming glow on the inner box she'd left in the middle of the desk.

Holding the small box, she once again began the process of discovering the cracks that revealed the way to open the box. An hour had passed when the box popped open. A small satin bag fell onto the desk.

Satin wasn't a cloth the ancient Maya would have had access to. She frowned and studied the bag shining in the light. The client wasn't going to be happy to find their ancient box had been tampered with. Would they think she stole the contents? Daddy would defend her, but why would someone play such a prank?

Plucking the bag from the desk top, the weight told her there was something inside. She pried the top open with her fingers and tipped the bag upside down. A silver ring inlaid with turquoise and diamonds dropped onto the desk, shimmering and blinking in the lamp light.

This wasn't ancient craftsmanship. She picked up the band, turning it and peering at the inside. An inscription was printed on the flat surface. *You are my heart.*

Her fingers shook as she slipped the band onto her ring finger. Tino had said that to her several times since they'd met. Tears trickled down her cheeks, and her heart felt too large for her chest.

Tino and Daddy had set up this "mission." Everything that had happened since receiving the call from Daddy now made sense.

Tino had found the perfect way to get her attention and deliver her present.

She slipped back into bed, pressing her body against Tino's, waiting for his arms to circle her and draw her closer.

She felt his arousal at the same time he kissed her.

"What are you doing awake so early?" he asked, moving his hands to cup her bottom as he pressed his arousal against her mound of curls.

"I couldn't sleep thinking about the box."

His body stilled. "And?"

"Thank you for the beautiful ring!" She kissed him long and lingering, transmitting her emotions to him through the kiss. Drawing out of the kiss she focused on another matter. "How did you find an ancient box to put the ring in?"

"It is not ancient." He kissed the tip of her nose. "I noticed the books you had on puzzles and took one to a master wood crafter. I asked him to build the puzzle box with the ring inside."

"But the Maya symbols on the outside box…They were carved so realistically."

"Remember the old man in the village in Guatemala who allowed you to read his tablet?"

Her mind buzzed with the memory and the honor the man had bestowed, allowing her to read and photograph the tablet. "Yes."

"I visited him and asked him to carve the saying."

The pride in Tino's voice and love twinkling in his eyes overwhelmed her senses. No one had ever taken the time to learn what made her happy. "That's a lot of trouble for a Christmas gift," she said as tears of happiness welled in her eyes.

Tino held her head in his hands.

"Ezzabella, the ring is more than a gift. It is my commitment to you. It is an engagement ring. I wish to marry you as soon as you pick the date."

Her mind stopped and her heart raced. *Engagement ring!* She knew his feelings for her surpassed any he'd ever had with anyone else. She'd hoped he would want to marry her someday.

He touched their noses. "Marriage is what you want, no?"

"Yes! I've wanted it since Guatemala, but I didn't want to pressure you into making a decision you weren't ready for."

"Querida, the ring tells you the truth. You are my heart. I would be empty without you in my life." He sighed heavily. "My only regret is that I was not by your side when you discovered the ring. I wanted to wait for the delivery of the box, but your father thought you would need the time to figure it out."

Isabella laughed. "Do you really like *A Christmas Carol?*"

"No. I only said that to get you to leave the box alone. I had hoped you would open it on Christmas Day."

She laughed until her sides hurt. "I'm sorry. You know how I get obsessed."

"Sí. That is one of the many things I love about you." He slid a hand down her side.

Her body shivered with anticipation.

"I would like to give you one more, early Christmas present," Tino's hands glided over her body as his lips caressed her neck and shoulder, moving lower toward her nipples. His hand stalled.

"But first." He slipped the ring off her right hand and picked up her left hand. "Dr. Isabella Mumphrey, would you marry me?"

She peered into his smoldering brown eyes and nodded. "Yes. Yes! I'll marry you!"

Tino pulled her down into the covers, dropping kisses down her body.

"This is my best Christmas ever!" Twirling the engagement ring on her finger, she knew her life with Tino would be as challenging as the puzzle box she opened and over-flowing with love.

~*~

About the book & Author

Thank you for reading *Secrets of a Hopi Blue Star*. This book was about Isabella finding her true roots and uncovering human trafficking at the same time. If you enjoy this book, please leave a review. It is the best way to repay an author. To continue on adventures with Isabella and Tino, look for book 1, *Secrets of a Mayan Moon* and book 2, *Secrets of an Aztec Temple*.

I also have several mystery series. You can find out about them at my website: https://www.patyjager.net

Paty Jager is an award-winning author of 48 novels, 8 novellas, and numerous anthologies of murder mystery and western romance. All her work has Western or Native American elements in them along with hints of humor and engaging characters. Paty and her husband raise alfalfa hay in rural eastern Oregon. Riding horses and battling rattlesnakes, she not only writes the western lifestyle, she lives it.

You can catch up with her at:

Website: http://www.patyjager.net
Blog: https://writingintothesunset.net/
FB Page: https://www.facebook.com/PatyJagerAuthor/
Amazon: https://www.amazon.com/Paty-Jager/e/B002I7M0VK
Pinterest: https://www.pinterest.com/patyjag/
Twitter: https://twitter.com/patyjag
Goodreads:
http://www.goodreads.com/author/show/1005334.Paty_Jager
Newsletter- Mystery: https://bit.ly/2IhmWcm
Newsletter- Western: https://bit.ly/2JVGe4j
Bookbub - https://www.bookbub.com/authors/paty-jager

Windtree
Press

Thank you for purchasing this Windtree Press publication. For
other books of the heart, please visit our website
at www.windtreepress.com.

For questions or more information contact us
at info@windtreepress.com.

Windtree Press
www.windtreepress.com

Hillsboro, OR 97124

www.ingramcontent.com/pod-product-compliance
Lightning Source LLC
Chambersburg PA
CBHW051051070925
32238CB00038B/557